Savage
Heritage

Savage Heritage

James McMurtry

ROBERT HALE · LONDON

First published in Great Britain 2008

ISBN 978-0-7090-8617-8

Robert Hale Limited
Clerkenwell House
Clerkenwell Green
London EC1R 0HT

www.halebooks.com

2 4 6 8 10 9 7 5 3 1

For Beverley Jane

Typeset in 10/12½pt Classical Garamond
by Derek Doyle & Associates, Shaw Heath
Printed and bound in Great Britain
by Biddles Limited, King's Lynn

CONTENTS

1

The Realist

The oak tree not the car-park connected her to the world. She parked her moped beneath it in the mornings, standing between the roots that dived into the ocean-earth like serpents. She peered up into the canopy through the synaptic maze of branches, imagining the history in the hundreds of years from sapling to aged splendour. Rebellion, emigration, Famine, struggles, troubles, freedom and war, she wanted to climb the tree and sit in its branches watching the world pass by, seeing history happen.

Orla Shea looked back into the classroom at her third years. Every year there was a class that made her vocation true. Here they were. Brendan had timetabled her the lowest group again because he knew what she would do with them.

Since September she had lost one to pregnancy, another to emigration and two to permanent exclusion. Those that remained could hardly spell their names or count on their hands; they rarely knew the day of the week or what they did yesterday, but she had to teach them enough about the history of Ireland and the world, for them to at least appreciate that life did not begin and end with television or Playstation or the estate where they lived.

'It was a long time ago Miss Shea. Do you know anyone who was alive during this Famine?' asked Sinead McAuliffe.

'It was over a hundred and fifty years ago,' Orla reminded, pointing to the wall and the timeline they had constructed during the previous lesson. 'How old do you think I am?'

'You're ancient, miss. You're over forty,' said Danny Mulroney.

'She's not. She's not thirty,' Sinead defended. 'Isn't that right, miss?'

Orla noticed that Sinead's collar was clean, her nails were scrubbed and she had fainter shadows under her eyes. Her new foster parents had already made a difference.

'I'm thirty-six,' Orla revealed, knowing they relished such confidences.

'You're looking old, miss,' declared Danny.

'I think you look lovely,' said Sinead, almost crying.

Danny asked, 'You have no ring, miss, are you not married?'

'Now Danny – you know that's private.'

A flurry of excitement followed.

'It's only 'cause he loves you, miss.'

'He'd marry you tomorrow. He said so.'

'Miss wants to marry Mr Flannery. I've seen them talkin'.'

Orla held up her hand and smiled and there was silence.

'Now . . . I'm going to tell you a story about a poor family who had to go to the workhouse.'

At the end of the lesson she walked to the window and looked out at the oak. The serrated leaves shivered with life.

Before leaving, Sinead approached and whispered. 'Are you married, miss? You can tell me.'

'I'm not, I'm afraid.'

'It's a shame, miss. You should be. Everyone knows that a woman on her own is desperate to marry a decent fella.'

Sagely she went from the room.

Only Danny Mulroney was left. He joined her and said, 'Are you looking at the Old Man again, Miss Shea?'

'Who?'

'The Old Man, miss. That tree there with the dead fingers and the twisted fat body with a face to stop the clocks.'

She laughed.

Primed by her approbation he added, 'Sean Fitzpatrick did it behind there with Bridget Grogan last week. Mr Flannery caught them.'

She withered him with a raised eyebrow.

'Sorry, Miss Shea.'

During the lunch hour the playground teemed and she sat at her desk reading a chapter of the latest crime thriller. She had become fascinated by translations of Scandinavian books with their snow-muted landscapes, so emotionless and untainted. She liked how the blood melted the crystals, how a fresh snowfall hid it all and how the cold numbed the pain. She also knew that the snows would melt in the sun, and in time all would be exposed.

But more than the forensics and gore, it was the difference she sought, the phrasing in translation, the habits and customs of another place, the places she had never known existed before.

After school she stepped under the canopy, out of the rain and touched the gnarled bark of the oak, imagining what the children would say, 'Like alligator skin; like fossils; like a dried river of tears.'

Against the slate sky, the grey playground and the terraced houses beyond, the season's cycle of the tree was her permanence, and just the thought of it was comfort since her grandmother's diagnosis.

Every evening she rode from the school, through the indifferent traffic and unsympathetic rain to Memorial Hospital.

Through the streets the cold rain soaked through her clothes and she contemplated taking a turn for her flat in Castle Road, but she knew she could not and continued on to the Memorial.

At a junction, a taxi rocked back and forth as the driver impatiently rode the clutch. When the lights changed he cut across her, forcing her into the gutter. It was all she could do to hold the moped steady and kick out at the rear of the car as it sped away.

She felt no fear. It was all she knew. Within her helmet the world could be far away, unravelling across the visor screen with the volume down. Within the helmet she was finally alone.

In the hospital car-park, when she took it off and the world rushed in, she realized that she was alone.

She was waiting by the lifts to the cancer ward, looking at the puddle forming at her feet when her mobile sounded. It was Martin.

'Hello.'

'Where are you?'

She clucked her tongue. 'I'm at the hospital.'

'No need to be crabby . . . What time will you be back at your place?'

'I don't know. It depends how tired she is. If she's strong today I'll be staying.'

There was a pause.

'Is it worth coming over tonight?'

'No. I'll be tired. I'll see you tomorrow. You can still take me to the exhibition.'

He sighed. 'If I come over tonight we can go online and book that weekend in Venice you wanted.'

'You wanted. I wanted to go to Rome.'

'Again? I just want to take you for dinner in St Mark's Square and then cross the bridges just like Katharine Hepburn. You said that's what you'd love to do.'

'Katharine was a spinster when she went.' She winced at the implication. 'I'd rather be Audrey Hepburn in Rome.'

'We need a bit of romance.'

'What do you mean by that?'

'Everyone wants romance,' he explained quickly. 'Following you around one ruin after another is not exactly appealing. Aren't you tired of all the broken statues of forgotten Caesars?'

'Not at all. I'll see you tomorrow.'

The more she thought about it, the more she wanted to go to Rome – alone.

Of all the cities, Rome was hers. She thought of the bubble that as a child she imagined she had. Within it she spun through time, visiting all the places she read about. From Elizabeth to the Easter Rising she had ached to see the light of other days, but most of all she had dreamed of witnessing for herself the macabre glory of Rome.

'So you definitely don't want to see me tonight?'

The lift opened.

'I've my evening planned. I'll see you tomorrow.'

The assumption that she should change her plans just to suit him still annoyed her.

On the ward, the duty nurse took her into a treatment room and demanded she change out of her soaked clothes. As the nurse took the sodden bundle away to the dryer, Orla managed to knot one tie on the back of the gown she was given. Craning to tie another she caught sight of her knickers and could not decide if the damp cotton was limp or her bottom was lumpy. Too exhausted to care or persevere with the second knot, she slipped on a robe and went to her grandmother.

Although the dread of Margaret's death numbed her soul, she longed for those last moments with her. The barren sterility, the machines, the weary sympathy were all insignificant when she held Margaret's hand. They could have been anywhere together, perhaps back in the kitchen in Wellington Street, just the two of them, laughing as they baked, or in the garden, Margaret pruning as she listened to Orla read from Nuala Phelan's *Stories of the Secret Gods*.

She could see her grandmother from the end of the corridor. Margaret would usually turn to her and smile as she approached and Orla liked to keep her eyes on her until she was at her side, but this evening Orla could not see her as by her bedside sat an elderly man. He was clutching her hand and holding his face close to hers.

Though she had been there almost every night for four weeks Orla politely tapped the open door. The old man and Margaret drew apart, dropped their hands and looked at her guiltily. Margaret smiled and the man gaped, blinking slowly. She saw his eyes were azure.

'Hello, my darling,' Margaret said weakly. 'I have a visitor . . . This is Donovan O'Meagher. He is a very old friend.'

Out of habit, Orla took off the robe and realizing what it would reveal rushed to shove it back over her shoulders.

She shook his hand and his grip lingered with warmth. Yet his eyes troubled her and she looked away. Deep in his face they seemed to search knowingly.

'Come and sit here,' Margaret instructed, patting the other side of the bed.

Orla complied dutifully.

'Where are your clothes? You look like one of us unfortunate souls.'

'The nurse is kindly drying them. I rode through the rain.'

'It's raining?'

'Pouring.'

'We hadn't noticed. Why didn't you wear your mac?'

'You know I look like a balloon in it.'

'Why didn't you take a bus?'

'It takes too long and it's always crowded and I have too many books to carry.'

'Didn't you know it was going to rain?'

'I saw no news because I was in late and I was up early.' Familiar with such interrogations Orla routinely arranged the bedside cabinet, ensuring the water jug was full, the cards upright and the tissues ready to pull.

All the while Donovan looked from one woman to the other. Ignoring him, Orla apologized. 'I'm sorry I couldn't be here yesterday, Nana. The parents' evening didn't end until ten. I telephoned the desk but they said you were sleeping.'

Margaret smiled. 'I knew. I knew and Donovan was here. He travelled from Cork to see me. I wrote to him and he came to me. We haven't seen each other in so long.' She was holding the old man's hand again. 'I thought of him so much and now he's here. He came all the way from Ballyanna – the valley of my dreams.' Her words carried the urgency of a confession.

'Has that made you feel better today?' Orla whispered.

Margaret wriggled upright. 'I have you with me and now Donny; it's almost a cure for the cancer.'

She laughed lightly, her eyes wide with joy and pain, and for the briefest moment Orla allowed herself to believe she could get better.

Donovan spoke then. His accent was a rich rolling Cork brogue; he spoke almost in a song.

'Does your mother know about the illness, Orla?'

Margaret interrupted. 'I've told him how long it's been since I found out. I told him I said Maeve should go home. The living should not wait for death and certainly not that of another soul.'

Orla smiled tightly, annoyed by her grandmother's denial in this. Her mother had been told to leave because she made them miserable. She had not wanted to be there and one evening, when she was shattered after school, Orla had sneeringly spoken to her mother of a life of selfish vanity. It was all the excuse Maeve needed to leave and they had not seen or spoken to her since.

Orla regretted what she had said – not because it was untrue but because it would arm her mother's anger. At best Maeve would deny it as merely a reflection of her daughter's resentment. Orla recognized that her mother was beyond her in all ways.

'She'll come back when she needs to,' explained Orla. 'Her husband has a business in London that demands her time.'

She saw that Margaret was thankful for the tact.

Donovan continued, 'And your father, Orla, do you see him?'

Orla looked away, perturbed by his knowledge of her. For her grandmother, she replied.

'He has been married again for many years now and he is happy with his family. He sends me cards but I don't see him. I don't really know him, Donovan. I wish him well though and I know he feels the same.'

Donovan seemed strangely satisfied.

'And is there a man in your life?'

Orla smiled then for it was ridiculous that this old man was questioning her so. She glanced at her grandmother who grinned girlishly and raised her eyebrows for Orla to reveal all.

'I have a man. His name is Martin.'

'He was a teacher but now he works for the government,' proffered Margaret with pride.

'A civil servant,' considered Donovan. 'What does he do?'

'He's an administrator for the Office of Public Works.'

Donovan nodded slowly.

'How long is it that you've been with him, Orla?' Margaret asked.

'A few years off and on.'

'Ages,' declared Margaret.

'So you have much in common,' said Donovan.

Orla thought about that. 'We travel together . . . Yes, we travel and visit and—'

Margaret came to her aid. 'But he is handsome and considerate and you are best friends.'

Orla shrugged. 'As a teacher I am very busy. Having been one, he understands.'

Later she would remember a bleak realization in that living moment that Martin did not understand.

Donovan was oblivious to her vagaries. 'So you go on romantic journeys?'

'Not really. I like museums and ancient sites and such. Martin is . . . patient. I'm usually too tired for romance.'

'Isn't the past romantic?'

'It's history. It's all too real.'

'But there is a sense of wonder still.'

'Oh yes. That's why I chose to teach it.'

'Have you considered marriage?' he asked bluntly.

Her grandmother simpered. Orla smiled wryly. She had not been subjected to such a barrage of questions since the interview for her post at The Holy Cross Community School.

'We've talked about it.'

'You've done more than that,' Margaret said. 'Martin has proposed.'

'Oh,' exclaimed Donovan, sitting straighter.

'But she hasn't said yes yet.' Margaret was reproving.

'She is considering it,' Donovan decided.

'She must not leave it too late or he will be off.'

Orla intervened. 'He didn't propose. We just talked about it and I said we should wait; I have been preoccupied lately – he understands, and anyway I'm happy living alone. I have my own things and my routine.'

Donovan did not seem to hear. 'And will you have children?'

'We both have careers to think of.'

'But it's not too late.'

'That's true – when the time is right.'

Donovan and Margaret shared a smile. Orla looked between them quizzically and Margaret realized her granddaughter's confusion.

'We corresponded for many years, Orla. That's how Donovan knows things about you.'

'Oh. I didn't know.'

'It was after the war and we wrote many letters . . . many letters.'

Orla was almost indignant. 'You never told me that.'

Margaret looked away sheepishly. 'It was a special friendship. It had to be secret, you understand. A woman couldn't write to a man like that.'

Recognizing what her grandmother had told was as much as she needed to know, Orla asked, 'How long are you here for, Donovan?'

'I'll stay as long as I am needed.'

Margaret nodded and her knuckles whitened about his hand. Margaret was alive again with him and even if it was for a few more days it was wonderful.

'I'll come and see you tomorrow then, Nana?'

She kissed her and left them there, conscious of them both watching her walk away down the corridor. She hoped her wet pants had not soaked through.

2

Indefinite Article

She awoke before the alarm after another fitful night and lay there listening to the traffic. She allowed herself to believe it was Margaret's imminent death that troubled her but she sensed it was much more.

Rather than dwell on it, she considered her day as she took a shower. She had planned it into phases – it was necessary at the weekends during the term-time to maintain a work-life balance. Organizing her leisure was a habit.

While eating breakfast, which consisted of fruit and fibre flakes with a sprinkle of bran, and drinking a cup of tea, she watched a half-hour of the television news cycle. She munched determinedly on the bran, annoyed with Martin, not so much for scoffing the last of her muesli, but for putting the empty packet back in the cupboard.

During the week, she allowed half an hour in the mornings to meticulously apply her make-up. She supposed it was a sign of age to take such a short time – for many years she had allocated at least one hour before the mirror before she could leave the house. Indeed, in recent years she had allowed herself the luxury of not applying make-up at all on weekends and so could afford to relax a little more.

Breakfast was phase one of the plan; to tick off phase two she got out the latest fitness DVD that Bernadette had recommended, ready to continue her new regime. She had done well with this one, already firmly established into a routine – this was the third session. She had missed the workout the day before because of the parents' evening, so in order to maintain the military discipline it was essential to adopt she would definitely exercise today.

She turned off the television, stretched and yawned and picked up the DVD case to read the blurb. This workout was specifically for the working woman. For just fifteen minutes a day it would attack the thighs, bottom, belly and waist. She stood, dropped her dressing-gown and looked in the mirror over the fireplace. Standing on tiptoes and stretching her body, she observed that on top it was not bad; it was down below that it all went wrong. She slowly twirled and then offered her reflection a wry smile.

'Ah, to hell with the world.' she muttered to herself. 'What do I care what anyone thinks?'

Of course it was not wrong; it was just genetics. Ample breasts, wide hips, sturdy legs, and all in a good size 12. She knew this was her shape and was satisfied.

'Motherly,' Martin had called her, but she did not take it as a compliment coming from him.

Womanly, she decided – all woman.

At least her auburn hair did not let her down. Although thinning more with every brush stroke, it still flamed between ginger and blonde.

She decided to swap phases and do the ironing first. She wasn't going to meet Martin until twelve, so she sorted out and loaded a pile of dirty washing and then started the ironing listening to Neil Finn. Looking out over the hedge to the road, she sang along at the top of her voice about bravery in suburbia and sad persistent thoughts.

There was a smell of singeing and lifting the iron she revealed a scorched imprint on the back of her blouse. She sighed and decided that keeping her jacket on would hide it.

She hung her trousers, skirts and blouses for the week on hangers and placed them in the wardrobe in the correct order. In the past she had ordered them by colour, style or size. Colour had not worked; she usually wore black or heavy autumn shades and on dark mornings she could not tell which was which. Sorting by style had proved as problematic; the fitted jackets and suits she preferred for work were so similar they rendered ordering useless. And she would never arrange by size again; the dimension spectrum simply reminded her of the weight she was when she was seventeen and all the sizes she had been since.

At the moment the order was determined by the day of wearing. She stood back and cast her eye along the rack. Although meticulously arranged, the clothes were no longer sophisticated and now, she had to admit, slightly staid. Perhaps a ruthless sort and a drastic makeover was necessary.

She closed the wardrobe door to the thought of tediously trawling through shops suffering the gum-chewing sales assistants wearing too much foundation and not enough flesh.

After making another cup of tea she went back into the front room to start exercising. She glanced at the blurb again. This workout was the easy answer to all her fitness needs. She could power on through her day, knowing she was in control and looking good. It was already 10.00 a.m.

The telephone rang. It was Bernadette. Orla sipped her tea and slumped on the settee. On the coffee table was phase four – the coursework she had to mark.

Bernadette was resigned. 'Why me? What's wrong with me? What do I do wrong?'

'So he's gone.'

'Yes!'

'Good.'

Bernadette gasped. 'Orla!'

'Bernie. That's why you've phoned. You know what I warned you about. You know what I think.'

'I thought it was different. He *was* different.'

'Don't be dense. What was different? He was handsome, vain and stupid. You're desperate and you were probably flutered. It's always the same.'

'He had a deadly arse.' Bernadette laughed.

Orla shook her head.

'I know what you're doing,' Bernadette claimed. 'You're judging me. You think I'm just as bad as they are.'

Orla laughed this time.

'I've told you, you should try a dating service.'

'No way. I don't need to do that.'

'You obviously do.'

'You're such a cow.'

'I would if I needed one. You can see what they look like—'

'Which is important.'

'But most importantly you can see what you have in common. I can tell everything you need to know about the men you find in those bars before I even step in one.'

'You're so cruel. You make it sound so cheap . . . I care.'

'Then find someone who cares as well.'

'Like Martin who you met by mistake?'

Prior to leaving the profession he had attended a training seminar at a Dublin hotel. When he realized he was sitting in the session entitled *The Innovative Teacher*, and not *Managing from the Middle*, he had been too embarrassed to leave. He later claimed he only stayed because he was sat beside her.

Orla ignored Bernadette's sarcasm; she could not accept her criticism of Martin when compared to the men she dated.

'I was lucky.'

'You share so much . . . I mean you have your dirty weekends so the sex must be good.'

'Bernie, you know I won't talk about that. It's private.'

'Are you sure there are no other handsome teachers at Holy Cross?'

'Who for?' Orla teased.

'For me, of course.'

'Bernie, I'm busy.'

'I don't care about their age.'

'You don't always need a man.'

'I'll even negotiate on looks.'

'I'm hanging up.'

'You're right, Orla. I am desperate. Help me.'

'I'll see you.'

She put the telephone down.

She had known Bernadette since they sat together in history class. Bernadette had copied designs from a library book for her project on Elizabethan court fashions whilst mooning over Mr Fallon. He had viewed Bernadette's chosen project with open cynicism.

'Short of Cromwell,' he had sneered, 'Elizabeth was the worst scourge of this island. Whilst those mannequins you're drawing there were writing sonnets and marvelling at potatoes, the people here, your people, were suffering.'

Orla had researched the Spanish Armada and imagined herself as Queen Elizabeth with the body of a weak and feeble woman and the heart of a king, and Mr Fallon had smiled and she had blushed and Bernadette had poked her with her pencil.

She wondered if it had always been that way between the two of them – the bickering and bitching and petty jealousies. She could not decide, but she knew she was tired of it.

Checking the time she calculated she could mark six essays in an hour. She took out the red pen and selected the first six. Her flat was on the ground floor and she had sole use of a small sheltered patio area at the rear. She took the papers there, laid out the marking scheme, and began to read.

Immediately, the fog of fatigue descended across her mind, but she was efficient enough to persevere and an hour later she graded the last one.

She sat back and caught sight of the exercise DVD on the floor. Going back inside, she nudged it under the chair with her toe. She then stood and turned before the mirror – with the right trousers and top she could still look good. She reached for her make-up bag – and just a little more enhancement would help.

Lastly, she lightly applied two dabs of perfume. The spiced citrus subtly reminded her of how her mother had smelled when she was a child.

Thirty minutes was how long it would take for a brisk walk into town. A stroll through Phoenix Park would be enough cardiovascular exertion for one day. She would adapt phase two and integrate it into phase five – that was flexibility. She was in control.

She phoned Martin.

'I'm walking into town so you don't have to pick me up.'

'That's a hell of a long way.'

'I want to walk.'

'I want to drive you through town with the roof down.'

'I'll walk. I feel like the fresh air.'

'Then go on holiday with me?'

'What fresh air is there in Venice?'

'The same as in Dublin.'

'Look, I want to walk.'

'We can go somewhere else,' he persevered. 'I don't care.'

'Well I do. We'll talk about it over lunch.'

She waited in the Garden of Remembrance by the sculpture of the *Children of Lir*. The children's human form was cast aside as they transformed into swans and soared into the sky. The sculpture always reminded her of being read to and transported through time on the back of one of those birds.

She was skimming through *The Irish Times* and not knowing why she bothered. Sometimes the news just made her feel frustrated and guilty. She closed it and folded it and shoved it in the bin. Taking out her latest novel she read until Martin arrived.

When he ambled along the path she checked her wristwatch and watched him over her reading glasses.

Although he was shorter than her, he was always immaculately attired and he carried himself with assured energy. When he smiled the shadows about his eyes faded and his perfect teeth were arrayed. She noticed two young women watching him as he passed but his aim was true and, to his credit, he did not respond if he noticed the attention in return.

Orla wondered what he saw in her. She did not make it easy. Perhaps she was grateful for the attention and it primed his vanity. Occasionally, with clumsy charm, he declared that she was gorgeous but she remained unconvinced. Bernadette claimed he should be telling her she was beautiful in every moment he could but Orla was a realist, and anyway, any man who did not worship Bernadette was not good enough.

She sighed, slipped in the book mark and took off her glasses.

'I love it when you look at me over your specs like that,' he declared. 'It's very sexy.'

'You're late.'

'We'd better get going then. Up you get.'

He kissed her and they walked out of the Gardens in silence. At the kerb she held out her hand for him to take but he did not notice.

'I'm sorry,' he offered as he checked the traffic. 'I had to find somewhere to park my baby. I can't just leave her anywhere.'

Orla pursed her lips to avoid a caustic comment; instead, she just glanced down at him with disdain.

He caught her.

'Are you wearing heels again?' he snapped. 'You know how that makes me feel.'

'I'm not.'

He glanced down. 'Oh, special shoes.'

'No; just comfortable,' she replied, shaking her head.

He had recently purchased a sports car and enthused about it being a two-tone blue Big Healey Mark II, declaring it an investment. She called it an insult. He had shrugged and laughed and informed her that his father had one; he had always wanted one and now he could afford one he was buying it. She had argued that it was uncomfortable and useless. He had given her an uncomprehending shake of the head and the conversation ended there. She had later realized it would have been the ideal time to argue about money and marriage but she felt no need.

'What is this exhibition?' he asked again as they crossed the road to the Municipal Gallery.

'It's a showcase for provincial artists.'

'So it's like charity for talentless bogmen?'

She sighed.

'I'm codding,' he assured her.

As it was the opening day of the exhibition, it was well attended and Orla soon lost Martin as he raced on through the rooms.

She appreciated the intense immediacy of the gallery. Her grandmother would take her there as a child and they would sit on the old leather couches absorbing the canvases, tracing the strokes and colours and entering the mind of the artists.

These new exhibits demonstrated an array of styles and forms and she was soon sitting again on a frayed couch immersed in a set of watercolours of Antrim hills. The wash of greys and greens, accentuated by jagged crags of black reminded her of the trip she had made with her grandparents shortly before her grandfather died. Because he had never been there, they had driven up to Belfast and along the Antrim Road to the Giant's Causeway. There had been few tourists at that time of year and she had stood with them both on the strange volcanic spur, contemplating his imminent death and the bleak horizon.

She was only halfway through the exhibition when Martin returned and stood behind her idly tapping his foot.

'Don't bother me now,' she hissed. 'Go on to the café and buy me a coffee. I'll be there when I've finished.'

He spun away dutifully and she moved on at her own pace, but by the next display, a collection of intense oils from Cork, her concentration was awry and she walked out.

At the table he sat licking his fingers and eying the bun he had bought for her.

Such boyish traits had once been fun.

'I only wanted a coffee, Martin.'

'I know that sure, but a bit of sugar will sweeten you up.'

She pushed the plate towards him and he seized the bun without hesitation.

'I'm helping you slim,' he said with a mouthful of icing and currants. 'I'm thinking of your hips.'

She splattered her coffee and had to wipe her mouth with her handkerchief.

'Martin!'

'What?'

She shook her head.

'And I know you ate all my cereal when you were last over,' she accused.

'What can I say?' he smirked dismissively. 'I love the stuff and what's the bother? I'll buy you another packet.'

'That's just it – you won't.'

'I will! Now, about that break,' he ventured, wiping the coffee drops from the table top with a napkin. 'I propose a compromise. I was thinking about Barcelona. There's the Gaudi architecture and . . . there's cheap flights now and—'

'But you've been there.'

He narrowed his eyes. 'But I've not been for years . . . I mean, I've been to Rome several times now so—'

'But now you want to go back to Barcelona?'

'I don't mind . . . Wherever you go is fine. I'm just making suggestions.'

It was tedious trying to guess what he really wanted. 'How about Oslo?' she said.

'What?'

'In Norway.'

'I hadn't really thought about it. Why there, of all places?'

'I've told you before that I'd like to visit.'

'Have you?'

'Yes.'

'Oh . . . But what's in Norway? Where's the romance?'

'I think it'd be different.'

'Well . . .' he said, his face twisting in a petulant frown, 'I suppose so.'

She sighed and smiled. 'Forget it, Martin. You surprise me. That's the way. Wherever we go it'll be great. It always is.'

3

Crying for the Day

The canopy of the Old Man was dense now and the wind danced through it as Orla watched from her classroom window. In the glass her wide eyes blinked wearily and she turned to the class. She was with her top set fifth year and realizing what she often forgot in the culture of bureaucracy and blame – that she truly appreciated the honour and joy of teaching.

'And you would think Southampton has a Titanic museum. It has not. There is a plaque on the pavement which you can stand on. It says that from this spot you could see the *Titanic* at the dockside – that is if you can see past the cranes and silos. The famous Ocean Terminal is gone and with it any remnant of what the town was.'

'But like you said, miss, the town was blitzed, just like Belfast. There can't have been much left.'

'But they have no value in their heritage. They have a memorial in the park and a model in glass in a small maritime museum down the road, and since the film they have put that sign up, but it's an insult to all those families who lost their loved ones. In some parts of the city, there would not have been a street without a merchant sailor who lost his life . . . Now, if you travel down to Portsmouth, they have a magnificent historical dockyard. There is the *Victory* and the *Mary Rose* and the . . .'

'But the *Mary Rose* is just old damp logs, miss. I have a cousin who's seen it.'

'Ah, but it's the artefacts,' she enthused, 'the small details. For the ship you must use your imagination, but when you have the shoes and bows and tools found as they were when the ship capsized, the past is there before you . . . Just like the cross section of the flagship helps us understand Tudor boat-building methods, the artefacts have given us a glimpse of the everyday lives of the people.'

There was a knock on the door and the runner came in. She handed Orla a note and waited. Orla read it and replied with a message on the reverse. As the runner left, Orla resumed her teaching, but now as an automaton.

She saw a few nudges as the pupils encouraged each other to keep her distracted.

'I think I should get back to the socio-economic breakdown of *Titanic*'s passenger list.'

'We don't mind, miss'

'We like it when you lose it about things that happened long ago.'

'Go on Miss Shea. You were giving it to Southampton.'

Orla looked away at the oak tree. It shook with life. A squirrel bounded up the trunk.

'Are you well, miss?'

She breathed hard but did not look at them. There was quiet in the room. The door opened and Brendan entered. He touched Orla's arm. She pointed to the textbook and the series of questions, took her bag and left the room.

Orla phoned her mother on the way to the hospital. There was crowd noise in the background and the line was faint.

'I think this is it,' Orla stated.

'How long has she got?'

'I've been called from work. I'm going there right now. You should be here.'

'I thought I had longer. I thought there would be time.'

'Did you?'

'What are you trying to say?'

'You should be here.'

'You don't know anything Orla. You don't know at all.'

There was static silence over the dissonant crowd.

'Keep me informed please,' Maeve instructed. 'I'll get there when I can.'

Donovan was sitting by the bedside when Orla arrived. He stood and went to her. She had not seen him there since their first meeting. He had been leaving before she arrived and she was grateful.

'Peggy suddenly took a turn for the worse,' he whispered. 'They say it can't be long. I think she has been waiting for you. Do you mind if I wait with you?'

As she absently slipped off her coat she saw the priest was also waiting. He gently touched her hand as she passed.

'Father O'Leary cannot come. Father Harrigan is the hospital priest.'

Orla hardly heard, but mutely shook her head as she took Margaret's hand. The fingers flexed lightly about hers and Orla cried. Margaret opened her eyes but there were no words; she could not speak but that was unnecessary now.

Orla kissed her grandmother's lips and waited while the priest gave the last rites. Donovan prayed.

When the last breath came, Orla was wide eyed with grief. She watched the breath seize Margaret's body in a weak convulsion that deflated with a soft sigh of liberation and relief. In that sigh Orla heard every word they had ever spoken together; in her cooling touch was every moment she had been in her arms; and her last smile was the same smile she had given all her life.

Orla held her head in her hands, the agony across her chest pulled out choking sobs.

And long after the machines had been turned off and the tubes removed Orla sat there remembering – and it was good; she knew there was nothing but good.

Donovan O'Meagher quietly left with the nurses and later Orla found him dozing in the corridor outside. She knelt before him and he revived.

'It's time to leave Donovan. Can I walk with you?'

His bleary eyes focused on her over his glasses, and he smiled. 'You can, of course.'

She wanted to be with him for a while longer. His connection brought Margaret closer. They walked to the taxi rank and did not speak. The memory and the feelings were too powerful to articulate.

'What about your motorcycle?' he asked.

'I'll get you to bed first,' she stated.

'I am grateful, but I think I should help you.'

'You are helping me, Donovan.'

At the hotel, he struggled to lift his legs and she helped to hoist him from the car.

'Are you well, Donovan?'

'I am. I just need to rest. These past weeks have been long.'

'Will you be staying for the wake and the funeral?'

'If I am welcome.'

She gave a benevolent frown.

'Ah Jesus. Margaret would want you there and I want you there and that is that. Would you like to help me make the arrangements?'

He nodded and blinked slowly. She helped him up the stairs, escorted him to his room and promised to collect him the following day.

She watched him ascend and then the taxi took her back to the car-park. By her moped she wept again; by the time she reached her flat she was almost composed enough to phone her mother.

Before doing so she opened a bottle of Chianti and sat on the settee. Her mother answered with a busy slur in her voice. Now there was music accompanying her.

'Speak to me,' she demanded, when Orla could not.

'Can you go somewhere quiet, please?' Orla managed to ask.

Maeve seemed to recognize the tone and shouted. 'I'll call you back.'

Orla drank another glass before the call came.

'She's gone, hasn't she?'

Orla inhaled hard to quell the grief and anger.

'Yes.'

'I should have been there.'

'Yes.'

'Like I said, I thought I had more time . . . Did she say anything?'

'No.'

'There's no need to be like this Orla. She was more to me than to you.'

'No! I'm here and you're there.'

Orla did not speak of love; it would be an empty word. There was a pause.

'When will you be back?' Orla asked.

'At the end of the week. Can you make the arrangements?'

'Yes.'

'Good. Thank you, Orla . . . I love you.'

Orla cut her off and cried again cursing herself for her weakness.

The church was well attended. Although Margaret had gradually withdrawn from the life in the city, declining invitations and avoiding visitors, she was remembered with affection.

Orla stood with Martin and Bernadette. Donovan O'Meagher sat praying at the end of the pew.

Orla was sure Father O'Leary was drunk. The priest had screwed up his face when Orla asked to speak during the service.

'Will it be from the scriptures?'

'No. The eulogy will be in my own words.'

He struggled into his vestments. 'It won't be anything frivolous now, will it? My service must be focused on God. A eulogy would be better at the wake than at Mass. I know what' – he coughed as he tried to remember her name – 'Margaret would want.'

'The church is where she wanted me to speak,' she said, quiet but emphatic.

He softened his tone. 'I just want to ensure sobriety and a sombre tone of the occasion so that . . . Margaret will receive the most holy and dignified ceremony.'

'I assure you father that my grandmother's memory will be remembered with absolute respect by me.'

'You can speak so.'

He began his speech and swayed a little, having to hold himself against the podium.

'Now I know that . . Margaret was a faithful wife and mother and that she was devoted to her granddaughter who is here before us. She was a woman who worked tirelessly for charities and offered her husband solace and comfort, and now she joins him. Her memory will live on.'

During the Eucharist the priest swigged the wine, visibly smacking his lips. Orla cast her eyes along the line, wondering if she was the only one witnessing the performance.

When it was time for her eulogy, the man gave a dismissive wave of the hand and petulantly strode off in front of the altar.

Orla stood for sometime looking out across the congregation and when she spoke it was without notes. She gazed across to the stained-glass window in which the Resurrection promised the light of Heaven.

'Margaret Tremayne was a woman of beauty, intelligence and integrity. She asked me to remember the laughter, so I did; she asked me to live on for her and I will; she asked me not to weep, but I did . . . I was honoured to have known her and I know that she would be humbled by your condolences.

'In every moment I shared with Margaret I knew her love was complete and unconditional. Always, when she looked me in the eye I knew she wanted to know what I thought. When she smiled I knew that she was simply delighted to be there with me.

'Margaret Tremayne was my grandmother and my mother; she was my sister and my friend. She gave me a sanctuary . . . she saved me.'

She closed her eyes.

'I remember reading with her on rainy days much like this one; I remember walking with her through autumn leaves, I remember the scents of spring in the air and her joy, but I will always remember her in summers without end. Perhaps we all like to remember the past in summer and in sunlight but when I remember Margaret I truly can.'

Her echoes faded, Orla opened her eyes and the congregation stood and clapped fiercely.

Outside the church, Bernadette whispered, 'Was the priest drunk?'

Orla giggled and nodded. Martin pursed his lips in disapproval and his hand tightened about hers as people approached.

Margaret was buried with her late husband Bertie Tremayne in Fair Hill Cemetery. The mourners stood within the small coppice which offered little shelter from the wind off Dublin Bay, but there was peace there.

Orla pressed close to Martin then, grateful for his warmth, all the while vainly hoping her mother would arrive.

Afterwards, they went to Rowland's Bar where a spread had been laid out in the function room above. Orla ensured Donovan travelled with her and by the end of the evening, after the condolences and reminiscing was over, she was alone with him. Martin had reminded her he had urgent deadlines to meet and she had told him to leave. Bernadette had gone of her own accord. There was an open fire in the room and after the tables were cleared the doors were respectfully closed on them.

'Can I come with you to the airport tomorrow?' Orla asked.

'Of course . . . You know, you're a fine girl. Margaret was blessed in the end,' he nodded.

It seemed strange to say such a thing. Afraid to suffer another bout of platitudes she nodded.

'Tell me how you met her?'

' 'T'was at the end of the war. I was walking along the Coastal Way near Ballybrannigan and there she was . . . Peggy was brazen, you know, and I was a little afraid I think.'

Orla chuckled. 'Brazen?'

'She was sure. And she looked for all the world like Bette Davis holidaying in secret. And Bette was a woman to be reckoned with . . . you have the same look about you.'

'Thank you.' She accepted the compliment. It had been said before.

'She was brazen because she was sun-worshipping as she used to call it.'

'Sunbathing?'

He nodded. 'And I walked by and I said she should fry exposing herself like that. I was an awful prude.'

'And what did she do?' Orla laughed.

'She laughed at me like you are now and just spread her arms wider. Then she put her arms up in surrender and asked me if I was the man from the Ministry of Sun.'

'And what did you say?'

'I was mortified. It's fair to say I was shocked by her in her underwear . . . and because she was a great beauty. I was obsessed. I laughed and she laughed and we got to talking and I sat down with her and that was that. We spent the rest of the summer along the cliffs. She was staying with her parents in Ballybrannigan. We spent our days in the fields and along the strands. I showed her all the places along the coast from Garrymore to Spanish Folly. We rode our bikes and walked and we laughed most of all.'

'She never told me about you.'

'And why would she? 'T'was long'go.'

'But it meant so much.'

'It did. But she had another life in the city and she went away. She never came back, but I think she wanted to. She married and we wrote to each other for many years.'

She looked from the flames into his eyes and saw he was crying. The blue intensity darkened.

'Did you ever read Nuala Phelan when you were a small girl?'

His questions no longer seemed strange.

'I did. Nana would read her to me. I loved to imagine the old gods and forgotten people. I still have the old book.'

'I sent you it.'

'You did?'

'I knew Nuala, you see.'

'You did not.'

'Sure, she collected all the stories from the valleys and made them her own. She had a beautiful voice in her writing and I knew you would not be able to resist.'

'You were right,' she whispered.

'If you ever come to Cork, perhaps you'll want to read them again.'

'I will.'

She held his hand and he took hers and kissed it.

'Thank you, Orla. You are a beautiful child and I am proud of you.'

She was moved by his gentle honesty and, by the fire with him, she felt calm for the first time since before Margaret's illness.

'Do you have children, Donovan?'

He hesitated. 'No.'

'Did you ever marry?'

'I did not.'

She wanted to say what a waste that was but it seemed cruel and who was she to talk of the single life?

However, he added, 'It wasn't unusual to be a country bachelor . . . Margaret told me you are a fine teacher.'

'I enjoy it. The children keep my mind young.'

'I've always thought it was a principled profession.'

'Yes,' she said. 'Yes it can be.'

'And it gives you meaning and purpose.'

'Sometimes,' she smiled wryly.

'Perhaps children of your own will give you that?'

'I don't think so.'

'Oh . . . then what will?'

'I don't know, Donovan.'

'Perhaps marriage will. When will you be married?'

She laughed then.

'Donovan, these are impertinent questions. Are you from the Ministry of Marriage now?'

'I am, and don't you know that Margaret was one of our secret agents?

She said you were her toughest assignment.'

Orla sighed.

'I don't know, Donovan. When the time is right I will marry, but when that will be, I don't know.'

'You're too busy with your teaching and travelling around Europe.'

'Yes, there's that.'

'It's a different Europe to the summer I met that girl on the cliffs.'

'It's a different world, Donovan.'

'Is it, but are the people really any different?'

That night as she lay awake she thought about what he said and she eventually descended into sleep with appalling images of marriage and children and a life that was not her own.

At the airport the next day as she waited with him for his flight to be called, he leaned towards her.

'You know this is only my second time in an aeroplane,' he revealed. 'The first was coming here.'

'Are you afraid?'

'I am not. Flying is a wonder. The things you can see . . . I saw the valley and the fields and the sea from a different perspective . . . There is still so much wonder in the world, Orla.'

She nodded, gulping the grief at his going.

'Thank you for being here,' she said.

He looked over his glasses at her, gently touching her face and kissing her on the cheek. She embraced him and then he had to leave.

When she returned to her flat her mother was waiting on the pavement. Despite marrying three times, Maeve Tremayne had kept her maiden name.

'It's more convenient when things go wrong,' she had casually asserted.

Maeve was speaking loudly into her mobile phone. When Orla passed, she held out her hand imploringly, blowing a thick kiss through over-painted lips and an insipid spiced-orange haze of Indian vetiver.

Orla ignored her but left the door open. Finally removing the phone from her ear, Maeve bustled in a few minutes later.

'You look ill,' she observed of her daughter.

'It's bereavement.'

'No. Your skin is grey and you've put on weight. You need sleep.'

Orla did not respond.

'I've contacted the solicitor,' Maeve continued. 'There will be a meeting tomorrow. I can stay for a few days, but I'll have to leave after that.'

'Would you like a cup of tea?' Orla asked flatly.

'Have you filtered coffee?'

'Only instant.'

'Then no.'

She put her case down and slumped on to the settee, idly scanning the room as Orla put the kettle on. She ran her finger along the dust on the television and smirked when she saw the workout DVD.

'What hotel are you booked into?' Orla asked.

Maeve's smirk straightened. 'I thought I could stay with you.'

'You can't. I'm too busy with marking. I've left it long enough as it is. I have to get it done.'

'They will understand if there is a delay.'

'Life goes on. Nana would want me to.'

'I won't get in your way.'

'It would be best for you to find a hotel,' she advised levelly as she poured boiling water on to the teabag.

Maeve gave a petulant twist of her shoulders and sat with her arms folded. Orla sat opposite her, staring at her as she sipped her tea.

Maeve folded her arms again. 'Have you checked up on Wellington Street?' she asked.

'Yes.' She reached into her bag. 'Here are the keys. You might as well have them.'

Maeve caught them and slid them straight into her pocket. 'Aren't you afraid that it will be all left to me and you'll receive nothing?' she asked.

'I know exactly what's in the will.'

'You do?'

'Yes.'

'Oh . . . So?'

'So you have no worries. Her home is all yours.'

'You know this for sure?'

'Yes.'

'And you won't contest it?'

Orla sighed. 'No. She wanted you to have it. It was what Bertie wanted.'

Maeve's chest swelled. 'Well, it was where I was brought up.'

'And so was I.'

Maeve ignored that. 'And her savings and furniture and valuables?'

Orla was patient. 'She has given me a few items that were special to us both – photographs, books and mementos. There was even that costume jewellery I wore as a child.'

Maeve frowned.

'They are of no value except to me,' Orla confirmed. 'She has left me enough to pay off my mortgage. If it was money I wanted then she has rewarded me well. What is left goes to you. It is of considerably more value.'

Maeve calculated. 'That seems fair. The house sale – do you think you could help to—?'

'There is nothing there of the family. It is just objects, furniture and such. Anything personal to me I have in my possession. Any professional house clearance service can see to the rest and I'm sure you have enough friends here in Dublin who will willingly help.'

'Can I see what you have taken?'

'No, and I didn't take it – I was given it.'

They stared at each other.

Orla stood up. 'Mother, I am tired and I have to work now. I'm sure those friends will want to see you and offer their commiserations. We don't need to see each other again while you're here.'

Maeve stood and brushed herself down.

'It doesn't have to be like this, Orla. Perhaps this will bring us closer. Perhaps—'

'If any documents require my signature have them sent to me and I will sign them immediately. Apart from that, what else is there?'

'I wanted to talk to you.'

'What have we got to say?'

'You hate me.'

'No, I don't.'

She wondered if Maeve understood how much her decision to leave her with Margaret and Bertie had changed her daughter's life for the good. Orla bore no bitterness for it, though perhaps she felt pity. Maeve had disappointed them all on so many occasions with her promises and lies. Bertie had smiled and denied and said Maeve was still the greatest girl, but Orla saw the true pain in Margaret's silence when Maeve didn't arrive when she said she would.

When she did appear, often after months away, the promises were forgotten with a gift from an airport or a newsagent. It was not for Orla to hate or love. She had long since accepted her mother for what she was and so the woman could find her friends or go to a hotel or the house.

'I want to talk about why I left, why I had to leave,' Maeve said.

'It doesn't matter now.'

'There are things that you don't know.'

'Does any of it matter now? I loved my grandmother and grandfather. You left me with them and they did their best. What could you say that changes where you were? Why would you want to? What harm did they do?'

Maeve cast her eyes down. Orla did not know her well enough to read her reaction. Maeve nodded, took her case and went from the place.

Watching her shadow fade beyond the blinds, she sat on the edge of the settee and wept again. Chastizing herself, she groaned to abate the tears, falling back on to the cushions and staring at the ceiling.

She tried to think of nothing, no family, no love, no school. It was warm in the room and she could hear the wind and the traffic in the distance, and slowly the mess of thought was diminished in her mind, until all she could think about was Margaret smiling through it all and smiling just for her.

Her mobile buzzed.

Her thoughts coalesced in the soporific stillness and she saw there was a sadness in the imaginary smile. It was sadness not caused by the estrangement of her daughter, or the loss of her husband, or even by the cancer.

The doorbell chimed.

It was the same sad smile she saw in a strange eccentric old man with whom Margaret shared a secret friendship that lasted years.

The telephone rang, but that was also unanswered because Orla was sleeping.

4

This Golden Thread

Martin lumbered into the kitchen, messy-haired and scratching inside his boxers. Orla winced behind her juice. She was hoping for more time alone before he got out of bed. That was always the problem with not enough chicken bhuna to absorb too much white wine. Always the opportunist, he had invited himself back, and always the optimist, she had allowed him to stay. She should have known that all that would come of it would be a headache and him. Sometimes she wished she had the headache the night before.

He farted. 'Sorry, Orla. That curry is taking its toll. I think I might have to block your cistern.'

'Do you mind, Martin. I'm eating.' Despite the years together, his over-familiarity still disgusted her. 'And go home if you're ill.'

'Won't you look after me in sickness and in health?'

'I won't if it's self-inflicted.'

'Wet the tea, will you?'

'I will not. Do it yourself; I'm not your slave.'

'No you're not,' he patronized. 'You're a fine thing to me.'

She took her toast into the front room to watch the news. He was still laughing when he joined her on the settee with a bowl of muesli. 'You know I'm bored with this stuff now,' he chomped. 'Can't you buy Sugar Puffs?'

'You're no more than a child,' she scorned. 'You've your own cereal at your place.'

'Jesus you're awful constipated in the morning. You need more of that bran.'

'This is how I am and I won't change.'

'Ah, now you're free from all your financial worries you have no use for the common prole like me.'

'That's not fair and anyway, you can lord it about now you have that promotion you've been so desperate for.'

'I didn't seek advancement; they invited me to apply,' he said piously; then he winked and put his feet up on the coffee table.

'Did you go to bed with your socks on?'

He shrugged and stated archly, 'You didn't notice.'

'You look a mess.'

'But don't I brush up well?'

Letters fell to the floor in the hall and she went to fetch them. He took his feet down reluctantly as she waited to pass. He turned the television to the cartoons, immediately laughing and choking on his cereal.

She took the letters into the kitchen, glancing down at him when she passed, disgusted by the hairs on the back of his neck.

At the kitchen table she sorted through the envelopes, immediately binning the junk. There was nothing unusual among the remaining correspondence except one letter with a Cork postmark. Taking a butter knife she meticulously cut it open. The volume Martin had increased faded as she read.

The first reading swirled like mercury across her mind. She read again, slowly this time.

He shuffled past. 'You've been staring at that letter a while. What is it?'

At least he was rinsing his bowl in the sink.

'It's from a solicitor in Cork. I am to inherit the estate of Donovan O'Meagher.'

He shook his head. 'Is he a relation?'

'He was a friend of my grandmother's. He was the old fella at the funeral.'

'Oh. The one with the grey eyes who did nothing but pray?'

'They were blue,' she said with exasperation.

'Jesus. What luck . . . If you marry me we'll have money and power.'

She smiled grimly.

'Mind you,' he considered, 'having an estate means nothing. It doesn't mean he was a landowner.'

'And not having inherited a penny, or being likely to, you're the expert?'

'It's probably some savings or something. But why are you looking so miserable?'

'Because the man is dead,' she snapped.

'But you hardly knew him.'

'I knew enough about him to know I feel awful.'

He waited a while before quietly asking, 'Will you accept it?'

'They want me to arrange an appointment with this solicitor to read the will.'

'You should go.'

'I don't know.'

Martin changed his tone. 'If I can help, you know I will.' He placed his hand on her shoulder.

She did not react. She was thinking of the flight down and the wondrous views she would see from the window.

*

Martin had suggested they take a city-break after the funeral but she had procrastinated. The thought of the journey, the sterile hotel room and walking between sites of often dubious significance held little appeal anymore. When he suggested they booked for even longer, she had refused outright. Instead, she arranged to fly down to Cork on the second Monday of the Easter holidays, deciding on a cheap flight and a hire car for the day. Martin had offered to accompany her – indeed he had tried to insist, but she had refused. She needed no crutch or company.

She sat in the airport car-park beneath the pristine new terminal for sometime, regretting how complacently she had assured the hire clerk that she would have no problems with the small saloon she was allocated when, in fact, she had not driven a car for at least a year.

It took several circuits of the car-park to fathom the controls. She stalled twice and several horns blared at her before she reached the roundabout that took her out of the complex.

Staying in the slow lane and leading an irate queue, she passed the scaffolds and cranes that were the stripes of the Celtic Tiger. She supposed the modern developments would be history making, but she expected this new history would be as bland and soulless as the architects and politicians who shaped it.

With relief she noticed the frequency of the building sites diminished as she drove along the dual carriageway out of the city.

Staying on the inside lane, she was able to relax a little and even admire the view across the mud flats and fields around Cork Harbour.

The solicitor's office was in the market town of Castleford to the east of Cork City. She found a space for the car by a well-tended river-bank park.

Across the flower beds willows kissed the water. On the other side, the faded façades of the three-storey town houses suggested their past affluence. After reapplying her lipstick in the wing mirror, she walked back down Main Street where the utilitarian shop fronts and agricultural traffic reminded her that any such prosperity had been lost in the incessant and unforgiving turn of the sod.

In the distance were the mountains of Tipperary, still shrouded in the cloud that had obscured them from the aeroplane and made the view mundane.

She was early, and to fill time, she paused at the windows of the shops on the way.

It was a typical farming centre, she supposed. To her eye, the fashions in the boutiques and the furniture were already dated and cheapened by poor materials and bad taste. There were tractors parked at the kerbside and all the road signs pointed to a destination far away – Cork, Waterford, Tipperary, even Dublin itself.

More than once she checked her reflection, satisfied that her suit offered a suitable city sobriety.

She entered the library and located the history section. There was the usual array of books regarding general Irish history, but little on the local area. She was disappointed. Perhaps this corner of Cork had escaped the ravages of rebellion or starvation or history in any greater sense than innovations in combine harvesting or hurling glory.

With a few minutes to spare she found the solicitor's office above a bait and tackle shop down a side street, and her arrival at the foot of the stairs was announced with the dull electric rattle of the doorbell. The door clicked open and she stepped inside, relieved that the roar and fumes of diesel engines receded.

Immediately, an old man in a stained suit that was frayed and too tight bustled down to greet her. She waited to decide if his impoverished attire was due his country practice or ineptitude.

She stood over him and he did not look up. He did shake her hand though, introduced himself as Mossy O'Sullivan, and invited her up to his office.

On the desk, he had laid out an array of papers. She accepted his invitation to sit and he looked at her at last as he eased into his own chair.

'I knew Donovan O'Meagher well. He was older than me and I lived out on the High Road then, by the Cross, but he was a kind fella. The pub was a little shop as well then and we would go there for pop and sweets.'

'The pub?'

'The Leaping Dolphin – it's gone now.' He waved his hand and continued to reminisce. 'He would always have time for us, taking us across the strands for the best places to fish or catch the crabs.'

She sat upright, adjusted her skirt and jacket and waited.

'Huge crabs there were then; man-eaters he would call them. He knew all the holes at the water's edge at low tide . . .' Mossy seemed to notice her again, smiled apologetically and stated, 'Donovan has left all his worldly possessions to you.'

'I really don't understand this. Can you say why he would do that? Why me?'

'Donny made it clear to me that he wanted you to find out for yourself. If you'll allow me to explain my instructions, I think it will all make sense. As I say, Donovan has left all he had to you.'

She sighed, resigning herself to the process. 'What would that be?'

'He has the cottage – An Doras. It's in Ballyanna . . . and twelve acres of land scattered about the area, savings amounting to ten thousand Euros and there's also all the objects within the property.'

She nodded very slowly.

'I must now apply for a Grant of Probate so that the estate can be distributed according to the will. I have taken the liberty of calculating the value of the inheritance for the Revenue Office – there will be inheritance tax to pay of course.'

'Are there no relatives who want to contest the will?'

'Donovan has many surviving relatives but none have contested.'

'So I will be in the lowest tax band as I am no relation.'

'You've done your research.'

'No. My grandmother recently died and it was necessary to know the law.'

'Oh. I am sorry . . . No. You will be in the middle tier.'

She frowned.

'I have been asked as a personal favour to give this to you Miss Shea.' He produced a scuffed leather satchel and placed it before her. 'In here you will find private letters and papers that Donovan wanted you to have on your first visit.'

'He was sure I would come?'

'Yes, he was, but I was also given instructions to send it to you if you stayed in Dublin.'

She unbuckled the satchel and peered inside.

'I have various papers for you to sign today so that the administration process can go ahead straight away. I will correspond with you regarding any other matters that arise. They will only be legal formalities. Unless you have any objection Miss Shea, I would like to leave you with the bag.'

'I've no objections,' she quietly replied.

'There are keys in there and maps with directions.' He stood looking down at her as she stared at the satchel. He quietly offered, 'I have no other clients this morning. I can escort you to Ballyanna if you like.'

'That won't be necessary – if I have a map . . .'

'Are you sure now? Those lanes are deceptive.'

'I think I can manage,' she smiled.

He laughed. 'That's grand.'

She frowned and he sat down again, looking her in the eye.

'Miss Shea. I told you I knew Donovan since I was a child, and though he was the kind of fella who would always talk to you no matter what, there was always a . . . reserve with him, as if something was hidden . . . or missing. There was some sadness . . . But I have to say that when he came here to me, to arrange this meeting, he was a changed man. He knew exactly what he wanted and when I had my instructions he sat back where you are now and seemed whole. I'd say he seemed satisfied.

'I tell you this not as his solicitor but as his friend, you understand. He was ill, no doubt, but the most well man I have even seen, if you know what I mean. That's why I laugh . . .' He stood again. 'You have so much to do and my number is among the details so you are not alone in this.'

She decided the man was neither inept nor relegated to a rural backwater – he was clearly where he wanted to be.

She stared at him and then asked, 'Mr O'Sullivan – am I related to Donovan?'

'How do mean?'

'Is he related to my grandmother in some way? Perhaps he is her brother?'

He cast his eyes down and reached into his jacket pocket. 'Lastly, here is a sealed letter which you should read first. I think it will explain more.'

Back at the river-bank, there was a moment of consternation when she thought the car had been stolen. It took a vague recollection that the car was blue, and a rifle through her handbag for the hire documents, before she was able to find the vehicle.

Sitting inside she watched the dancing willow leaves make battling ripples on the water. The solicitor's words echoed in her mind like a Mass in an empty church, rebounding through the rafters, overlapping and colliding and making the meaning indistinct. With a nail file she delicately tore open the sealed letter and heard Donovan's song-voice as she read.

Dear Orla

You showed me kindness on my excursion to Dublin and I was grateful. The way you were at such a time – showing such grace and care, made me proud. I have been tired and lonely for many years, but I have carried on as if I knew I had an unfulfilled purpose. When Peggy wrote to me at last, I went to her and I knew my purpose was found.

In the bag you will find the keys to the doors and cupboards and boxes in An Doras, my home for all my life and my family's home for over two hundred years. I wanted Peggy to share it with me but she could not.

Search the cottage and try every key. All of what you find is yours now and I want you to know it. In one particular place you will find the letters that Peggy and I exchanged, and some that were never sent. Please read them all Orla. I want you to know; we want you to understand.

Donovan O'Meagher

She forced the realization of what this meant out on to the periphery of her mind and sat there for sometime looking across the river but not seeing to the other side. It was warm through the windscreen and though she thought of so much she could not remember what.

There was a rap on the window and she was startled out of her vague reverie. A traffic warden with a face, Orla thought, like a bare arse in a nettle patch, stabbed the pane, indicating that the parking ticket had expired. He then thrust his thumb over his shoulder. Orla brushed the papers off her lap and gave him the thumbs up. As she pulled away she then gave him her middle finger and saw in the mirror, with some satisfaction, that he had noticed.

She pulled over outside of the town and studied the map, eventually tracing a route from Castleford to Morroe, a village on the way to Ballybrannigan and Ballyanna. Setting off, she found the ways were signposted well, but after passing the cavernous empty grain warehouses of Morroe, she was soon lost in the lanes beyond that narrowed and wound dangerously around blind bends and forked without warning.

She stopped and asked directions of a farmer in a tractor she was stuck behind for a mile or so, but even after she had deciphered his drawled instructions, she was lost again, and then, by chance, half an hour later, she suddenly saw a signpost for Ballyanna at a crossroads. She braked hard and sat there breathing fiercely, more from frustration and relief than from shock.

There was a narrow parking area on one corner of the junction, with a post box and picnic bench. She pulled in there and looked to where the sign pointed, switched off the engine, slowly unbuckled her safety belt and stepped out of the car.

The sign pointed down a lane that led into a dark avenue, where there were farm buildings among the trees. Beyond, perhaps half a mile away, she could see the glistening sea between deep valley sides.

She glanced about her, wondering if this was the Cross Mossy O'Sullivan spoke of. Where she stood there were more houses set back behind trees and hedgerow, but apart from her there were only cows and crows.

Then she heard the distant whine of an engine moving rapidly through the gears and saw a shining four-wheel drive speeding over the hill towards her. She pressed against the car door as the vehicle roared past and was gone again around the opposite bend. She shook her head. It did not matter where you were, she thought.

Slowly, she drove down into the valley, first of all passing what she now saw was a sprawling half-derelict dairy farm. Its vast sheds were dilapidated but the fine house was in good repair. She continued through a long avenue of trees, at the end of which, before a bend in the road, was the gate to a second smaller farm. Its sheds were clean and chickens and geese roamed across the yard and out into the lane. Most of the fowl fluttered into the ditch as she passed, but one flew up on to her bonnet. She hit the brakes again and the bird struck the windscreen. She was relieved to see it immediately revive, and then appalled when it began pecking at the paintwork.

Orla pressed the horn but the chicken just clucked. She got out and clapped, and the bird attempted to run, making scratching steps over the bonnet. Thinking of her rental deposit, Orla leaned over and shoved at the bird, shooing it as she did so. It fell on to its rear, spun around and fell over the passenger side. She rushed to see if it had been damaged, but it was already lost among the other birds in the ditch.

She straightened and brushed her hands together and felt rather pleased with her swift reactions. She did, however, glance up and down the lane to ensure her prowess had not been witnessed.

Passing several cottages along the lane she eventually reached a long house opposite a narrow boreen. The boreen ascended through the fields over a humpbacked bridge above a stream. Orla parked at a low wall where the lane split in two; one fork continuing down a steep slope to a strand and the other curving to the left up to a cluster of farms obscured by the hedgerow and trees along the hillside.

She stepped out of the car. The air was crisp and clear off the sea. She saw how the barren fields were emerging from winter, and as she breathed deeply, her thoughts turned to imagining the verdant beauty of summer.

She walked down the slope to the water. The lane cut between the cliffs to a crumbling slipway at the cusp of a wide bay. The tide was out, and the wave cut platform exposed. A lone fisherman was working out in the bay that expanded outwards along high sheer cliffs. To her right there was a small stony strand, on the other side of which were steps leading up to a cottage on the cliff edge.

Back on the lane above, she took the photograph from the satchel and matched it to the house opposite the boreen.

An Doras was long, perhaps the length of three town houses. At about halfway there was a porch. At the nearest end there was another door, but the windows each side had been boarded. The roof was new and so was the paintwork. Donovan had certainly invested in the building in the years before he passed away.

She took the single key from the bag and went to the door on the porch. Her hand was shaking as she pressed the lever, ducked down under the low frame and entered the gloom. Passing deep walls she inhaled the old cold earthen odour of open peat fires and damp.

Taking two steps up, she stood in a wide living-room on a solid stone floor. Light filtered in through a small window at each end. In a warm stasis of peace, the moment pulsated at her consciousness, but was lost when she found the light switch.

All around her, on dressers and shelves and occasional tables, was an array of plates, framed photographs and books, and of china and pewter ornaments. The open walls were crowded with paintings and prints in oils, pencils and watercolours. Many were faded and foxed. All depicted unnamed ruins, dramatic coastal views and archetypal portraits in traditional dress; they were the images one found in bazaars and thrift shops across the world.

Over the chairs and settees there were quilted and crocheted throws. The seating was arranged around a huge fire place with a circular belt bellows. Directly in front of the hearth was a reading chair under an ornate glass lamp stand.

She stood there for some time, absorbing the intense array, the age of it all and the absolute stillness.

She went to each room, standing at its centre and turning, weaving Donovan's presence with hers. The spaces spoke of a life lived for books and knowledge and perhaps unknown wonders. She thought the damp was the taint of his sadness.

She saw that the beds had been stripped and new linen folded on them. The windows had been left ajar and the place had been cleaned thoroughly. She almost regretted that there was little visible dust.

At the back of the cottage, on the other side of the living-room, there was a door, about three feet high. She stooped low to go outside and there gasped, for it led to a secluded garden.

Before her, about ten feet away, there was a stone wall supporting the bank of the field above. This wall curved around the cottage and was strewn with a hanging fuchsia bush that sheltered an intricately planted rockery. At the far end, a rose bush had been trained into a narrow arbour over the gate.

Among the stones, plastic labels had been inserted into the earth. She immediately recognized the flowing hand as Donovan's. She walked along rockery, reading the names: December Dawn; Rock Rose; Lanarth White; Bleeding Hearts, imagining the plants in the bloom.

She stood there listening to the sounds of the birds, wanting to name them. A cow lowed and a tractor spluttered across a far field. She could even hear the sea lapping below.

There was an ornate iron bench set into the flower bed and she sat down, trying to assimilate everything she had seen. If this was to be hers she would need to understand.

The solicitor's words remained in her thoughts, indifferent to her shock.

She went back inside and examined the bundle of keys. Some were labelled and she began to eliminate them, testing drawers and doors, each time checking for the bundle of letters. All she found were sets of photographs, stamps, books, porcelain, ornaments, postcards, and more books and paintings.

In one dry leather hat box she found an array of old letters dating from the nineteenth century, and received from America, Australia and England. Although sensing she was an intruder, the letters beseeched her to read them. Perusing a few random pages, she was drawn into the fears and passions of these dead souls.

Her eyes fleeted about the room, seeing it as it was, seeing a hundred lives passing through.

She sat on the bed reverently holding the brittle paper between her fingers and deciphering the graceful strokes in the faded ink.

. . . They came for you again in the night. They would not believe that you had perished. They would not believe that you could escape. The people secretly rejoice that the landlord is dead. It is more dangerous now but I think we will persevere. There is much talk of the Black Feather. Some say they have transformed into crows and flown to America . . .

. . . I think of him always, though I know it is forbidden. I feel no shame . . .

The letter was written to Brede Houlahan and signed by Frances Roche. It was dated 1846. The long dead names resounded in her consciousness and she sensed she should know them.

These personal items were what made history real to her and, as she sifted through other papers, she was compelled to read more, but forced herself to put them aside to resume her search.

By Donovan's bed she found a series of notebooks written by him. She skimmed the pages and found that in his fine hand he had recorded many folktales of the locality. She read a tale of a city beneath the sea, entered through a magical labyrinth. The stories of Nuala Phelan echoed in Donovan's words.

She found bundles of photographs and postcards. Sitting down once more she reverently looked through them, trying to visualize the people, their thoughts, their desires and their lives in those moments.

More and more the voyeurism was supplanted by a sense that she knew these people, or least wanted to. It was how she accessed history, moving beyond the grand scale of battles and politics and reigns, to imagine the human needs of love and survival.

By the open fireplace in the living-room, there was a door. Finding the key, she unlocked it and stepped through into a darkened room that was twice the area of the living-room. Feeling for a light switch she flicked it and saw what had been hidden behind the boarded-up windows.

It was clearly the disused pub.

There was a wide open space with a small bar to her left. In the far corner was a grandfather clock that reached the ceiling and opposite her was another substantial soot-blackened fireplace. On the low slung beams was an inexplicable series of metal rungs. There were a few tables and toppled sugan chairs, and on the shelves various artefacts were mouldering in the damp. The entire area was coated in a layer of thick dust and cobwebs, and the smell of wet soot and damp dirt pervaded. She could almost hear the people laughing and cheering and shouting.

It was at such moments she thought, that she would like to have her bubble on a thread through time and space, on which she could travel back, just to see it all as she could only imagine.

She closed the door and was once again within Donovan's space, feeling as if he was still there.

Outside on the porch she phoned Martin. The reception bars on her mobile were low and fluctuating; when he answered she could hardly hear him.

'It's a cottage by the sea,' she said.

'That's grand.' He immediately became businesslike. 'Now I want you to think about its rental potential, or its use as a summer retreat.'

'Or a home.'

'Someone might buy it and make it a home.'

'That's not what I meant and anyway, they'd have to love the country. It's way out in the countryside.'

'Are you coming back tonight?' he asked.

'I don't think so.'

'I thought you flew so that you could be back in a few hours.'

'I've changed my plans.'

'What's that?'

'My plans have changed.'

'Orla Shea has changed her plans?'

'Yes,' she smiled wryly.

'So when will you be back?'

'Tomorrow. I think I want to stay. You must see it Martin. It's all so . . . weird. I have these letters and it's like . . . I don't quite feel right receiving these things from a stranger.'

'I can't hear you. I'll see you tomorrow. I can't wait to see you and this magic cottage.'

She followed a crow across the sky. It landed atop a telegraph pole where it seemed to watch her.

5

Some One or Other of Their Sons

Strolling down to the stormwall she saw that the tide had risen and the lone fisherman was rowing back into the bay. Again, the sun broke through the cloud cover and was splendid across the bay. She decided to phone Bernadette.

'Where are you?' Bernadette's voice was faint.

'I'm stood on a cliff top looking down on a beach and a small bay. There are fields and farms all around me but, apart from a fisherman rowing towards me, the place is deserted.'

'And what have you inherited?'

'A cottage and land. It's an old place – very old, and you'll be pleased to know that there is a pub but it looks like it's been closed for years.'

'So I'm unlikely to find a fella there. Do you know why he left it to you?'

Orla reflected. 'There's so much to take in, Bernie. I'll talk to you when I come home.'

She snapped the phone shut and walked down to the strand as the fisherman rowed through the channel to the shore. When she reached him, he was out of the dinghy and dragging it through a bank of stinking wrack and kelp.

Tall and unshaven he glanced up and nodded as she approached. He did not smile but looked quizzically at her with narrow and deep-set eyes. She smiled though and grabbed the side of the dinghy, immediately gagging on the stench of decaying weed, fish guts and bilge. On the slats within the dinghy was a plastic container holding fresh lobsters and edible crabs.

'You don't have to do that, but thanks anyway,' he said.

'It's no bother.'

'No really, I'd rather—'

Staving off the nausea she pulled hard and slipped on the loose stones. Slumping on to her backside she slid into the weed at the water's edge.

She screamed shrilly and then sat there in shock for a moment before noticing the fisherman was now standing in the water in front of her.

'Are you all right?' His voice was high, fast and harsh, and he frowned as he held out his hand. 'Have you hurt yourself?'

She looked down at her shoes and skirt, stained and soaked through with filthy seaweed. Screwing her face in disgust, she began to brush away the weed with jagged futile strokes.

'You should have listened to me,' he reproved.

'I was trying to help.'

'Do you see anyone else here? How do you think I manage on my own?'

And despite the flecks of grey through his closely cropped hair, he could not have been much older than she was, yet he scolded her as if she was a child.

She shrugged and ignored his hand. Clinging to the dinghy, she pulled herself up.

'See the winch there,' he pointed past her as if the rusting contraption made it all clear.

'I was trying to help,' she repeated flatly, grinding her teeth and vainly brushing away the slimy weed.

'And I thank you for the thought,' and seeing no more than her pride was hurt his tone softened, 'but if you're not used to the strand you should be careful.'

He waded back to the other side of the dinghy. Like one of the pupils she reprimanded in the playground, she turned away, cursing under her breath as she trudged across the stones.

In An Doras she took off the shoes and skirt and with livid twists she scrubbed and rinsed them in soap powder she found under the sink. Hanging the garments outside in the back garden, she slipped on a pair of Donovan's trousers she had come across earlier. She then sat down in the reading chair by the fire with a glass of water, cold feet and a distinct dislike for the surly fisherman. She stared miserably into the cold grate, trying to assess all that happened.

There was the crunch of footsteps approaching from the strand and through the nets she saw the man carrying his bucket in one hand and his oars over his other shoulder.

As he had passed she heard a voice in the lane addressing him. She craned to see who it was but could not get an angle past the thick walls and small aperture. When he stepped out of view, there was a harsh exchange of words. Straining to hear, she could not discern what was said so she scurried through to one of the other rooms to get a better view. Holding back for fear of being seen, still she could not hear properly.

As she went back through there was a knock at the door and she opened it immediately. The other voice stood there smiling.

Unlike the other's hard features, this man's eyes were wide and he smiled easily.

'That was quick. Hello there. Is it Orla?'

'Yes.'

'Grand. Donovan asked me to make you feel welcome as best I could so here I am.' He held out a basket. Inside was a selection of wine, cheeses, bread, coffee, tea and milk.

'Thank you.' She took the gift. 'Please come in.'

He followed her inside.

'I'm Jack Callaghan. I own Ballygarry, the farm up by the Cross. You would have passed it on your way down.'

'The one that's half-derelict?'

'That's the one,' he laughed. 'The milking is done at another location now and the sheds no longer have any commercial use. They are too expensive to maintain and too expensive to clear. I try to keep the house tidy though.'

'I saw that . . . Please sit down.'

She pretended to study the contents of the basket whilst eying him. He was dressed impeccably; his tweed suit, that was crisply tailored, accentuated his imposing shape. His hair, she noticed had been cropped but well styled and his sideburns pointed emphatically down his jaw.

She quickly focused on the basket again.

'This is just what I needed. I was sat here with a glass of water wondering where the shops might be.'

'You'd have had trouble finding one. There's a store in Ballybrannigan and a garage in Garrymore, after that, the nearest is Morroe.'

'That's not much is it?'

'Well, it is the country.'

'Yes but there must still be many people . . .'

'Ah well, so many of the houses here are empty. They're holiday homes now.'

'But those people who are permanent. Where do they shop for this?' She glanced at the basket. 'This doesn't come from a garage.'

'There's farm produce and they all have cars now. They go to the supermarkets in Castleford and Dunfrae and Cork as well. It's all very modern.'

'I saw the developments on the way here.'

'It's what the area needs. They're about to open a new shopping complex in Castleford. It'll even have a multiplex cinema.'

She sighed freely, smiled and looked him in the eye. 'Will you have a cup of tea, Jack?' she asked.

'I will of course. Can I help?'

'I can see where everything is but thank you.'

She stepped into the kitchen.

'What do you think of the old place?' he called.

'The bathroom and kitchen are not so old.'

'Donovan spent some of his savings on that before he . . . He wanted to leave it habitable like. 'T'was my contractors who did the work.'

'I don't know if I'm pleased about that or not.'

'Well, there was no toilet or kitchen and now there is.'

She laughed.

'Now I'm delighted,' she assured him. 'I heard you arguing outside. I met your man on the strand earlier. He was . . .' She hesitated.

Jack stood in the door frame. Orla pulled a face.

'Ah, then you've met Patrick McLeavey.' He pursed his lips. 'I think it's fair to say that he was . . . angry – angry that Donovan left his home to you, well, to anyone but him.'

'Ah, no!'

'He saw me with the basket and you can imagine what he said.'

His slow and sincere phrasing made it easy to like him. She consciously suppressed the acknowledgement that he was handsome as well.

'I often brought Donovan vegetables – spuds mainly. He was kind to me as a child and I never forgot. He used to keep boxes of sweets to sell to all the children in the summer. Then, for the rest of the year, if we tormented him enough, he would give the local children what was left . . . You know he told me your name, but I didn't imagine . . . you.'

They held each other's gaze and she shivered.

'It's cold in here,' he said. 'Do you want me to set the fire?'

'That would be great.'

When she brought the tea in, the flames were high and casting a spectral hue about the room. Jack had put on the reading lamp and was on the settee, slowly feeding coals to the fire. On the reading chair was a pair of thick socks.

'For your feet,' Jack said.

She put the tray down and hurriedly slipped them on.

'There're peat blocks out back and there's a few sacks of coal . . . Here, I have this.' He held out a key.

'More keys,' she laughed.

His brows creased curiously. 'Donovan gave me a key,' he explained, 'when the work was to be done and towards the end so he didn't have to get up like.'

She took it from him.

'Did you know him well as a man?'

Jack shrugged. 'I think I did towards the end but he was very private and I think I was always in awe of him.' He smiled. 'There was something . . .

holy about him. I think he was to be a priest but he changed his mind. He would sit where you are reading his books and writing. People loved to talk to him outside there on the porch . . . He had so many stories about the place and the past. He could name every rock and stream for miles around . . . But in the end, as I say, he sat by the fire and had no more to say. When he came back from Dublin that was it. He saw you in Dublin?'

'He did, but he was there for my grandmother. They were friends during the war. They would write to each other.'

'They must have been close.'

'Um.'

'I mean, for you to have been given such a gift.'

She nodded, unsure of what to say.

'Ah . . . I can show you where he is buried. It is nearby.'

'I'd be grateful.'

'You'll have to wear something on your feet. You can pad out a pair of Donovan's boots with more socks. Why is it you're not wearing your shoes?'

Her feet were warming now.

'I fell into the water on that strand,' she explained.

He laughed.

'And who can blame you? It's steep, stony and slippery – but you've survived. You see, you've already a story of your own and you've only been here seconds.'

They walked together over the humpbacked bridge and up the steep boreen opposite An Doras. About halfway up, the lane leaned left sharply, and where it reached the seasteps above the strand, there was a cottage on the cliff top. There, the boreen turned back on itself in a hairpin bend and led up to a farm, the roof of which could be seen over the rim of the valley.

At the hairpin was a stile. Orla paused there and looked down across the bay and valley. From that vantage point she could admire the scale of the scattered homesteads and appreciate the wild beauty.

Jack took her over the stile and along an overgrown path to the western tip of the bay.

'Apart from for the funeral, this section of the Coastal Way is rarely used. Several of the cliffs towards Mourne Head have fallen away and it's not safe.'

'But we're safe?'

'Y'are of course, and you're with me.'

They followed the path to the end of the headland. It was high there and she noticed that just below the path stood a stunted tree, deformed by the wind into a witch's hand.

'That tree,' she exclaimed.

'I'd say the whole cliffside needs to be burned back,' Jack decided.

'But don't you imagine how long it's suffered there?'

'It's just a tree . . . I suppose it's something that the goats and gales didn't finish it off as a shoot.'

As she bemusedly shook her head she studied the vague lines in the grass on the slopes.

'What are those?' she asked.

'Slippage maybe.'

'They look like furrows.'

'No way. Who would plant there?'

He shrugged.

From the crest of the headland she could see into the next valley. It was a small inlet and above it, there were shallow hills. At the foot of the first hill there ran a stream that fell as a waterfall on to a small strand. On the second hill there were the four scorched walls of a ruined chapel. Beyond that, on the far slope, was a small walled cemetery.

'This is Andreenmacotter,' he explained. 'The chapel there was burned.'

She expected him to say more but he did not.

They walked between the gravestones and he pointed to one. As he stepped away Orla knelt beside it. She saw Donovan's name and her soul ached. Among the other graves she saw the O'Meagher name, and in her mind, the stones were remnants, a history she needed to know.

Jack was strolling down to the small strand. He was throwing stones into the sea when she approached.

'Thank you for that,' she said.

' 'T'was no bother; I didn't know what to do up there so I . . .'

'No. It was right. I'm fine. Thank you. This waterfall is beautiful.'

He shrugged again. ' 'T'is.'

She followed the stream across the sand and into the sea. The sound of the waterfall and soft waves were the only sounds in the serenity. It was fine place to rest, she thought.

On the way back she questioned Jack about Donovan's family. 'Did Donovan not have any closer relations here?'

'He did. The house there is owned by his sister, Anne McLeavey.' They were approaching the house at the hairpin bend above the strand. He stopped, turned and pointed. 'Through the trees there is Annamat. That's where McLeavey sits and plots.'

She could see a rooftop within a copse further up the valley.

'Is he that bad?'

He blew a sigh. 'Just be careful. There were some terrible shenanigans before you came, with weeping and wailing about what right a stranger has to the land.'

'Surely someone would contest it if they felt that strongly.'

'I'm told they tried, but they did not want to pay out the legal fees or maybe they knew that it was not theirs to expect. Donovan always said his people hated the outside world. He said they didn't know the world had changed when they hadn't. He was sure the valley needed to change and here you are.'

'I can't change anything.'

'We all can if we choose to.'

'The place must have changed by itself over the years?'

'It has but not enough. Take my farm. I own a fair amount of acreage but I no longer farm the land directly. There's a greater profit in others doing it, claiming my subsidies and making investments. I've had to change but I welcome it as well. These people here want to live in the past and waste the land. They own fields that have not been planted in decades. It's backwards but that's the European Union for you. It's a waste.'

'What do you invest in?'

'I've a few houses here and there which I've repaired and brought up to a modern spec with the traditional values like. The past wasn't all it was cracked up to be. It was hard and lonely out here. I see my job as bringing the past back to the future.' He chortled. 'People who come to the country want the appearance and the amenities. You saw my home. That's what I try to do . . .' They stood in the lane outside the long house. 'So what do you think of the place so far?'

'The valley remains old.'

'But the future will find it. It will change.'

'You misunderstand – I hope it stays the same.'

'Oh. And what of the house?'

'It's . . . dark,' she smiled.

' 'T'is,' he laughed.

'There are so many shadows, even in the garden.'

'I think Donovan wanted you to make it your own, to bring the light back in. Are you sure it's for you?'

She shrugged. 'I truly don't know. I don't even know if it's mine to take.'

'I think that is why he gave it to you.'

'I think there's more to it. I think there's a secret I've yet to discover.'

'Well I can't help you there. He told me nothing except that a Dublin girl would have it all. But, if there's any other way I can help you all, I will.'

She looked at him and he smiled sincerely.

'I appreciate that, Jack,' she said. 'I think I'll need it.'

He left her at the porch and promised to meet when she next returned. She thought of phoning Martin again but decided not to. Instead she went back inside, banked the fire and lay on the settee wrapped in a quilted blanket, staring into the flames. It was darkening outside and she was soon asleep.

She awoke in the night, hearing male and female voices passing on the lane. She was tearful as the couple shared laughter that faded into the stillness. Then there was only the crack of a log falling into the embers and the faint whisper of the tide. She felt apprehensive, staring at the shadows and fumbling for her mobile.

'What is it?' Martin groaned.

'I've just woken. I needed to hear your voice.'

'So there's nothing wrong?'

'It's very dark and quiet down here.' She could hear a siren in the distance over the line.

'It was quiet here too until my phone rang. Now I'm bloody wide awake.'

'Do you forgive me?'

'No.'

'Do.'

'All right I will, but only if you're on that flight back tomorrow.'

'I will be. I'll see you.'

She stared into the fire a little longer and was soon asleep again.

6

Then Voyeur

In the morning she smiled at the thought of Jack's kindness as she made herself tea and toast and walked to the stormwall. Through squabbling gulls she saw McLeavey's dinghy was still up on the stones and wondered if Donovan's faith in her would be enough when set against the animosity of this man.

Standing there made her feel on the edge of all things, perhaps too far away from what she knew; perhaps too desolate a place to know and feel part of; perhaps the family's antagonism would be too difficult to negotiate, but for all that, she wondered if all those souls who had gone before her saw it as she did – savagely beautiful.

She went back inside to pack her bag, find the letters Donovan wrote of and go home.

An hour later she sat in the reading chair with her packed bag at her feet, frustrated she had not found the hiding place, and resigned to driving to the airport to wait out the time in the terminal.

Then she saw it.

There was a door behind the bellows, obscured by the coal bucket. Working through the few remaining keys she opened the door to reveal a square toffee tin. Its surface was faded but pristine and on the lid was an old painted image of the General Post Office in Dublin Town.

She sat back in the chair and in the cold light through the window, prized the lid open. Inside there were two folded notes, a bundle of letters tied with a black ribbon, a selection of photographs and a black feather.

The photographs had clearly been taken outside An Doras, on the strand and along the cliffs. In them Margaret and Donovan laughed and held each other. She wondered who had held the camera. The last photographs made Orla gasp. One was of her mother and the other of Orla herself. Both women were girls again offering the shy gap-toothed smile for the school photographer.

She put the photographs to one side and studied the two individual notes, immediately recognizing Donovan's fine hand on one and her grandmother's on the other.

It was beginning to rain outside and the darkening sky was drawing the light from the room. Orla turned on the lamp and read the note from Margaret. The hand was uneven but still strong, clearly written shortly before her death.

My Darling Orla
I need no more words to express how proud and privileged I was to have you as my granddaughter. We shared so much and all that I said to you was true, but there were things I could not say even to you. Now you have found the letters and photographs you are beginning to understand why.

I have instructed Donovan to reveal to you all that was hidden. Please forgive me; those unspoken words were too painful to say, but I know you will listen now and try to understand.

My Love Always

There was a pain across her brow as the tears fell. Slowly she opened the next note, wiping her eyes with her sleeve.

Dear Orla
You know that Margaret and I met in 1945. Margaret was holidaying here and I was working in the fields. We attended dances, searched the strands and talked through the night, and we fell in love, but at summer's end she returned to Dublin and we exchanged letters. I loved your grandmother and I believe she loved me but our love was forbidden and it was a secret correspondence.

Meeting you has proven to me that my love for Margaret was not in vain and that I feel no shame. Please read these letters in the order they are dated. And I hope that it will help you understand the gift I have given.

Donovan

Orla breathed heavily. The revelation of love was less shocking than the admission that Margaret had kept a secret, even from her.

Untying the ribbon she sifted through the letters. They were postmarked Cork and Dublin and some were unsent. Carefully checking the franking she saw the first letter was postmarked Dublin and dated 1945. She slipped it from the envelope and gently unfolded it.

Dear Donovan
I am sorry for leaving without saying goodbye and I am writing because I want you know that all those things we spoke of, all the dreams we shared and more, were all real to me. I know I should feel shame but I feel only joy when I remember. Yet I was not honest with you because I knew that if I told you the whole truth the joy would end sooner and I did not want it to.

I am engaged to be married and I have been so for the past year. My fiancé is a fine man and our families are close. His name is Bertie and we have known each other since childhood. It was always expected.

I have sinned enough, Donovan, and I know you would not want me to suffer, nor I you. You are too fine and there will be another girl who deserves your kindness, your beauty and your mind. I only regret that it is not me.

Margaret Kavanagh

Orla read the letter again, almost feverishly, the words of suffering and shame resounding. She rubbed the heavy paper between her fingers, trying to imagine herself there, trying to understand.

She quickly read the reply, postmarked a few days later. The elegant hand was quick and long and desperate.

Dear Margaret
I waited on Cromwell's Hump for hours hoping you would come to me, and then I went into the village to discover you had returned to Dublin. I wanted to follow you and bring you back. But I realized I knew so little of your life there, and even less now.

I beg you to reconsider. What we shared cannot be for nothing. This man may be your friend but can he know you? Do you truly want him to? Is it too late?

There is no sin or shame in love, Margaret. We have done nothing wrong. How can you say there will be another? You are gone and I am broken. Heal me. Come back to me. I will wait for you.

Donovan

Orla folded the letter into the envelope and saw that Margaret had replied a few weeks later.

Dear Donovan
When I received your letter I could not cry because I have cried too much since returning. Tears were not enough. All I have left is the promise I made before I met you. I cannot betray my family or my fiancé when they are entirely innocent. I am resolved to marry and more so because I am pregnant with his child.

I meant every word I said to you but there are choices that must be made and I have made mine. Please do not follow me. If my infidelity were known, my life as my word would mean nothing.

I will never forget you or the love we shared. Our love was real, Donovan, but you must forget me – for me and for us.

Margaret

Orla's heart beat faster as she read on.

Dear Margaret
I know the child is ours. Tell me it is not so and I will trouble you no more.

Margaret, this love, this pain, is more than anything I have ever known and I will never forget you. Your words mean everything. You have honour but you also have courage. I will wait for you.

Donovan

Orla stopped, carefully straightened the pile and placed them in the satchel with the other items. It was raining hard outside now and she noticed how small the room was and how darkly the shadows fell. She sat there for sometime, thinking about what she had read; all the desperation and the naïve passion. She thought she knew how it would end but she wanted to respect their memory and their love and read the rest with time and solitude – in her own space.

Martin was waiting at arrivals. He looked fine, she thought, and though she immediately sensed a vague and elusive inadequacy, she laughed giddily and embraced him at the barrier.

'I've missed you,' he whispered.

She kissed him and ran her fingers through his newly cut hair.

'Very neat.'

'I told you I brush up well.'

He took her bags and led her to the car. They spoke of her excursion and she described the cottage and the cemetery and the views from the cliffs. She did not speak of the letters or Jack Callaghan.

'So the country crowd are angry,' he reflected. 'They'll be chasing you back to the city with pitchforks and scythes.' He laughed at his own joke.

'I just don't think they expected it to be a stranger. The house has been in the family for over two hundred years and then it was given to me.'

'Do you know why?'

She had rehearsed her response to this question. 'I think it was more of a gift to my grandmother than to me. He loved her all his life it seems.'

Martin sneered. 'And he never married?'

'No.'

'Jesus, what a waste of a life. Margaret had a good marriage with your grandfather.'

'She did,' she agreed.

'He must have been mad.'

She did not respond to that.

At her flat, Martin carried her bag. Flipping off her shoes she smiled to see the bunch of freckled pink lilies on the coffee table. As she stroked the blushing petals Martin handed her a box of chocolates.

'It has the pralines and the truffles you like. It was very expensive.'

'Which means I won't be able to resist.' She was both annoyed and impressed.

He went to the fridge and chose a bottle of wine while she cut the flowers over the sink. As she arranged them in the vase she inhaled the scents and thought of a hidden rockery in summer.

Martin uncorked the bottle and chose two glasses. Orla watched him in the mirror as she placed the vase on the mantelpiece, resentful of the way he moved about her home with familiar ease.

He embraced her from behind. 'When I said I missed you, Orla. I really meant it.'

His hands caressed her thighs and he pressed against her. She smiled at him in the mirror and turned and held his hands firmly down.

'I'm going to have a bath and then I'm going to bed.'

'To bed?'

'Aye, to bed,' she said.

'To sleep?'

'Yes.'

'Oh.' He looked over her shoulder at the flowers. 'Will I see you tomorrow?'

'You will, of course.'

'What about the wine?'

She kissed him. He narrowed his eyes and stared at her, trying to gauge the level of rejection.

'I will see you tomorrow,' she reassured as she walked away. He slapped her bottom and took his coat.

'You're lucky I love you.'

'I know,' she said.

'You would crush a lesser man with your will.'

'I know that as well.'

He grabbed her then, kissed her and left.

Orla stood alone in the hallway, still fraught after the two days of her expedition and all its expectations. It was then she made a decision. She finally knew what she wanted.

She wanted a bath.

She took the bottle of wine and a glass and went straight to the bathroom where she opened the taps. She poured in vanilla foam bath, dimmed the light and fetched the satchel. She then stripped, but just before stepping into the water, she remembered the chocolates.

Clutching her breasts she scurried through the flat, seized the box and was soon back in the bathroom slowly easing herself into the water. The water was too hot of course, and she quietly yelped as, by slow degrees, she immersed herself until she was finally down, inhaling the familiar scents of home, just glad to be back.

With a mouthful of truffle chocolate and a sip of wine she opened the next letter to the heady rush of earthen flavours and alcohol. It was dated several months after Donovan demanded to know the truth of the child's paternity.

Dear Donovan

You are wrong. It is too late. I have no honour or courage. I was married last month and the love I should feel is tainted by my weakness. My baby is becoming heavy within me and I am afraid. Everyone smiles and so do I, but my soul is shrivelled; my heart is empty. I live with the meagre consolation that you are in the world and you know that I think of you.

Please don't think ill of me. If we cannot be together, please help me. Be a friend, a voice, a hope.

My love, Margaret

Orla sipped the wine and took another chocolate. In that moment her heart was full: for Margaret, so much younger than she was today, such passion, such desperation; and for Donovan alone in Andoras.

Again, Donovan replied within days.

Dear Margaret

I am sitting in Andreenmacotter above the waterfall and my tears are falling into it. I know you are good, that fate is cruel and that my love for you will never diminish. I will be your friend; that will always be so. Did we not laugh every day? Did we not speak beyond words? Did we not leap with joy from rock to rock, falling together into the sea, holding each other beneath the waves, being as one in those moments? Perhaps this pain will end. Perhaps we can help each other.

Donovan

Orla slid back and doused her own tears. Under the water she held her breath, imagining the two of them beneath the waves. It was difficult to believe how the fervour of youth could last a lifetime. She tried to remember her own passions but there was none so enduring. Perhaps she cried then because of that.

She emerged; sipped more wine, bit into another truffle and read on.

The two of them began an affair of words – but there was nothing salacious, nothing unfaithful and never mentioning the accusations and demands the early letters pleaded with. Instead their exchanges settled into a familiar pattern of news and views, from the mundane to the extraordinary, and all confessional. It seemed neither had another in their life with whom they could share such intimacies. Their love was never again mentioned, nor the passion or the time they shared together one summer.

Donovan would write of his family's tribulations: the loss of his grandfather to tuberculosis; his sister Anne becoming a widow at the age of twenty four; his estrangement from his brother Seamus; the death of his mother and shortly after, his father. He would tell of the struggles on land and at sea, of crops and catches, of the perpetual seasons and eternal stories. And although he would never admit it, Orla sensed the world he knew was being lost to him as traditions were forgotten and celebrations ignored.

She read again his account of the day Maureen O'Hara visited Ballybrannigan. She laughed aloud as he described her fiery hair and wicked eye and how she took a launch to see the strands along the Imokilly coast. She even came ashore in Ballyanna, and of all the crowd of people who ran the Coastal Way, following the boat to meet her on the strand, it was Donovan who had carried her on to the stones.

When I held her in my arms I could have been Errol Flynn. She smelt as exquisite as she looked. She smelled of the darkest rose and the purest lily.

They had walked up to the Leaping Dolphin for a pint and there she told her tales of Dublin and Hollywood. Orla imagined them in that forgotten room with a fire cracking, the clock ticking and all the locals crowded in silent awe at, as Donovan put it, the star that had fallen to earth.

Margaret's letters were from a parallel world it seemed. Where Donovan dwelt in dank caves and on wild cliff edges, she inhabited a landscape of terraced streets, tended gardens and stifling respectability.

She wrote of the birth of her daughter and how she named her Maeve. She revealed how her daughter's coming transformed her despair to joy. She spoke of her husband's stoic care, and her affection for him that deepened over the years and anaesthetized the pain of regret and guilt.

Her life was as it should be. Her family prospered and she had it all until, in her words, Maeve gained her own mind. From a precocious child to a petulant adolescent, Margaret wrote of her sense of failure with her daughter; how she could no longer engage with her, and yet, her father, who idolized her, indulged her whenever he could, was in turn worshipped by the girl. She wrote of the increasing arguments about reprimanding Maeve's wayward exploits, and how Margaret was cast as the tyrant for expecting more. Orla chuckled wryly and shook her head when Donovan even gave advice.

These dances and the music are full of flavour, but the taste will last as long this gum they chew. I say take her aside and talk to her. Tell her the facts and if she will not listen then have her see the priest. He will know what to do.

Orla suddenly shivered, realizing the water had cooled. Leaping from the bath she stood there, dizzied by the speed of exertion and several glasses of wine. Catching sight of herself in the mirror she breathed in, trying to lessen the aesthetic corruption of more than that night's wine and chocolate. It was no use, and after the wine, she would leave caring until the morning. She quickly wrapped herself in several towels and gathered the letters in the satchel.

Then, because she was alone and would not be taken advantage of, she decided on another glass of wine.

In the bedroom she changed into her cotton pyjamas she never wore when Martin was there and went through the usual routine of checking the windows and doors so that she could curl up in bed to continue reading. Her stack of half-read detective fiction by her bedside would wait.

With the bedside lamp on, her teeth brushed and the rain against the window, she read of how Maeve was now seventeen years old and refusing to acknowledge her mother's existence, let alone her authority or advice. Margaret's letters carried an increasing tone of desperation.

Dearest Donovan

More and more I think about how far we have come and the choices I made as a girl not much older than my daughter now. I think about how I was so afraid of shame that I chose this life, this lie, and yet Maeve fears nothing. You know she is a stranger to me. I disgust her. She sees me as just a wife and mother and no more, but I am more, Donovan, you know that.

The old pain has returned. Bertie is a fine man and I cannot harm him, not now, but if I am nothing to her and he is all, it is unbearable. I want to scream. I want to tell them all the truth but I cannot – I am still a coward. So I must tell you and only you that he is not her father. I was untouched before I met you. You were the first.

I tell you this now because I need you to know. I need to know that the truth can be spoken.

All my love, Margaret

There it was. Orla exhaled and shook her head. She, too, wanted to shout at her grandmother for her foolishness. Not for the choices, but her motives in telling Donovan as she did.

She lay back on the pillow tracing the cracks in the ceiling. She realized that she knew what the letters would eventually reveal – she had known in the solicitor's office. Donovan and even Margaret had known she would understand if she just went to Ballyanna.

She sifted through the letters trying to find the reply but there was none. The next letter was again from Margaret and dated the following month.

Donovan

Why did you come here? Why did you do it? I told you the truth because I thought we could help each other and still have hope, but you almost destroyed everything.

When she came to me and spoke to me I did not know at first why and I searched for the words. I did not realize until she asked who you were and how I knew you. I denied it all, of course, but I am sure she was not convinced. The way she looked at me filled me with fear.

It was wrong to come here, Donovan. It was cruel to us all. There would have been a way but now she is even further from me – from us. She even spoke of the meeting to Bertie and he asked me to explain. I have lied again and what is worse is that he believes me; he has always believed me.

I have sent you pictures; I have informed you of the events in my life here; I have told you my thoughts, but you should not have assumed you had the right to anything more.

I don't know what to do now. I don't know if I can go on. I don't know.

Orla tried to think of the woman she knew, possessing such confidence and kindness and strength of will. It was hard to envisage her as this young mother. Donovan promptly replied.

Dear Margaret

You must go on. I am sorry for what I did. When I read your letter I took my coat and hat I left the valley. I sat on the train and all I could think of was the two of you – the three of us together. You are right; the photographs and the letters made me think that I was part of it all and I am not.

I am ashamed to say that I saw you on the Sunday. You were all together as you came from church. My God, you are so beautiful and I felt as I did on the cliffs that summer.

I waited at the end of your street and when Maeve walked towards me I had to speak to her and to know her. I, too, searched for the words when those I had rehearsed were suddenly preposterous. I was in a place I had never been before, talking to a child who knew nothing of me and making her afraid. It was ridiculous and cruel. You were right. She and her father are innocent. It is enough that I have seen her and she has seen me.

Orla lay back against the pillow, her soul swollen with the guilt and love in these letters. In her mind the confirmation swirled confusingly.

She thought of her grandfather. Until his death he had been the most gentle and kind person she knew. His patience and laughter had made her what she was. She remembered his funeral and Maeve's violent grief as Margaret had stood silently with Orla. Now Orla was beginning to see it differently.

She awoke before the alarm, startled and ready to go to work, but, realizing it was still halfway through the holiday she settled back. She was unsure of how much sleep she had had. She had read for hours. The letters were scattered on the bed and floor.

She had a headache.

But she could not decide if it was the truth of her heritage or bingeing on the wine and chocolate that had dulled her thoughts and thickened her veins. She lay there for some time trying to ignore her swollen bladder and thinking that her new diet would start that day.

When she eventually climbed out of bed, she struggled through her ablutions, had breakfast and watched the news.

Gradually reviving, her thoughts turned to what else the letters would reveal and she turned off the television and went back to the bedroom.

Gathering and ordering the letters again, the next had been posted several years later.

Dear Donovan
I know you have respected me all this time and I am grateful, but I am despondent without your words. Without knowing you are there, there is only emptiness.

Please write to me to let me know about you as you used to do. I will begin by telling you that Maeve is to be married. She is pregnant and claims to be in love with this man. I have urged her to look in on herself and question that love. She says she has and she is adamant. I do not want her to be afraid as I was, but she will not listen.

Even if you do not write, I will think of you and understand.

After his long silence, Donovan replied immediately.

Dear Margaret
I remain here. I think sometimes that life is passing me by. Where others have their families, my family is dying and I am alone. I have nothing but regret, but I have chosen this life. To the world I laugh and smile and pass the time of day but when I am alone, I think of you.

These feelings have not diminished. I thought they would if I stopped writing, but you are more precious to me now than you ever were. I want to believe again.

And so they settled into another bizarre routine, writing letters every few months or so. Orla cried again when she read the letters concerning her birth.

Her name is Orla. She is healthy and strong but her mother is bleak and will not tend her. I go there everyday and change and feed the baby and Maeve lies there. The doctor has assured us that it will pass.

There was the letter containing a photograph Orla had never seen. It had been taken on her first birthday.

I enclose a picture of Orla taken in my arms. I am looking at you. Can you see how beautiful she is?

By the time she reported her daughter's marriage breakdown, Margaret's relationship with Maeve was only cordial. Although she claimed to pass no judgement, it was clear Maeve's dissatisfaction with her marriage extended to her life – Maeve demanded a life of her own. To be trapped with a husband she did not love and child she did not want was too much.

Orla remembered the day her father left. He was a reticent man, distant and severe. She did not remember his touch at all, and then he was gone. There was no violence and no arguments; he just became absent.

Maeve took her daughter to her parents' house in Wellington Street. Orla sat in the front room while her grandparents went into the kitchen with their daughter. She remembered Maeve speaking imploringly of freedom and pain and a wasted life and that there was another man. Orla had gone to the kitchen door to see Margaret collapsing and crying and her grandfather consoling her – at last turning away from his daughter.

Maeve had passed her daughter in the hallway and went from the front door without looking back or touching her. Orla never lived with her mother again; it was Margaret and Bertie who ensured that their granddaughter had love and opportunity.

And while she lived, Margaret never spoke of that day to her granddaughter.

Maeve wrote a few letters from England and sometimes she would arrive around Christmas clutching envelopes containing cards with kisses and money. Sometimes she brought a friend; much later she was accompanied by a husband.

Orla had cried for her at first and then ached for her, and when she would arrive Orla would embrace her with childish desperation, pleading with her to take her with her. And Maeve would stroke her hair dutifully and say it was impossible. Orla remembered being consoled by the subtle scent of her perfumes and the perfect lines of her make-up when she smiled and denied her.

As the years passed and the visits became less frequent, Orla felt only guilt for her secret admiration and her desperate need, and she admired more her grandparents' patience and infinite love. When her mother's vivacious confidence became a hollow excuse, her make-up became overdone and her perfume overwhelming, Orla understood that whatever Maeve was searching for she had not found it in the other man or the next man or the man she married.

Orla feared making the same hollow excuses in her own life, yet more and more she wondered if she had.

Margaret wrote with pride about Orla's transition into womanhood, her obsession with history and her decision to become a teacher. Although, on wet Tuesday afternoons in front of a classful of uninterested fourteen-year-olds returning from PE, Orla had questioned the decision many times, Margaret had not.

And yet for all that she shared with Donovan, when she was finally free, Margaret did not send the letter that told him of Bertie's death. More than once Orla had to stop reading because of the pain in her chest and the tears in her eyes. But she did read and understand that when Bertie died it was in love and with love. She considered Margaret's reasons for not going to Donovan. Perhaps it had been too long; perhaps she was a coward; probably the grief and guilt over her husband were too much.

For his part Donovan continued to write. He claimed it was out of habit but his words were still heavy with the old love. He told of how the annual Ceremony of the Rest he had been planning in the summer before Margaret left was to be no more. He wrote of marriages and divorces, of the coming to the valley of Seamus McLeavey and his wife, of the birth of Patrick. He wrote of Roberto's return and the hope that the valley would be revitalized by their youth.

And then Orla reached the last letter. It was postmarked two weeks before Margaret's death.

Dearest Donovan
I write to tell you now that I no longer feel shame. I've had a good marriage and tried my best as a mother – I could do no more. All those people whom I did not want to disappoint are gone now and the world in which sin crushed my soul is almost forgotten.

Bertie is dead. He never knew our secret, and the guilt I feel is tempered by the years I gave him.

Maeve lives away from me now but Orla is here. She is still a fine and beautiful girl, faithful, intelligent and strong and I see you in her. I still remember you walking towards me along the Coastal Way; I could always see it was you from so far away with your straight back and long stride.

Donovan, I am dying. I am dying and I am alone. If you are able, please come to me so that I can see you once more.

For sometime, Orla sat on her bed. There was warmth in the room, a living warmth. It was still raining outside and she listened to the cars hissing by. The love in those letters revealed the indifferent cruelty of the world.

She smiled; there were no more letters except to her. Donovan had travelled to Dublin after receiving the last one and she had met him there and she was glad.

She was glad, but she sat there and cried into her pillow for a long while. She cried for the two lovers, for her grandfather, for a life unlived, for the death and the secrets and most of all she cried for her own loneliness.

That afternoon, she telephoned her mother. It was unusually quiet at the end of the line. Maeve was guarded, clearly, still resentful after their last meeting.

'I've been reading through some old letters Nan gave me,' Orla explained. 'Do you remember a man by the name of Donovan O'Meagher?'

Maeve did not immediately reply. 'Yes.'

'And what do you remember?'

'I met him once. It was just before I was to be married to your father.'

'Why do you remember him?'

'Because he claimed to be my father.'

'Nan didn't know that.'

'I didn't tell her.'

'Why?'

'Because my father was Bertie Tremayne. He still is.'

'Did you believe Donovan?'

'It didn't matter.'

'Did you believe him?'

'Yes. It was obvious.'

There was a long silence.

'Why?'

'Because my mother never loved my father – I know. I know because I lived with men I never loved . . . but I was not going to hurt Bertie, not even to hurt her . . . I loved him too much . . . So I didn't want to talk about it . . . And there's another reason,' she laughed. 'Like I said, 't'was obvious, I saw myself in him . . . In those letters – did Mum admit as much?'

'Yes.'

Orla could hear the smack of her lips as she heavily exhaled smoke into the receiver.

'The house is being sold by the way.' Maeve digressed. 'The firm I've employed is highly professional.'

'That's good.' Orla was not to be diverted. 'How do you feel about knowing Donovan is your father?'

'Not much. Does he want to meet me again?'

'He's dead.'

'Oh. Don't you want to know how much the house was valued at?'

'No.'

'Oh . . . I'll be free to do as I want now.'

Orla could not resist. 'Haven't you always been?'

There was a silence.

'I'm sorry, Orla.'

Then the phone went dead.

Orla squealed angrily. Maeve had done it again. She had given an apology without explanation. She had thrown it at her and expected it to be enough, like a pound note in a Christmas card, or a doll or a dress.

The scent of the flowers was strong in the room as she watched the rain fall. She thought about a loveless marriage, a life lived as a lie, of loneliness. She wondered whom she was most like. Was she like her father, distant and severe? Was she like her mother, wilful and selfish? She did not know, but she knew that she had to find out for herself.

7

The World Comes In

When the summer term began, Orla busied herself with planning and gathering resources. Finding new and stimulating material for revision was always difficult when most students wanted ways to avoid rigour.

One lunch-hour she had finished preparing a worksheet and was sat staring out across the playground at the oak tree, hoping to see the first yellow catkins. Smoke wisped about the trunk and she smiled to see Brendan stride across the playground and haul out a pair of likely lads.

She was thinking of Ballyanna. Her thoughts often turned to the cottage and the cliffs and she knew she wanted to go back again to explore the world in the letters. Perhaps Donovan had desired that.

There was a knock at the classroom door and she beckoned Danny Mulroney in.

'I've something to show you Miss.'

'Oh?'

He rooted in his rucksack and produced a box.

'My granddaddy gave it to me. He said he was given it by his grandma who was at a post office.'

Orla laid the forest green sash out across the desk.

'That was the Easter Rising of 1916,' she said.

He looked at her, blinking slowly. 'My ma says we could sell it on eBay and make a mint.'

Orla chuckled. 'You shouldn't do that. This is a rare artefact, but you won't get much I'm sure. It must be kept in the family . . . or in a museum. Your job is to keep it safe.'

'You have it, miss.'

'No. It's yours, but thank you.'

'I love the history, miss, but only because you teach it. All the other subjects are boring. All they do is make us copy.'

'I don't want to be hearing that now and I know it's not true.'

He shrugged and smiled.

'But I'm glad you have such an interest,' she added. 'Did your father tell you any stories about your . . . great-great-grandmother?'

'He said she met a man called . . . Collins.'

'And what did he say about him?'

'He said Collins was a fierce bollix from Cork but they are all like that down there.'

She laughed out loud.

'I have these,' she said, and took out her diary. In it she had the photographs of Donovan and Margaret.

Danny slowly scrutinized them.

'That's my grandmother and grandfather in a place called Ballyanna . . . in Cork.'

Impervious to irony, he observed, 'They're happy.'

'That they are. I'm finding out all about their lives and that place there.'

He shrugged incomprehension and she smiled as she folded and handed back the sash. 'Why don't you do some research on these things and the Post Office and write a presentation for me?'

'Writing?'

'You can use the library and download pictures and the writing from websites.'

'You really want me to?'

'Of course.'

'I will. I'll go to the library now.'

'But talk to your father about it as well. Find out what else your family knows,' she called, but he was gone.

She returned to her tuna sandwich and bottled water. The tuna was repulsive and she threw it in the bin. It sometimes seemed that her troubles were skewed – keeping to a size 12 often seemed more important than finding purpose in life.

She made a decision in that moment to travel down to Cork at the weekend.

When she informed Martin, he offered to go with her, as did Bernadette, but Orla wanted to go alone once more.

She took the train to Castleford on Friday evening and watched the light fade across the fields until her face was reflected against the dusk. She read the rest of the way, entering another frozen murder scene where a detective, a recovering alcoholic, failed husband and abandoned friend, was meticulously unravelling the forensics.

In Castleford she managed a circuit of the superstore before taking a taxi the rest of the way, arriving in the darkness, tired but exhilarated. Dropping her bags in the porch she walked to the stormwall and looked back up the valley at the scattered lights. The moon was on the water across the strand below. She sensed the serenity. In the city it was so easy to feel dislocated, to be in crowds and yet feel apart. More often it seemed that life was ephemeral, and most people had little sense of their past when progress was to be made and entertainment to be had. That her people had walked this way for centuries made her feel part of it all. She imagined their shadows all about her.

Inside An Doras she set a fire, made tea and revelled in unpacking a selection of her favourite books she had brought with her, placing them on the high mantelpiece. The fire was strong now and she sat before it, watching the flames and feeling quite content.

In the firelight she began to read more of the old letters she had discovered. These were from Brede to Frances Roche, telling of her struggles in Boston. After fleeing the Famine and escaping the noose it seemed as nothing to her life in the New World.

. . . Though we have suffered we considered ourselves lucky. The captain was merciful and ship was worthy of its crew. I was near death but Jack was with me always. 'Where else had I to go?' he said . . .

. . . These barracks of Paddytown are a hellish place and not fit for good people. The rooms are airless and dark and filled with fear. There is much drinking and fighting and cursing, but we have loyal friends and no one will come near us to take what we have. They have tried but we are one . . .

. . . The people are no more than slaves. The politicians and the money-men as we call them are a canker one and all, but they are afraid of us and they should be. We are out of the Barracks now and as it was in the valleys our power is the night and the eternal light . . .

She fell asleep dreaming of her savage heritage and the following morning she was up with the first light, feeling charged, feeling as if she could have been one of those distant daughters.

After a walk to the stormwall with a cup of tea she was back inside emptying all the kitchen cupboards and wiping them down. On the shelves she stacked her usual shopping fare of rice and pastas, dried herbs and spices, tins of chopped tomatoes and soya chunks. When the meagre fare was arranged she stood back, realizing how crude her culinary skills were. She supposed it was a lack of time, her grandmother's expertise and too many take-aways that had crippled her in the kitchen. She supposed all she needed was someone she wanted to cook for.

She placed several neatly packed cardboard boxes of loose tarnished utensils and cracked crockery in the outhouse. There, against a collapsed fireplace, draped in web and ivy, she noticed a rusting bicycle. From the cracked leather saddle to the flat carry frame before the handle bars, the uncompromising contraption scorned her comfortable life. Tentatively, she touched it, touching the past, knowing it a little more.

Very soon after this, she was back inside and had set upon the bathroom, knowing that until she had cleaned completely, she would never settle. On her hands and knees, scrubbing every corner, she was disappointed to discover the linoleum was poorly cut, the sealant messily applied and the cistern cracked and leaking. Indeed, despite the scour of bleach there was still a faint odour of waste, and she made a mental note to ask Jack about the drains.

In the shower afterwards, she stood for sometime in the soft flow, allowing herself to feel both cleansed and at ease at last.

Only then did she have breakfast, sitting in the reading chair and studying the maps from the satchel.

There were two: the first was a printed section of the immediate area around Ballybrannigan Bay; the second was a hand drawn affair of Ballyanna and its environs. The letters were in Donovan's fine hand. On it, the twelve acres of land she had inherited were marked. She decided she would walk the fields and find them.

Before leaving, she tied her hair back and took out her cosmetic bag. Pulling at her face in the mirror, she was able to ease out the subtle lines. She began her make-up routine with the powder but immediately paused as Patrick McLeavey strode past outside.

Blowing a quiet raspberry, she clipped down the powder puff and put it away. Then, whisking on eye liner and lipstick she declared herself ready.

She followed the stormwall up to the stile which led on to the Coastal Way. Jack had told her the path was popular with walkers and she followed it past the western cusp of the bay to the headland beyond.

On the way her mobile rang. She saw it was Bernadette and hissed a curse.

'What a night,' declared Bernadette.

'What happened?' Orla asked, assuming it was just another man.

'The speed dating.'

'Ah Jesus, Bernie.'

'I told you all about it.'

'No, you didn't.'

'Yes, I did.'

'You didn't because you know I would have discouraged you.'

'Well, I'd have taken no notice and I'm glad I did it . . . I have to tell you. I went round the room, thinking it was no use and he was the last one I spoke to. It was destiny.'

' 'T'was desperation.'

'I think this is it.'

'You're faint. We'll speak later.'

She turned the mobile off.

On the local map the she saw that the small cove there beneath her was marked Guileen, and the headland on the far side, Cromwell's Hump. It was to the summit she climbed and at the peak took out Donovan's letter and read it once more as it flapped in the wind.

He wanted her to know and understand, and there, between the sea and the sky, she turned and turned, thrilled as the wind rushed against her.

At her feet was a lichened depression in the rocks. She stepped into it and knelt out of the wind. It was warm and silent there and the isolation was intense. In the letters, Donovan had written of the Hollow he and Margaret would lie in, and she was sure she had discovered it.

She stepped out and looked from the map to the ground, getting her bearings. Three miles away along the coast were the three islands called Lir's Tears, clearly marked on the larger map. Trying to hold the smaller map straight in the wind, she saw that beneath the headland, there were submerged rocks called Manannan's Fingers. She smiled, remembering again Nuala Phelan's retelling of Lir's grief.

It seemed the first of the twelve fields was beyond the headland, past the slopes of heather. Martin was always the one with the map, striding determinedly through the city streets as she followed. She had encouraged this; it allowed her to do what she was there for, which was to absorb the scenery and appreciate it all undisturbed. It was the same when it came to the car. She would never drive when he was with her. She told him it was because he was so assertive on the road and he intimidated her, but it was only because she wanted to admire the views and maybe read a bit and then doze if she was tired enough. However, when she suggested they buy an old Dormobile and drive around Europe together, Martin had asked her if she appreciated the distances, and more, would she be sharing the driving duties? She had said there was no way she was driving on the wrong side of the road, and so he had instantly and adamantly refused.

As she considered the best path to take, a woman approached along the path. She was about her age and clearly pregnant. Orla waited and greeted her.

'Are you lost?' the woman asked, smiling easily. To Orla, her freckles and tousled red hair imbued her with innocence, but her eyes were fierce and defiant.

'Not yet. I'm looking for this field.'

She showed her the map.

'That's Donovan's map . . . You're Orla.' She held out her hand. 'I'm Saoirse Cesare. I'm married to one of Donovan's great-nephews.'

Orla was guarded.

'I'm pleased to meet you. It's only my second time down here and I thought I'd explore.'

'If you follow the path along, take a left where it splits and it'll take you up to the field. You can't miss it; there's standing stones there.'

'Thank you. I see you're pregnant. When's the baby due?'

'In August.'

'Is it your first?'

'Oh yes. These O'Meagher babies are monsters, I am told.'

'Should you be out over these hills in your condition?'

'Of course! I was just turning the carrageen moss. I've been collecting it and laying it out since Donovan died. He would sell it to Killybeg House. That's where I work. There's no money in it but they like it that it's local which has got to be good.'

'And what do you do there?'

'I work on the estate and I guide the visitors through the gardens in the summer. I tell them the history and I give advice about the planting. This year though . . .' She patted her belly. 'What do you think about what has happened with the inheritance?'

Orla recalled Jack's warning about the extended family. It was difficult to believe this woman was resentful, but she was reluctant to reveal too much about herself.

'I've not really come to terms with it yet. I'm still absorbing it all. That's why I'm looking around, you know.' There was a silence as Orla averted her eyes.

Saoirse said, 'Donovan used to say that this hill was where Cromwell's men threw children from, and down there is where we fish in the summer. They say that when you snag a rock it is the children's grasping hands.'

Orla smiled grimly and Saoirse waved.

'I'm desperate for a pee so I'll be off now.'

'Thanks for you help.'

' 'Tis no bother. If you're passing please drop in. We're in the workshop at the bend in the road, before the trees. Perhaps we'll see you.'

Orla took the left path that led on to a wider tractor path curving over a hill into the upper fields at the eastern edge of the valley. Where the path ended was a gate to a wide pasture. She looked across and saw the standing stones on the opposite side. On the map they were named the Damanta Stones. She opened the gate and went to them.

There were three pitted stones; one still upright, one fallen and the other leaning against it. They reminded her of a world far more ancient than a few transient centuries.

The fallen stone made an ideal seat and she saw by the muddy pit at the base of it, that others had sat as she then did looking back across the valley. The sun cast a clean and pure light that morning, flowing across the farmsteads and fields, and she thought she was beginning to know the place.

The sun was warming as she held her face up to it. She took off her shoes and just listened to the silence.

For many minutes she simply sat there, thinking of nothing, until eventually she shivered, suddenly appreciating that it was too exposed on the hill.

So she sat on the grass where the stones offered a break from the wind. Soon she was asleep dreaming vividly.

She awoke with a gasp; the sun was hidden and she was in shadow. Her dreams had began as an amorphous array of situations with Donovan and Margaret, and from their love denied, her dream had weaved away through time, back to the Black Feather and shipwrecks and soldiers without mercy.

She sat up startled when she realized Jack Callaghan was standing before her. Peering up at him, she was reminded again of how squarely handsome he was and how it was slightly intimidating.

'How are you?' he asked.

'Fine,' she croaked, quickly gathering her senses, touching her hair and straightening her jacket.

'I saw you from the boreen. I thought you would be off exploring the fields. I hope you didn't mind.'

'Not at all. I hope I wasn't snoring.'

He laughed.

'Just a dribble there.'

She wiped her lip.

'Only joking,' he quickly admitted. 'I hardly recognize you without the make-up.'

'Is that good or bad?' she asked, appalled by her own coyness.

He just smiled and she blushed and looked down to the map at her feet.

'I see you have the map.'

'The map?'

'I helped Donovan draw it. I can show you the rest of the plots if you like.'

She was irked by the intrusion. 'Actually, I'd rather explore at my own pace.'

'Oh . . . Well, what have you found so far on you explorations?'

'Just this field and these stones.' She indicated to the map and he glanced at it. 'I think it's part of Donovan's land.'

' 'Tis. It's the best site in the valley – a prime location. Can you imagine a house up here? What views?'

'I can't imagine building here at all. These stones must be sacred.'

He laughed. 'Whoever put them up saw the same sight . . . Listen, would you like another kind of tour? I'm off to Ballybrannigan and I can take you there and show you a few other places.'

Cold and with her bladder aching, she accepted and so they walked together down to his Range Rover outside An Doras.

As they drove through the lanes she noticed the interior was yellowed.

'I didn't realize you smoked,' she said.

'Do you?' he asked.

'No.'

'Well, I've given up,' he said.

Further on, he pointed out various properties and fields and they stopped occasionally to see the views. On the hill above Ballybrannigan she stood for a moment contemplating the bay and the mountains beyond. She then cast her eye along the single road through the whitewashed village along the western edge of the bay to the lighthouse in the distance. Below the grand church on the high ridge above it all, the houses were pressed against the hillside like ancient spume.

'Over there, the church is called the Star of the Sea. It's where Donovan attended Mass.'

'It's a beautiful village.'

'But it's dead.'

'Oh.'

'It's not what it was. Locals are leaving because they can't afford the house prices and the people who can are only here for a few months of the year.'

'There must still be life in it.'

'The world is changing too fast for it, I think.'

'There must be a way to revive it.'

'We could build more houses . . . cheaper houses.'

They drove slowly through the village, passing a pub, the post office, a pristine shrine, disused dancehall, a hotel and a lifeboat station. With the holiday homes empty, the place possessed a forlorn beauty. Jack parked above the pier by the Compass Pub.

'It's a different place now,' he explained. 'When I was a boyeen there were ten pubs but now there are just the two. Maybe it's a good thing. They have music back at the Laughing Gull. Perhaps you'd like to go next time you are here?'

She nodded.

'Many people from Dublin have bought homes here. Do you intend to move here, or sell, or. . . ?'

'I don't know.'

He changed the subject.

'Over there is Garrymore. The sandy beaches curve around the bay for miles.'

They sat there for sometime as he pointed out the places she already knew.

On the way back they stopped at the post office beside the general store. She browsed around the shop while Jack went next door.

With delight she found they had a selection of Nuala Phelan books. Included among them was a reprinted collection of short stories she remembered from her childhood in Wellington Road, but this new edition included exquisitely painted images of the old gods. Both monstrous and human she saw that Lir, Anu, Manannan, Nuada and all the facets of the Morrigan were there. She went to the counter.

She stout shopkeeper stared at her. His rolled-up sleeves revealed an array of faded tattoos.

'Ah. She was read to you as a child no doubt.'

Orla laughed. 'She was, and I've always loved the stories. They live in my imagination still.'

'Sure, you know why we sell her books?'

Orla shrugged, not quite understanding.

'Didn't you know she's from here?'

'I knew she's from County Cork. Do you mean she's from Ballybrannigan?'

'From this very shop.'

'Get away.'

' 'Tis true. I'm not codding you. The Phelans owned the place. She was their only child.'

'And where does she live now?'

'She has a house along the coastal road near Mourne Head, but she's no stranger. She comes and goes. She's a fine girl. They say she's in America at the moment.'

Orla stood shaking her head and grinning rather foolishly.

'You should have a plaque to let the people know,' she enthused.

'Ah go'way. Now, you're a Dublin girl, are you not?'

'I am.'

'I can tell by your speech. Now tell me, do you know a man by the name of Noonan? Gerald was his first name.'

'No,' she said. 'No, I don't.'

'Are you sure now? He was about this tall with a shock of white hair. He looked like a ghost with great big eyes . . .'

She purchased the book along with a fresh loaf of bread and waited by the car, remembering the heavy book that had arrived one Christmas, knowing now that it was Donovan's gift.

When Jack returned her to the valley she thanked him.

'It's not a problem, Orla. You know where I am.'

She sat there for a moment, not knowing why, and then thought he leaned towards her, but she was unsure because she had opened the door and was on her way out of the car. She stood in the lane and watched him go, wondering what she would have done if she had stayed a moment longer.

Elannat had been built into the hillside at the top of the seasteps. Occupied by the coastguard for fifty years it had been purchased by the O'Meagher family at the turn of the century, and from its high vantage point the generations since had continued to watch the sea that was their life and death.

At the end of the house was a conservatory which commanded views over the bay. Having decided to introduce herself, Orla knocked on the windows there. The blinds were half-drawn, but she could see faded wicker chairs inside and a pair of binoculars stood upright on the window sill.

The door within opened and, possessing the same fierce blue eyes and arch expression as her brother, Orla immediately recognized the woman who approached her.

It seemed Anne McLeavey also recognized her.

'Orla,' she whispered, coming out to her and taking her hand. Orla took it and the woman drew her close. 'You have come home to us at last. Please sit down.'

The chairs were comfortable and it was pleasantly warm in the conservatory, but as Anne spoke Orla found herself distracted by the sight of a cloud shadow racing across the waves.

Anne smiled. 'I have been fortunate to see this view every day. Others say it never changes, but I've never tired of it. I see it changing from moment to moment. If you look at it enough the colours, the light, the sea and the land – they are never the same.' Anne's eyes were fixed on her and Orla was perturbed. 'I've seen you at the stormwall.'

Orla looked away and did not know why.

'In the past people would stand there and gossip,' Anne said. 'We didn't know what was true and what was not, but we laughed all the time. I think Donovan even laughed at times . . . Over the cliffs was where he liked to be most of all – walking, waiting, searching . . . He could name every crag, cave and cove along the coast.'

'I'm sorry I did not come here before,' Orla offered. 'There was so much to do. No . . . I just didn't expect it to be the way it was.'

'I understand. Donovan was determined for you to come here. Did his scheme work?'

'What do you mean?'

'Before his death he talked to me of his hopes.'

'What did you say to him?'

'What could we say sure? He knew his own mind; neither I nor Patrick could change it, and I think we knew him best. We were with him to the last and he was adamant.'

Orla did not know what to say.

'Are you thinking this could be your home?' Anne asked.

Orla frowned 'I don't think after . . . Dublin is my home and there is the inheritance tax.'

Anne waved dismissively. 'They let you pay it in instalments. Speak to Mossy O'Sullivan.'

There was a silence in which Orla could hear the wind softly singing around the eaves.

Anne smiled. 'I saw you up at the Damanta Stones this morning as well. You know there's a spell cast for anyone who sleeps there. You didn't take forty winks now did you?'

'What sort of spell?'

'To trap you here forever.'

'I did sleep a little.'

Anne laughed and so did Orla.

'Have you had trouble sleeping in An Doras?'

'Not at all. It's very comfortable. The sheets and pillows were pristine.'

'I changed the linen again when you left last time.'

'Oh. Thank you . . . I didn't realize.'

'Donovan asked me to.'

Orla smiled uncertainly.

'You have made friends here already,' Anne stated, still staring at her.

'I think I have. Jack Callaghan has been very helpful.'

She saw Anne bridle.

'That is good,' Anne said. 'He is charming. He will help you, of that there's no doubt.'

'Is there something I should know?'

'I'm sure Jack has told you all you need to know.' There was an uneasy silence which Anne broke. 'You know I'm the last of Tadhg and Shelia O'Meagher's children. All my brothers and sisters are gone.'

'Are you lonely up here?'

'Not at all. I'm always having visitors and I have my grandsons and my son of course.'

'And a great-grandchild soon.'

'Yes!'

'Can you tell me about Donovan?'

Anne seemed to relax again.

'He was a religious man – some say spiritual. Do you go to Mass, Orla?'

'Um . . . Yes. Um . . . I do.'

Although Orla had lied, Anne shrugged, seemingly satisfied.

'People also said he was a queer hawk.'

Orla was bemused.

'Strange,' Anne clarified.

'And was he?'

'He was not. A more kind and gentle man you wouldn't meet. They said he was foolish, but he knew his own mind . . . and now you are here.'

'Foolish because he never married?'

'And he could have, many times over. He was tall and athletic and his mind was sharp, but he chose to be alone.'

'You know I met him in Dublin before he died.'

'He told me so. He was very proud . . . but his time in Dublin changed him. He had been weak for a while and after he came back, after your grandmother died, he had no will . . . He was always going to the church, down the strand or just sitting on the porch talking to passers by, but when he returned he stayed inside . . . He stopped reading, eating, setting a fire, or even talking. He wrapped himself in his blanket, wrote his letters and waited to die. He only let a few people in. Patrick and I went down there often.'

Orla looked at the old woman.

'Did you ever meet my grandmother?'

'I did. I thought she was a grand girl altogether. She was older than me and from the big city and so I was in awe of her. I thought she was like a film star . . . People came and went all the time in summer and we thought nothing of it, but after she left, Donovan was darker. Perhaps only I saw it, but he was.'

Anne made tea and they talked on about the valley and the past and Orla listened with relish to the tales of the place; many she now knew, but Anne's perspective gilded them.

But the more she listened the further away the old woman was. Her words were of another world, a world Orla could never know.

After an hour Anne announced that Saoirse and her grandson Roberto were to take her shopping in Cork City. She invited Orla.

'Thank you but I think I'll walk over to Andreenmacotter,' Orla decided.

'You know the way over Gortagort?'

'Gortagort?'

'The Famine fields. You can see the ridges on the slope where the people planted. It was the only place left to them.'

Orla realized what she had seen on her first visit. 'I'd like to go to explore more of the place by myself,' she said.

Anne opened a drawer and took out an old brass telescope. 'Explore away so. And take this with you. It was Donovan's for when he would come up here and watch the ships.'

Orla examined the antique brass telescope, admiring the patterns etched into the rims and imagining what had been seen through it. At one end were the initials *J.B.*

'It's yours now.'

Promising to return, Orla left Elannat and set off westward along the Coastal Way.

The wind was light as she strode through the heather and stopped at intervals to absorb the bay. Alone in the afternoon she was struck by the desolate beauty of the place, but more by the thought that she could be part of it. She thought that perhaps she was closer to the world Anne described than she realized.

From the rocks below, cormorants dived, the gulls scavenged and she even saw a hawk hovering in the field. What most delighted her were the seals basking in the meagre sun and out in the bay, a pod of dolphins breaking the waves.

Through the telescope there was an even greater peace; only the sight of Patrick McLeavey pulling lobster pots broke it. She watched his rhythm as he heaved at the lines and inspected the baskets. She folded the telescope and walked on.

Below her she again traced the lines in the cliffside and noticed that where they ended there was a vague path that led down to the raised spur on which the twisted tree clung. She followed the gentle slope down and discovered that on the other side of the outcrop was an aperture obscured by bracken. She crouched, pulled the plants aside and peered within.

The hole was high, and wide enough to take a stooping adult. At the lip, steps which disappeared into the darkness had been dug out of the ground. She also noticed an old ship's rope was tethered to the wall and this too followed the steps down.

She could hear the hiss and boom of waves below.

She smiled, imagining she was Persephone and descended. Even more, she wondered if this was the entrance to the Otherworld that Donovan wrote of.

The wind moaned despondently through the tunnel and she steadied herself on the rope. It was adventurous not knowing what she would find. The darkness deepened, but as her eyes adjusted she could detect a faint light below; although vague, it filtered across a wide chamber she stepped out into.

Even in the gloom she could see the jet striations and wet coloration on the walls. The roof arched in a crude hemisphere across which faint stars of light seemed to flicker. The cold air was heavy with shadows and she closed her eyes, feeling as if she was among an invisible multitude that silently clamoured and called out to her.

'Hello,' she called, her voice falling dully against the darkness. 'I'm here . . . I'm here,' but the sound seemed to slide between the rocks, lost forever.

On the other side of the chamber she saw a hue of light from another way in, and she went to it. As she did so her knee struck the edge of a stool and an old lamp fell on to the damp sandy floor. Replacing it, she knelt over the edge of the hole and saw she was above a gully at the base of the cliffs. Now she could clearly hear the sea beyond.

She sat there momentarily between the darkness and light, between the decision to go back the way she had come or to explore further. Feeling girlish and daring she decided she was enjoying herself too much and so she swung her feet over the ledge and dropped down the six feet on to the soft sand.

There she stood in a narrow gully between two high sided rock faces. Where the rocks sloped into the waves, a seal she had seen from above took one last glance at her before splashing into the water.

She walked to the water's edge and was able to see Cromwell's Hump on the other side of the bay. However, though she craned her neck she could not see the strand. Apart from her footprints on the sand and the limpets on the rocks, the place was barren and she decided to climb back.

At the cave entrance she gripped the ledge above her head and tried to haul herself back up and could not. She stood there, only slowly realizing what she had done.

Feeling foolish she waited a while then stepped back to find another way out. There was a way up the cliff side if she could climb out of the gully, and so she ran her hands along the sheer rock faces, looking for handholds, but there were none. In frustration, she tried to ascend anyway, cramming her fingers in the small striations and cracks but getting no more than a few feet from the ground before slipping on the wet surface, striking her knee on the rock and falling on to her backside.

She sat on the sand caressing a deadened knee and feeling slightly weepy, but not yet fully able to appreciate her predicament.

She studied the waves rushing in and out of the gully, trying to determine how far they would reach and whether the tide was coming in or going out. She did not know.

She then saw a walker traversing Cromwell's Hump on the other side of the bay. She waved and shouted to no avail. Taking out the telescope she focused on the figure and helplessly watched it disappear over the ridge.

It occurred to her that she could swim back to the strand or, better still, climb the rocks from where they entered the sea. Taking off her shoes and socks and rolling up her trousers she began to paddle out, but the waves were up to her knees by the time she was six feet out – more, the water was numbingly cold and she knew there would be no swimming for her.

As she turned to trudge back through the tide she heard the splash of oars. McLeavey rowed into view.

'Hello,' she called, forcing a smile but actually elated.

He stayed his paddles on the rowlocks and stared at her there.

'I think I'm trapped,' she admitted, grimacing now.

He shook his head in exasperation.

'Is there a way you could help me? Perhaps send someone down to the cave back there and give me a hand up?'

He continued to shake his head. She was losing her temper now and also the sensation in her toes.

'I was exploring,' she found herself explaining. 'I think I was too adventurous.'

She laughed nervously: he dipped his oars and rowed on.

'Will you help me?' she called, her voice echoing against the walls. 'Where are you going? Can you send someone? Please! I need a rope or a ladder or something.' Out of the water again she paced back and forth, reviving the circulation to the toes by digging them viciously into the wet sand. 'So ignorant; so ill-mannered; so bloody superior,' she accused.

Flouncing against the rock wall she continued to curse and even cry a little. So much for adventure; all she had found was a damp and dark gully, and she did not even know what she was looking for.

'If you give me your hand, I'll pull you up this way.'

She gasped and turned. Silhouetted above her was McLeavey. He had clearly climbed up from the next gully. His hand hovered. She sniffed and looked away, composing herself and calmly, indeed slowly, put her shoes back on.

His lean hand was calloused and strong as he heaved her up. Her feet kicked and slipped on the rock face and she hit her knee again, letting out a little yelp as he pulled harder and lifted her over the edge with ease. Standing on the dry lichen, the sun seemed to break through the cloud and she could see his dinghy tethered in the next gully. Glancing down, she could no longer see the cave entrance.

Patrick stood on a ledge a foot or so below her so they were eye to eye.

'Thank you,' she offered ungraciously.

She noticed that his hair had grown out since their last meeting, but he had clearly made no effort to tame the dirty blond tangle.

'There's a rock just under the water there.' He pointed into the gully and she could now see the submerged form. 'I didn't want to damage the dinghy.

You came down through the Deep. What were you doing in there?'

'The Deep?'

'The cave is called Houlahan's Deep.'

'Ah,' she realized. 'I saw the entrance and I explored it.'

'You shouldn't be up on Gortagort alone. You don't know the place.'

'Jack Callaghan showed me. I was confident I knew the way.'

'He should know better. He should have warned you.'

'I spoke to your grandmother and she didn't say a thing about it.'

'I've no doubt she thought you'd stay on the path. If you'd have slipped in the tunnel—'

'There was the rope.'

'I know; I put it there.'

'I was quite safe.'

He raised a reprimanding eyebrow and stared.

'The tide is coming in and it reaches the entrance there. What would you have done then?'

She ignored the question and was haughty. 'I think I can climb back up from here.' She looked for the path that was less distinct now.

'No, you can't. That would be just as stupid. You wouldn't get ten feet before you fell back into the gully . . . and you've hurt your knee!'

She stopped rubbing it. 'I'm fine.'

'I'll help you down.' He held out his hand again and she took it reluctantly.

As he rowed back into the strand, he was looking over his shoulders to navigate the narrow channel. She tried not to look at him, but found herself grinding her teeth with both grudging admiration and galling embarrassment.

When the dinghy scraped up on to the stones she jumped off into the stinking weed and waded ashore.

'Can I help you?' she asked, through her clamped jaw.

'No.'

'Then thank you again.'

He nodded and she turned away and instantly back again.

'I do respect this place,' she declared.

He shrugged.

'And I am grateful.'

He nodded and looked at her then, straight into her, as if for the first time, his blue eyes searching and she had to look away.

8

Emotional Landscapes

A few weeks later, over the weekend before she planned to return to the valley, Orla and Martin were watching films together at her flat. Although Martin lounged too languidly over her furniture it was better than the alternative which was to watch it at his place.

They had each chosen a film. She had picked *Il Postino*. He had resisted watching it with her for the entire time they had been together and so she was surprised and slightly suspicious when he finally acquiesced. He did complain about the subtitles but she did not care.

She did however immediately regret in return agreeing to watch *The Great Escape* again. She supposed she appreciated their endeavours to be free, even though watching Steve McQueen jump the first fence clean, when the second was not to be, made her despair.

After *Il Postino* she was choking on the tears. Martin yawned and shrugged.

'Totally unbelievable,' he declared.

'What?' she gaped.

'I didn't believe any of it and I didn't care.'

She was so disgusted she did not even want to discuss it.

'Do you want me to open another bottle?' he asked.

'No.'

'Well I'm having some more.'

Even watching him shuffle to the fridge could not diminish the image of smiles like butterflies.

He returned to the settee, uncorked the bottle, filled his glass, took a swig and swallowed hard.

'I am looking forward to going to the cottage with you though,' he said.

She smiled thinly.

'The thing is I won't be able to make it this weekend.'

'Why not?' she gasped.

'I've a report to complete.'

'How long have you known about this?'

He was sheepish at first. 'Not long.'

'How long?'

She knew his deadlines.

'A few weeks.'

'What?'

She was furious. She accepted that his work demanded long hours, but this delay in telling her seemed deliberate and the manner in which he told her was too much.

'And I suppose you've left it to the last minute.'

'It has to be done. I'm not a machine like you.'

'I'm no machine. That's unfair. You make me sound like I've no emotions – no life even.'

'That's why I got out of teaching as soon as I could.'

He had taught Design and Technology.

'You just didn't like children.'

'At least I knew when it was time to leave.'

'What are you saying?'

'You should leave and we'll have more time together.'

'Why should I leave? I like teaching. I like children.'

'Come on. You don't have a life. You don't relax like me . . . or with me.'

'I do have a life,' she asserted, but even she was unconvinced.

'Come on, Orla, you know what you're like.'

'Do I? Perhaps I don't. Explain it to me.'

He hesitated. 'I haven't everything organized like you, that's all. Not many people have. You're always in control. Even when I do stuff for you it's because you've allowed me to.'

As he spoke he placed the disc in the DVD player.

Her eyes narrowed. 'You spend too much time talking when you should be working.'

'You know me, Orla. I like people. I can't lock myself away.'

'I work from the moment I arrive to the time I leave. Being conscientious is not being obsessive.'

'And I meet my deadlines and the work is done well enough.'

'Well enough is not good enough. What if things go wrong?'

'Nothing does.'

She loathed it when he was dismissive.

'Leaving things to the last minute is not complacent if it's done on time,' he argued.

'No, you're just complacent with us. Enough is nowhere near good enough when it means my plans are ruined, when our time together is affected. I was looking forward to this and you know it. You must have known you had this to do.'

He slithered off the cushions and crawled to her. She remained with her chin up in disdain.

'I'll go down with you at the start of the holidays. We'll make a week of it, perhaps even longer. You're right and I'm sorry.'

She nodded once and he rolled back on to the settee, winking at her as he puffed his cushions and pressed play.

'Anyway,' he said, 'I can't change the way I am. I won't change, just like you won't. Aren't we too old to change the way we are?'

She shook her head and stared at the screen, feeling her life ebbing away with every frame that flashed.

Half an hour in her patience was waning. 'You can fast forward this bit,' she said.

Martin made no response.

'Are you really enjoying this again?' she persisted.

He was motionless.

She turned on the light and threw a cushion at his head. He snorted awake.

'What?'

'You were bloody sleeping and I was watching it on my own.'

'I was awake.'

'What's just happened?'

'They were trying to escape.'

She threw another cushion. 'Jesus, Martin. Turn it off. You can watch it at home.'

She went to the kitchen to wash her glass and poured the wine he had left down the sink. When he eventually returned from the toilet she manoeuvred herself to the opposite side of the table. He was unable to get to her.

'I've ordered a taxi,' she stated.

'What? Why?'

'I'm tired. I've marking to do tomorrow.'

'I said I was sorry.'

'I heard.'

'You are a robot!'

The next day she met Bernadette for lunch in a café by the Liffy. When asked directly, she admitted what Martin had decided.

'He's not going with you?' Bernadette exclaimed.

'He's busy.' That was all Orla wanted to offer.

Bernadette shook her head, staring Orla in the eye and waiting.

'He has work to do,' Orla stated.

Still Bernadette was silent.

'We're going down together for a week in the summer.'

Bernadette suspended the sugar spoon over her coffee and raised an eyebrow.

Orla gave in. 'He's an arse and I still haven't forgiven him.'

Bernadette added the sugar and then another in celebration.

'How about I come with you to keep you company?'

'You would?'

'Of course – I'd like to see what you've been going on about. Will there be unmarried men?'

'What happened to your speed date?'

'Everything he had to say he said that night.'

'I thought you saw him again.'

'I did, and everything he could do he'd done, and I knew I didn't want to see him again.'

She giggled; Orla shook her head.

So, Bernadette asked again. 'Are there any available men?'

'A few. The one who has the dinghy I told you about – he's available, I'm told.'

'Not him. He sounds awful. What about this Jack?'

'What about him?' Orla heard her own petulant rhetoric.

'Orla! What are you thinking?'

'Nothing!'

'Right. I'm going if only to save you from yourself.'

Bernadette refused to take the train, and on the flight down, she was still enthusing about the farmer.

'So he's definitely single?'

She was speaking too loudly and Orla was embarrassed.

'Yes.'

'With no obvious physical defects?'

'How do I know?'

'And you're sure he's not gay?'

'Look, he's breathing. That's all you usually need to know.'

Bernadette was oblivious. 'I need to be sure of all the vital statistic before I make my moves on him.'

The jet banked right as it circled into Cork airport. As it did so it descended in the long curve along the Imokilly coast. Orla could clearly see Lir's Tears and Cromwell's Hump and then Ballyanna Bay itself. It gave her a thrill. She nudged Bernadette.

'There it is.'

'Where? I can't see a thing.'

'It's gone now.'

Bernadette hired the car and Orla was delighted she was driving. However, her friend demanded to meet Jack that very night, so when they turned at the Cross and saw the lights on in Ballygarry she demanded Orla pull on to the forecourt.

Jack came to the door.

'We saw the light and decide to say hello,' stated Orla apologetically.

Jack smiled widely and stood aside. 'Please come in.'

'This is Bernadette.' Orla glanced at her friend who was already simpering.

He took their coats and they went into the lounge where an open fire blazed. He hurriedly gathered his paperwork that had been spread across the coffee table.

'I was just working though some business proposals.'

He directed them to sit and tipped a full ashtray into the fire. 'Would you like a drink? I have wine or something stronger.'

'I don't—' began Orla.

'Yes please – wine,' said Bernadette.

As he fetched the wine Bernadette gave Orla an excited thumbs up. When he returned she was arch.

'You keep the place so well,' she said coyly. 'You must be very domesticated.'

'I have a cleaner, Bernadette—'

'Bernie.'

'Bernie . . . and I don't like mess.'

'Has your family always owned this farm?'

'No, my family still live in Ballybrannigan. When I came back to the area about fifteen years ago, I bought it. It was bankrupt. The farmer here had boozed all the money away. I built it up again and made it economical. I was able to sell some of the land and develop other parts. You have to diversify.'

'So are you still a farmer?'

'The farm is still working, but put it this way – I don't have to work anymore.'

'A man of leisure,' she purred.

'I don't have to work but I chose to.'

'I went to see Anne McLeavey,' Orla interrupted.

'Oh.'

'She said she and Patrick were with Donovan a lot before his death.'

'They were, but only to torment the poor old devil. I would often find the old man in tears after they had been there. He would beg me not to let them in, but what could I do? I couldn't stay there and I couldn't change the locks. Ask anyone. Sure, they know what it was like.'

'She seemed so sure, so adamant about things.'

'She's wily. I mean I get on with her, but she's sharp and won't take any messing when it comes to money.'

Orla was enraged.

'I want to go up there right now and confront her, confront them both. What right have they got?'

Bernadette placed her hand on her arm. 'There's no need, Orla. Their anger is enough. You've got what they wanted that's all they see.'

'She's right,' agreed Jack. 'The best way is to be careful and watch what happens . . . Just be prepared, is all I'm saying. Don't be deceived and don't be surprised.'

'I won't,' she said. 'Look, I'd love to stay a while Jack but I want to get down to the cottage and settle in.'

'Of course,' he agreed and stood. 'There's music in the Laughing Gull tomorrow. I'd like to invite you both if you'll come.'

They agreed with a toast and returned to the car.

Orla stopped above the strand. The moon was in and the darkness was deep. A single light shone in Elannat.

'Jesus, I can hear the sea,' Bernadette exclaimed. 'You're that close.'

'As close as I am to the road in Dublin.'

'But apart from that there's nothing?'

'Nothing at all in the night.'

Bernadette shivered and giggled. 'I don't know if I'm afraid of the dark or giddy over meeting Jack Callaghan.'

'Or a little drunk, and I think he'll soon be afraid of you if you get too amorous.'

Bernadette held her close as they crossed the lane to the cottage. Inside, Orla turned on the reading lamp and Bernadette gasped.

'Jesus, it's lovely.' She was drawn to the cluttered shelves. 'But all these things . . .'

'I've already started to box up some of the clothes and clutter. Donovan collected everything and threw nothing away. There's a charity shop in Castleford that will think I'm an angel. I had a mind to ask the relatives if they want to inspect it, but after what Jack said.'

'Just get rid of it,' Orla advised. 'To hell with them if they don't respect you or his memory. And what's that smell?'

'It's the smell of the country.'

'It smells like . . .'

She followed Orla to the bathroom.

The foul odour was stronger but on close inspection the cistern and floor were clean.

'I'll scrub it again,' she said.

They sat by the fire until the early hours, drinking a little more wine.

'You know Jack was looking at you and not me,' Bernadette admitted.

'He was not. He couldn't see past you.'

'It was obvious. Are you sure you and him haven't. . . ?'

'No!' Orla was indignant. 'I've Martin. I'm not interested.'

Bernadette pulled a face.

'What is it with you and him?' Orla asked.

'Nothing. Except – what is he to you is the question? I mean really?'

'He's my fiancé.' When she said that she wanted to make it true but she only felt guilt.

Bernadette was unconvinced and had drunk enough wine to bait her.

'Why him?'

Orla's eyes widened. She spoke emphatically, still determined to deny. 'He's kind and funny and we get on.'

'Can that be enough?'

'I don't think I want to take advice from you, Bernie.'

'Or talk to me about it at all?'

'I don't know what you mean.'

'We talk about everything except you and men. If you don't talk about it, then you'll go on being miserable. I'm your friend; I can't allow it.'

'It's not your place.'

'It is my place.'

'I'm not miserable.'

'Not here. I can see that. It's the first time I've seen you at ease in ages.'

'Really?'

'You're always so snappy these days and when you're not giving out you don't seem to care at all.'

'I do care.'

'I know, and that's why it shows sat here with you now.'

'Coming here has changed everything,' she revealed.

Bernadette sighed. 'Do you love Martin?'

Orla hesitated. It was against all her instincts to discuss such matters, even with Bernadette.

'Bernie I . . .'

'You don't, do you?'

'I do.'

'In that case, do you even know what love is?'

'If that's your argument, I can't win. And what do you know about love anyway?'

'I like being alone. I do what I want. I like men and they like me. You say I'm shallow. I say I'm waiting for the one and while I wait I have a great time. thank you very much. When the one comes along and I'm helpless – then I'll know. But it hasn't happened yet.'

'But what if he's there and you don't see him because you're too busy loving yourself?'

'Then at least I've lived life.'

'That's an awful way to live. The men you meet and the times you have, the sex . . . there's no love.'

'Does there have to be?'

'Yes there does.' She balked slightly when she said that, sensing her own doubts. 'I couldn't bear it if I didn't think there was more than just that moment. There has to be more. If neither of you know each other and neither care then you might as well . . . well, you might as well masturbate.'

Bernadette laughed at Orla's prudish embarrassment.

'You don't know them,' Orla asserted, 'and that can't be enough, and it can never be the same as being with someone who knows you intimately and with whom you're going to share the rest of your life.'

'And that's what you have with Martin?'

'Yes!' she claimed too forcefully.

'Do you even know him?'

'We have shared so much.'

'There you go again. What have you both got in common?'

'We travel and we watch films.'

'Does he care about history?'

'He does, in his own way.'

'Does he appreciate art?'

Orla shrugged.

'Does he read?'

'Not really.'

'And I know he resents you doing so.'

'That's not true,' she argued, but even she was unconvinced.

'Do you like sport?'

'No.'

'What's the sex like?'

'You know I don't talk about that.'

'Jesus, you're a prig.

'I'm private. That's too personal.'

'But you'll listen to me talking about it.'

'Do I have a choice?'

'No,' Bernadette smiled, but she was not ready to concede. 'So do you really know him?'

'Of course I do.'

'Do you really love him?'

'I don't know.'

'Well . . . What?' Bernadette took a deep breath. 'You don't know?' she whispered.

Orla raised her eyebrows, realizing what she had admitted. There were no tears.

In the morning Bernadette complained bitterly about getting up before nine o'clock but Orla made her tea and toast, wrapped her in an overcoat and chivvied her down to the stormwall.

Bernadette chomped sulkily more annoyed than awed.

'What do you think?' Orla eagerly asked.

'It's a bleak place.'

'Really?'

'It's just rocks and grass. There's not even any sand on the beach down there.'

'Don't you think it's a perfect haven?'

Bernadette sipped her tea and was slightly revived. 'Why not?' she exclaimed. She looked from the panorama to her friend. 'You see, that's exactly what I mean, Orla.'

'What?'

'You've changed. You're like a child here.'

Orla giggled.

Later, they drove to Castleford where they trawled through the shops and Orla hauled her into the hardware store where she purchased a pair of wellington boots.

Bernadette bought a new dress.

'I had a pair in Wellington Street when I used to help my nana with the garden; Nana used to laugh at me because I was so confused about the coincidence in the name. I thought they were named after the street . . .'

Bernadette stared at her blankly as she reminisced.

Orla caught the look. 'Anyway,' she coughed. 'I think they'll be great down on the strand and when I'm weeding.'

They visited the museum in the local distillery and had coffee there. Orla gave Bernadette her free tot of whiskey.

'I hate the stuff,' she sniffed.

Bernadette smacked her lips. 'And I can't get enough.'

They returned to the cottage and Bernadette immediately went for a nap. Orla emptied her bags. In the charity shop, where she had given the first boxes of old suits and shirts, she had found an intricate silver photograph frame. Behind the glass she slipped a photograph of Donovan and Margaret and placed it on the sideboard.

In the photograph they were riding a bicycle down the boreen – she could see that now. Donovan rode and Margaret sat on the carry frame on the handlebars. They were laughing and she was stretching star-wide with abandon.

While Bernadette slept, she put on her new wellingtons and went out into the rockery where she weeded. After that she continued sorting through Donovan's belongings.

Passing the bedroom she saw Bernadette had simply flopped across the bed and so Orla fetched a blanket from the chest of drawers. As she pulled the blanket out she noticed a long leather-bound spine beneath it. Unfolding the blanket over her friend she took the book and returned to the living-room.

Opening it on her lap she saw that it was a ledger of family trees. The first tree was for the O'Meagher line, the next Geraghty, followed by Houlahan and Byrne and Spellissey and so on. Where each tree was related to another Donovan had inserted a code in coloured inks. The names resonated in her mind, through the letters and conversations and beyond. And when she saw that the last tree was her own, she laughed to herself wryly, wanting to believe that she had always known she was connected.

She was tidying again when Bernadette emerged from the bedroom and stooped under the door. Her bleached hair was in a frizz and her roots were showing. 'You'll be a bent old crone before you're forty,' she complained of the low frames.

'I'll get them raised.'

'Have you got a CD player?' Bernadette asked indifferently.

'No.'

'I'm sure I saw it when I came in.'

'I haven't got one down here,' Orla lied. She did not want poodle rock anthems at full volume.

Bernadette shrugged and walked through to the kitchen humming 'Livin' on a Prayer'.

Two hours later, by the time Jack was due, Orla was still sorting. Every cupboard now hid neatly piled or boxed books and ornaments, but Orla had found herself persistently waylaid and engrossed in the objects.

She was particularly captivated by a selection of film annuals from the thirties and forties. As she perused them she was trying to imagine how, among such harsh austerity, Donovan had perceived the flawless glamour of Hollywood.

Indeed, after her toils, the box of objects she intended to take to the charity shop contained no more than musty clothes and a pile of dog-eared and foxed western genre paperbacks.

Bernadette had helped for a while but quickly lost interest and, aided by a bottle of cheap Riesling she had insisted on picking up on the way back, she set about getting herself ready for the evening ahead.

Realizing the time, Orla ran to the bathroom, brushed her teeth, slipped into her jeans and sweater, brushed her hair and pinned it back, and put on lipstick.

Martin always complained that pinning her hair back made her look like an unmarried schoolmistress, but her neck was long and she liked to think she looked like Uma Thurman.

Bernadette approached her at the mirror. She was straightening the new dress. It was well cut but her ample waist was testing the seams.

'You're not going in that,' Bernadette stated, seeing Orla for the first time.

'Why not?'

'Make an effort.'

'I have.'

'I'll look over-dressed.'

'You always do.'

Bernadette shrugged. 'That's the consequence of having style. Here help me with this.'

Bernadette held the dress together as Orla struggled with the zip.

Jack arrived late and drove them into Ballybrannigan. Out of the 4x4 Bernadette led the way, taking him by the arm. The Laughing Gull was thronging but they found a corner and Jack went to the bar.

It was an old pub, low-ceilinged and yellowed by tobacco, the walls cluttered with faded photographs of lifeboat crews, trawlermen and proud farmers with their prize bulls and tractors. She read the photocopied poster for the band – *The Open Hearts: Personal and Universal* and she wondered where she'd heard that phrase before. On a small stage in the far corner the band was set up to play fiddle, bodhrans, accordion and guitar.

She sat by the open window and the air was warm as it ebbed against her. She could see across Ballybrannigan Bay. The mountains in the mist seemed to separate her from all she had ever been certain of in her life.

Bernadette was laughing too loudly and she was attracting the attention of several men. Orla could not decide if it was desire or derision. She watched Jack weave away through the crowd, observing how he walked with a pugilist stoop, his shoulders swaggering defiantly. At the bar, he conversed and laughed with ease, and she could not help but notice how other women there looked over their glasses at him. She immediately felt embarrassed by her envy.

'I hope you're going to behave,' she said to Bernadette.

'I might not. I might get flutered.'

'Ah, don't show me up. I don't know anyone here and I don't want them to get the wrong idea.'

'Don't worry. Relax,' she replied, whilst looking sidelong into the room.

Her dismissive tone irked Orla. 'This isn't some place in the town you can get drunk and make a scene and no one will know or care.'

Jack worked his way back through the crowd and placed the drinks on the table. Bernadette reached for hers too soon and they slopped into Orla's lap.

Though Orla gasped, Bernadette didn't seem to notice and it was then that the band took the stage and ignited the audience with 'We Shall Be Heard', 'This Night Will Last Forever' and 'Irish Love of Mine'.

Bernadette was immediately up and clapping and singing. She had a fair voice but she did know the words.

'I'm sorry,' Jack said in Orla's ear.

'It's not your fault.'

'It's just that you look great in what you've got on and your hair . . .'

Orla hid her blushes behind her glass but Jack had joined in the singing with Bernadette who was by the end of the first set croaking out of tune.

During the break, after several more rounds, Bernadette declared she needed the toilet.

'I'll go with you,' Orla offered.

'That's all right. I think I'll go outside for a cigarette. Do you fancy a ciggie, Jack?'

'No; I don't smoke.' He glanced at Orla. 'I've given up.'

'Oh.' Bernadette shrugged.

As she swayed away Orla apologized then. 'I'm sorry, Jack. She likes you, I think.'

'I've given no indication . . .' He considered and was then gracious. 'I'm flattered and she's a fine girl.' He grimaced coyly. 'I'll have to be careful. I'm not used to such attention.'

'Are you sure now?'

He looked at her and his smile dropped.

'I am.'

Orla looked away not knowing what to say, not wanting to betray anyone. Jack leaned towards her.

'Orla I—'

One of the women she had watched before leaned between them. 'I think you better get into the ladies,' she said. 'Your friend may need some help.'

Jack smiled awkwardly and followed Orla. They found Bernadette on her knees in the cubicle with her head down the bowl. Orla wiped her face, flushed the chain and lifted her up. In the corridor, Jack took her without a word and carried her out through the side entrance.

Orla sat with Bernadette in the back with the windows wide open as Jack drove back to Ballyanna. He said nothing as Bernadette moaned.

Outside An Doras, he carried her inside and while Orla put her to bed he stayed in the living-room, reviving the fire. When she came out he had made a pot of coffee. She sat with him.

'I think we've given the gossips something to talk about tonight,' he said.

'You don't strike me as the type of man who would care about gossips.'

'I don't for myself; it's just I don't want people talking about you because of Bernie.'

'She's a lovely girl and a good friend. She got over-excited. She needs to find the right fella, that's all – someone who she's in love with, who isn't a complete arse.'

He smiled. 'I know that sure, but it will be you and me they'll be talking about as well.'

'Oh. Why?'

'Because we've been together every time you've been down.'

'They're already saying that?'

'Yes.'

'Well there's nothing to it.'

'Still, they'll talk.'

'Let them.'

'It's not like in the city, Orla. Here the gossips are rampant and people's opinions are changed by them. It's all they have to do . . . I heard about your journey to the centre of the earth.'

'What was that?'

'The escapade in the cave.'

She blushed.

'You can be sure your man McLeavey had a laugh on you.'

She thought about that and she remembered the look he gave her.

Jack put down his coffee and stood up.

'Well, I'll be off. I've a business trip in the morning.'

She looked up at him, wanting so much more in that moment.

'Thank you Jack.'

'Ah, it's nothing. We're friends, aren't we?'

She looked at him directly then. Yes,' she said and it was he who looked away.

After closing the front door, she saw Bernadette had slipped from the bed and was splayed across the floor moaning again, her white hair matted with vomit. Orla fetched a warm wet flannel, heaved her up and gently chastized her as she cleaned her face.

'You're too old to be getting so drunk.'

'You're right,' Bernadette slurred. 'I'm nearing forty. I live with my cats and I have nothing. I am desperate. I'm lonely. I'm mutton. I'll end up a barren old spinster.'

Orla had to smile; she had heard it all before.

'Do you think Jack is the one?'

'Would he want you after such a carry on?'

'Do you think I'll ever find him?'

'You try too hard.'

'And you don't try at all.'

'And what do I have? I don't think I know what I want. Do you really think I'm any different to you?' she asked, but Bernadette was asleep.

She knew they would leave the following day, but she knew even more that she would return.

9

Carborg

She did not return to the valley until the beginning of the summer holidays and this time, as promised, Martin accompanied her.

He insisted on driving to Cork. They left on the Sunday and the weather was fine. He folded the roof back and put the music up and they were winding through the Tipperary Mountains in a few hours.

She watched him stroking the steering wheel of the Big Healey and was reminded again of her conversations with Bernadette in An Doras. After the episode in The Laughing Gull, they had not discussed what she had admitted to her about her feelings for him, though Orla had thought about it. It made her afraid and a little ashamed, but she knew the truth could not be ignored; she had accepted that much. She had decided this time together, away from the city, was to be the opportunity to find the truth.

It had gone well so far. She insisted on listening to Neil Finn on the way and he had reluctantly agreed. He was still euphoric after hearing about Bernadette's antics in the pub.

'The woman is a menace. At her age – acting like a teenager.'

'She was embarrassed. That's enough. I wouldn't have told if I thought you were going to gloat.'

'She deserves it. You know she doesn't like me.'

'That's not true.'

'Right there, in your voice; I can tell you're lying.'

'Just because you're not her type doesn't mean she doesn't like you.'

'Any man is her type.'

'She's not that desperate.'

'Yes she is. I don't know what they see in her.'

'She's fun and kind and anyway, she's my oldest friend.'

'She's loud and leathery and your only friend . . . I don't know what *you* see in her. She's nothing like you.'

'Are you saying I'm not fun and kind?'

He gave a teasing smile. 'You're more . . . aloof and indifferent.'

'What?'

'On the surface, that is.'

'I am not.'

'It's a good thing.'

'To be cold and uncaring?'

'It means you don't easily get hurt.'

'I get hurt. You're hurting me right now.'

'But I know what's underneath it all. You're a boiling cauldron of fire,' he mocked.

'You make me sound like a repressed witch.'

He was floundering now. 'Not at all. But Bernadette is a witch . . . For you, I meant the fire of desire – passion, like.'

She folded her arms and he concentrated on the winding road.

'Do we still have to listen to this?' he asked flatly. 'There's an Oasis CD in the glove box.'

'I'm not listening to them.'

'I've listened to this since we left.'

'I can't listen to them. It's music for adolescents – all that posturing and ignorance. Who cares except spotty boys who hide in their bedrooms, or journalists who have never grown up? It's bland and hollow and I hate it.'

He was wide eyed, unused to such vehemence. Orla even surprised herself – and about something as trivial as pop music.

'They've sold millions and I don't think it's just the adolescents who were buying it,' he stated condescendingly.

They'd had this argument before and she thought it inane but he had annoyed her and she could not resist.

'You're saying record sales equate with talent?'

'I'm just saying—'

'Well don't say anything; it's a puerile and unintelligent racket and I'm not interested.'

When they reached the lanes of Imokilly he was accelerating though the blind bends.

'Slow down,' she ordered in the wind.

He pressed the accelerator, but when she did not react he eventually eased off.

'Is there anything about me you respect?' he asked irately.

'I respect you completely.'

'It doesn't feel like it.'

'I could ask you the same question.'

'I've never—'

'The money you wasted on this car could have gone towards a house together.'

'I can sell it for more than I paid for it,' he scoffed.

'We should be making plans not buying toys.'

'There you go again, respecting nothing of what I am. I need this car. It says something about me.'

'You're not wrong there. For those who know you, it says you don't have enough money and what you do have you waste.'

He was glib. 'You only live once.'

'Ah belt up with the clichés. You're a cliché. It's a car. Is that all there is for you? Is that what makes you complete?'

'At least I know what I want. It's you who has nothing. Isn't that why you're off to this cottage trying to find meaning where there is none? Look at yourself.'

She thrust her chin up and looked the other way.

He leaned over to the glove compartment, fumbled open a CD case, ejected Neil Finn and slid in his Oasis CD. He even punched the air when the stolen power riffs burst in.

Orla said nothing. She put on her sunglasses, tied her headscarf and leaned to the left where the wind rushed at her face. She was trying to imagine she looked like Audrey Hepburn but could not quite do it with the Beatles pastiche blaring.

'You look like an old crone at the gate in that scarf,' Martin shouted over the music and the Healey roaring through the gears.

She tightened the knot and shook her head, choosing to ignore him. For the rest of the way she only spoke to point out a turn here and there.

Passing Ballybrannigan she could not tell if the twist in her stomach was anger, or the anticipation of being in the valley again.

At the Cross above Ballyanna she shouted for him to stop and the car skidded to a halt in a shower of grit and dust. She leaned over and turned the volume down. He immediately turned it up again.

'Turn it down, please. You don't normally have it that loud.'

'That's because you don't like it.'

'I've let you play it for the past half an hour.'

He was petulant. 'You let me do nothing. I did it myself.'

She gave an exasperated sigh.

'Is this it?' he asked.

'Turn here and go straight on,' she pointed.

All the way down the lane they took turns to switch the player on and off. It was only when they passed the workshop that Orla became conscious of the childish game.

On the roof above the place she saw Patrick McLeavey with another man. Having slowed for the bend in the road, she saw how their laughter stopped as the music burst in full blast again. She turned the music down and finally

Martin did not react.

'Is the one with the evil eye, the fella with the attitude?' Martin whispered out of the side of his mouth.

'Yes.'

In the wing mirror she saw the other man thump McLeavey on the arm and then the two men resumed their laughter.

Martin drove slowly now.

'I'm sorry,' she said.

'Me too,' he replied, and he leaned over and kissed her. She was relieved that they could start again.

Eager to show him the views she directed him to the stormwall above the strand. Standing there, it felt like she had always known the place. The letters had made it indelible in her mind, and she liked to think she was seeing it through the eyes of all her ancestors.

Martin approached from the around the car, rubbing the paintwork on his way, and embraced her from behind, kissing her neck. She shivered and smiled. He smelt good. He rested his chin on her shoulder. She squirmed to dislodge it. He straightened.

'Where is this magnificent view you promised me?'

She looked out to sea.

'There.'

'Rocks and sky and sea – I'm astounded by the beauty,' he said drolly. 'Can we go into this haven you have inherited? Which one is it?' He looked around the rim of the valley, at the farms and homesteads there.

'There,' she pointed at An Doras just behind them on the lane opposite the humpbacked bridge.

'Oh. I thought . . . It's close to the sea, like you said and it's white and it has a low roof and small windows. It's every bit the country cottage.'

'It's mine and it was given to me by my blood grandfather. That means something.'

'It would if you knew the man and if he was any part of your life.' He was walking down to the porch. She followed and opened the door.

Inside, she stood in the living-room and he leaned over her shoulder, peering down his nose at the remaining miscellany of Donovan's life, cluttered in the meagre light through the window.

'Does the place have running water?'

'Yes.'

'Good. Put the kettle on. I'm gasping and I need warming up.'

'You should have kept the roof up on that car.'

'What's the point in buying such a vehicle if I can't show it off?'

'There is no point in buying it except to show off – I told you that.'

She was conscious they were bickering again and decided she would avoid it – or at least try to.

'The place smells of damp and something else . . .' He sniffed. 'You'll need to see about that. My asthma will give me problems if it gets bad. I'll get the bags.'

'I'll make you a coffee and set a fire to get you warm,' she said, but he was already outside.

When he came back in he dropped the bags and watched her turning the bellows.

'What a contraption. You could invest in central heating. You'd have none of that nonsense and it'd get rid of the odour as well.'

'This is all part of the experience.'

'But you'd soon tire of it if you did it every day.'

The flames were climbing through the paper and kindling.

'Couldn't you at least do that with those firelighter things I've seen?'

'You could, but there's no art to it.'

'I'd rather save time than be an artist. You could be making the coffee that you promised. You'll be using flint and sticks next. I say flick a switch.' He stood in the centre of the room with his hands on his hips scrutinizing the dim corners. 'You know, I'd knock this place down and start again.'

She gasped.

'It was functional during the Famine no doubt, but now it has no purpose except as a place to wallow in the past. It's so . . . dingy.'

'But I've plans.'

'Oh yeah.'

She took his hand and led him to the door beside the fireplace. He stepped with her into the old pub tentatively.

'Jesus . . . I just thought these would be spare rooms with more clutter.'

'It was called the Leaping Dolphin and it was a pub when there was a community here.'

He stood at the centre of the room, slowly scanning it. She remained at the door. Their voices echoed.

'If you're not going to demolish the place, this should be the front room.'

'I've room enough through here and I have other ideas.'

'What?'

'What do you think of me opening this place up to the public in the summer as a heritage centre? With all the stuff Donovan has left I—'

'Do you realize how much work would be involved?'

'But if it was what I wanted to do. . . ?'

'What would be the point?'

'It would mean so much. It would be perfect.'

'What about your teaching?'

'I haven't thought it through yet, but what do you think of it in principle?'

On the periphery of her consciousness she was disgusted by her desire for his approbation.

'I think you're mad.'

Appalled, she went back into the living-room and stood staring into the fire.

He retreated for the rest of the stuff. She was in the kitchen when he returned.

'Where am I to park the car?' he asked.

'On the lane.'

'You're joking. Have you not seen the state of the surface? The paintwork will be ruined by all the salt and dust.'

'This is the countryside.'

'And I dread to think what all the lose chippings will do to the finish.'

'I know a farmer up at the Cross; perhaps you can park it in one of his barns.'

'And what about the mud in a farmyard?'

She took a deep breath and handed him a mug of coffee. He took it through to the bedroom.

She sipped her tea and stared at the rough whitewashed wall. She touched the stones and smiled and then felt the vibration of a heavy thump. It was followed by a scream and a tirade of curses.

She rushed through to the bedroom to find him on his knees before the bed. His coffee was spilt on the stone floor and he was holding his head and crying.

She knelt by him. 'You need to bend down through the doors. I should have said.'

'Don't talk to me!'

'Let me see it.'

'Don't even look at me.'

He was doubled over now.

'Go on. Leave me alone. I've split my head open.'

'There's no blood. I'll get a wet towel.'

He shrugged her off and she paused at the door and watched as he whined, struggled to his feet and rolled on to the bed.

She returned and gently placed the cold towel over his forehead. He sniffed and she soothed him.

'Sorry for shouting' he said. 'It really hurt, Orla.'

She smiled and set about cleaning the spilt coffee. She then made another mug, took it to him and left him there for a while. She went out to the car, put the roof up and emptied the boot.

After bringing in more boxes of condiments and clothes she sat by the fire reading. Just as she felt herself easing into the place again she heard Martin scream. She ran to find him standing precariously on the bed. The towel was wrapped around his fist. He was waving it feebly.

'What is it? What has happened?'

'There,' he squealed. 'There! It's huge. I reached for my coffee and it ran out from under the bed. It's as big as my hand. There!' He thrust the towel. 'It's a bloody tarantula.'

She saw the spider scurrying across the rug, and taking her water glass from beside the bed, she dropped it on the creature. As it reared up inside, she slid a piece of paper underneath and thrust it at Martin who was watching intently. He flinched and flattened himself against the wall.

'You're a disgrace' she mocked.

'I don't care. When it comes to spiders, I hate them.'

'It won't harm you. You'll harm yourself first.'

She threw it outside the window and Martin bounced down and slumped back on the bed.

'That's no good. It'll get back in for sure.'

She had no sympathy. 'There's probably ten more around this room alone,' she added.

He leapt up and was immediately searching, pulling back chairs and cupboards.

'And they're all watching you right now, waiting for you to go to sleep so they can suck your blood.'

She left him there. Only when the scraping and thudding had ceased did she go back in. He was lying down with a pillow over his head.

'What's wrong?'

'I've a headache after banging it and my dust allergy is giving me hell.'

'Have you taken your antihistamine tablets?'

'They're in my bag,' he replied feebly.

She fetched them and he swallowed one with his coffee. Soaking and wringing the towel again, she placed it on his forehead.

'I don't mean to be a pain.' he conceded. 'I'll get used to it here.'

She smiled. 'Have a sleep and we'll decide what to do after that.'

He nodded.

'Did you lock the car for me?'

'You don't need to down here.'

'Do it anyway.'

She took her coat and went out into the lane. The day was overcast as she walked to the stormwall and imagined Donovan alone amongst his neighbours' laughter. Staring out over the sea she considered Neruda's advice to the Postman; 'Walk around the bay slowly and look around you.'

Leaning against the lichened wall she breathed her bay, understanding at last.

Hearing footsteps on the path she turned to see Saoirse Cesare and the other man from the roof approaching arm in arm down the lane. He wore an overall tied by the arms about his waist and his black hair was cropped short. His skin was dark but she was unsure if it was grime or genetic.

Orla was struck again by Saoirse's hard beauty and her softly swollen abdomen.

'Hello, Orla,' said Saoirse. 'I'm told you drove down with your husband.'

'Not my husband; my . . . partner.'

'Oh. This is Roberto.'

He grinned widely and held out his hand.

'So you're Donovan's great nephew?'

'I am and so I'm your second cousin.'

'You're English.'

'You could say that, but I've been here longer than I was ever there.'

'And Roberto is a fine English name as well,' she said, shaking his hand.

He laughed easily.

'That's another story altogether.'

'Be careful,' warned Saoirse. 'Once he starts talking he won't stop. No one passes the workshop without a word or two thousand.'

Roberto winked blithely.

'What do you do in the workshop?'

'I build boats. The house used to belong to Pearse O'Meagher – Donovan's younger brother. I was his last apprentice and here I am still . . . with my beauty queen here.'

Saoirse pursed her lips disapprovingly. 'Is your partner around?' she asked.

'He's lying down. He drove all the way and struck his head the moment he stepped inside the house.'

'Poor fella, but he'll have to get used to it.'

'We're just off down the strand; will you come down?'

'Another time. I think I'll go back and see if he's still with us.'

She watched them descend, still uncertain of their intent; even so, the romance of it all was perfect.

Her thoughts then turned to Martin.

Inside, in the lamplight by the fire, she settled to read more of Brede's letters to Frances.

. . . They have killed Jack, murdered him in the street for no more than believing him to be me. They will know the touch of the Black Feather. This is my struggle. How I wish you and Juno were with me in this . . .

She was cross-referencing names in one of the letters against the ledger of family trees when there was a knock on the door. It was Jack Callaghan. She was embarrassed, suddenly disregarding the letters and realizing that in all her imaginings, she had not considered the two men meeting. She hoped Martin would stay in the bedroom.

'Jesus, that's a fine car you have there, Orla. It's no hire car. You're a surprising and a sophisticated woman, that's for sure. I didn't think it would be your style.'

'It's not. It's not mine.'

'Oh.'

He looked past her.

Martin emerged from the bedroom, still caressing his head. He held out his hand.

'This is Martin,' Orla introduced. 'He's my fiancé. Martin this is Jack Callaghan. He's a local farmer. He's been very helpful.' Martin walked to the fire and sat there forlornly.

'And how are you finding the place?' Jack asked stiffly.

'It should come with a health warning,' Martin suggested.

'The low door frames,' Orla clarified.

When Jack looked directly at her again, she was downcast. 'I only stopped by to say hello,' he said. 'I'm glad to meet you, Martin.'

He stepped back outside. Orla followed, only to see Saoirse and Roberto pass by. They smiled as she waved but did not respond to Jack when he nodded over his shoulder.

'You're engaged,' Jack said in low tones. 'You never spoke about it.'

'I'm sure I did, Jack.'

'No, you didn't. I would remember that. I know I shouldn't assume but I didn't expect it.' There were tears in his eyes.

'I'm sorry, Jack, if I've—'

He smiled. 'No. I'm sorry. I'll see you soon . . . Remember, if you need anything you know where I am.'

Mute with confusion she watched him walk away. Martin was reading the letters when she returned to the room.

'What are you doing?' she asked coolly.

He cast them aside and shrugged. 'They were here and I had a look.'

'And what do you think?'

He yawned and stretched. 'I think that world has gone.'

10

In Me Now

That evening they sat by the hearth drinking wine. Orla watched Martin in the firelight and in a euphoric haze she remembered how beautiful he was to her. He caught her looking and in mock shyness returned the gaze from under brows.

'That's the trouble with you,' she said. 'You know what you look like to me.'

'Just to you?'

'To any woman.'

'What do I look like?'

'You're a handsome devil.'

'That's why we go together – because you're as fine to me.'

She blushed then for a moment allowed herself to believe that it was enough.

'Have you thought about what we were saying?' he asked.

'What was that?'

'About marriage like.'

'You have no money. You bought that bloody car, remember?'

'We've wealth enough in love.' He caught her frown. 'And I'd sell it in an instant if—'

'And resent me for it.'

'I would not.'

'So you would give up your baby out there for children?'

'I would.'

'That's too easy to say now.'

'Look, what else can I do? If you want to get married; I'll marry you. If you want children, we'll have children? It's all up to you.'

She wanted him to demand it; she wanted him to declare his love forever, yet she did not know what she wanted. She smiled tightly and changed the subject.

'What do you really think of the place?'

'If it can be renovated then it is an investment. You could sell it for a fortune being so close to the sea.'

'I won't sell it.'

'Then what are your plans?'

'I imagine living here one day.'

'When did you decide that?'

'I've been thinking about it for a while.'

'That's all very romantic but what about your life in the city?'

'Life changes.'

'But there's nothing here.'

'Doesn't that depend on how you look at it? You could see it as having everything.'

'How? Where are the restaurants, the buses, the theatres and shops?'

'Cork is an hour away and there are towns before that. I'll be showing you them.'

'All the same, we have so much in Dublin. I mean, take the theatre – what shows will come here? You have to go so far.'

'Wouldn't that make you appreciate it more?'

'You're right. I've only been here a few hours and I'm appreciating the city much more.'

She would not be baited. 'I'll show you tomorrow.'

Conflict loomed on the periphery of her senses. Determined to deny it she put down her wine and leaned into him, kissing him on the lips.

'Shall we go to bed?'

He withdrew slightly.

'I'd like to. What with the wine and the head banging and driving all the way, I need to sleep.'

'Don't you want to make love to me?'

He hesitated. 'Not here, Orla.'

'Why not?'

'To tell you the truth this place gives me the creeps. When you showed me that old pub I was half-afraid. So many shadows – I feel like I'm being watched all the time.'

'Go to bed then,' she said, turning away from him.

'Orla, nothing's changed. I just can't relax. Not yet. This place will be fine once you've made it your own, but there's too much of what it was here.' He stood up. 'I'll see you in the morning, or you can come now and keep me warm, perhaps protect me from those spiders and ghosts.'

'I'll sit by the fire for a while. I'll be along later.'

As she listened to him climb into the creaking bed she considered his fear. She felt nothing of it. In the walls and shadows, all she felt was the presence of history and her place in the timeline. For her it was pride not fear.

She left him in bed in the morning and drove the Healey to the store in

Ballybrannigan. There she purchased bacon, eggs and sausages, milk, bread and butter and returned to cook him a breakfast.

She was singing along to Neil Finn, hoping rather than being certain that there would be no more empty self-possession between them.

The place was alive with the rich smells of the grilled meat when Martin came through to the kitchen and turned the music off.

'My head,' he said.

She placed the breakfast before him. 'I went to the shop earlier. I know you like a cooked breakfast now and then. And we're going to be out in the air all day.'

He grimaced. 'I can't face it, Orla. It looks lovely, but I'm not up to it. You eat away though. I'll have a cup of coffee.'

'I've been up for two hours this morning preparing for this. How do you think you got the paper?'

He stared blearily.

'I'm sorry.' He broke the egg yolk, cut the end of a sausage, dipped it and chewed with deliberation. 'That's good,' he smiled.

She nibbled at a slice of bacon and watched him read the paper and sip coffee and then sneer distaste. 'You should get a percolator,' he suggested. 'It says here that house prices are rising up in Dublin. You know that if you leave, it might be impossible to afford to go back.'

She pulled the top of the newspaper towards her with her fork.

'Do you think I would even consider that?'

'It's what it says.'

She sighed. 'What do you want to do today?'

'You can show me more of the marvellous scenery or the wondrous sights.'

She thought the sarcasm unnecessary.

'You choose,' she said.

'I saw some fishing rods through there. They have hooks and things. Why don't we find some rocks and go fishing?'

'I didn't know you could fish.'

'It'll be fun.'

'Where is the tide?'

'That doesn't matter.' He waved his hand. 'You just find the water's edge and away you go.' He slapped the paper shut and went off to change.

Half an hour later she was leading the way across the Coastal Way to Cromwell's Hump.

'Jesus these cliffs are high,' Martin complained. 'Are you sure these paths are safe?'

'They have been for centuries but exactly now is the time the cliff will collapse and the sky will fall in.'

They came to the shallower cliffs around the guileen and she took a grassy path that led down to the sheltered cove. There were a series of drops above the rocks, which they negotiated by working together, passing the rods and taking each others' hands as they slid down the grass ledges and jumped across eroded fissures. Eventually they found themselves on the black outcrops opposite Cromwell's Hump.

Martin led then, but went tentatively between the sharp edges. More than once he slipped and struck his shins, casting venomous looks to Orla, daring her to offer some platitudinous pity, but she serenely looked the other way and made sure he didn't see her smile.

When they reached the water's edge, he straddled the rocks and set about untangling the line and the rusty spinner from the reel.

'You go over there with yours,' he instructed.

'I think I'll watch you to see how it's done . . . Do you really know how to use it?'

'Just aim and cast it as hard as you can. I've seen it on the television.'

The line eventually fell free and he gave out a small gasp of relief.

With the spinner dangling at the tip of the rod, he unclipped the reel, leaned back and thrust it forward. The reel immediately clicked shut, the line stopped unravelling, and Orla watched the spinner fly back in a dangerous arc to strike her on the chest before she could react. Yelping, she fell to the ground. The three-pronged hook was snagged on her sweater. Martin dropped the rod and went to her.

'Jesus, I'm sorry. You were in the way.'

'I was not. You don't know what you're doing.'

'I do. The line jammed on the reel. See it's all tangled.'

She shoved his hands away as he tried to grab at the hook. Gently she prized the barbs from the wool and threw it back at him, but he had already turned away and was untangling the line.

She sat there for fifteen minutes while he worked on the knots. Slowly she was able to forget the snag on her sweater and absorb her surroundings. She gazed over the rocks that seemed to pulsate with the life and history of the place. They were sheltered there but she sensed the merciless might of the sea beyond the guileen, and the subtle threat excited her.

Again she imagined centuries of her people on the rocks, fishing for their lives. A warm breeze rushed past her. With only the sea and the air and the sky she felt at one. Only Martin's breathing and his occasional curses interrupted her reverie.

'There,' he exclaimed, holding up the rod. 'That will fly now.'

He stood and so did she, stepping back out of range. This time he launched the line and the spinner flew out into the water. He whooped with delight and started to reel it in. As he did so he glanced at her over his shoulder and winked triumphantly.

Then the line went taut.

'Jesus! I have one! The first cast and I have one!' He reeled furiously and the line thrummed. 'Oh shit.' He tugged the rod, bending it this way and that. 'If I give it a good yank then it will— Oh.' The line went flaccid as he reeled it in. The spinner and hook were gone. He paused for thought. 'Give me yours,' he said.

She handed him her rod and he checked the reel, deciding to bite off the spinner and knot it to his remaining line. As he bit and spat, Orla caught sight of something in the clear water a few feet below the ledge where they stood. It was a dogfish and she squatted to see it more closely. It was marvellous to her to see its sleek and subtly mottled body gently curving through the weed.

'Look at that, Martin. Isn't it beautiful?'

'Don't do anything more,' he ordered. 'I can get it.' And so he stood there dipping the spinner, trying to entice the dogfish.

'Don't do that, Martin. Let it be.'

'What are we here for?'

The dogfish ignored the spinner and went deeper until its shape was almost lost in the kelp bed. Martin dropped the line again just over the fish and yanked hard. The hook missed, caught a weed, tightened and broke.

He fell on to his backside. Orla laughed. He cursed. But when she pulled him to his feet he began to laugh with her.

Picking up the rods they turned to make their way back to the path, only then noticing how the tide had risen several feet, and the lower reaches of the way they had come were now submerged.

He held up his hand. She did not know if it was to stop her speaking, or if he imagined he was taking military command. He stepped down in the water, straddling the rocks and nodded manfully as he lifted her across.

He then spent the next ten minutes on the slope above wringing out and drying his socks and trainers.

At An Doras they changed and Martin decided that visiting a few of the local places of interest would be as stimulating and safer. Orla, however, was indifferent. She could have gone on exploring. In the warmth of the house, out of the air and sun, her skin prickled pleasantly and her legs ached comfortably from climbing.

They drove to the outskirts of Morroe and took the tour around Killybeg House where there was a renowned restaurant.

Saoirse Cesare was on duty, leading a party through the gardens. She waved when she saw Orla.

'Who's the heifer?' Martin whispered.

'Her name is Saoirse. She's married to my second cousin and she is pregnant.'

He chortled as she shook her head and knelt to smell the herbs and flowers. Sensing her disdain he dutifully bent to share the scents.

When they came to the rose arbour, she stared at the Great House against the hills and beyond, seeing the terrible beauty. She asked Martin to take her picture in the dappled shadow by the blood-red blooms.

In the café, he relaxed. 'This is more like the city living I like,' he declared over tea and cakes.

She was scrutinizing the evening menu. 'And more like the cost of it, as well,' she said.

'Ah, you pay for quality and service.'

She shrugged and looked out over the exquisite gardens. She supposed she was paying for such pristine beauty and so did not mind much.

'And don't you think this place has style?' he enthused.

She followed his eyes to the waitress, unsure if he was referring to her mock Edwardian costume or the figure it curved around. Either way, she was surprised to realize she did not care.

Before leaving she purchased several trays of pansies, lobelias and geraniums, cultivated from the greenhouses of the Great House.

'For the garden,' she explained to him.

'Why do you need a garden when you have all that wild space at your door?' he asked.

'It'll be my own space beyond all that and I want to learn.'

In Morroe itself they drew up beneath the Norman round tower. Martin was whistling loudly as they crossed the road. She thought it irritating and uncouth.

'If you must whistle, whistle a tune,' she suggested.

'It's the nerves.'

'What are you nervous about?'

'The thing looks like it's going to fall.'

Between the post office and bakery, the Imokilly History Society ran a small shop selling genealogical materials, second-hand bric-à-brac and postcards, old and new. She browsed through the books on Morroe Cathedral, the Great House and gardens, and the surrounding villages. It was with some delight she saw that tickets for the tower could be purchased there. She immediately paid for two and followed the curator up the rusting steel ladder to the entry hatch. Orla always felt a thrill at such times, but halfway up, in the close and heavy air of the stairwell, Martin apologized, 'I have to go back,' he said.

'Why?'

'I feel closed in and I don't like it and I'm wheezing with the asthma.'

'We're nearly there,' said the old curator.

But Martin was already retreating.

She remembered the long climb around the dome of St Peter's in the Vatican City when he had stopped at intervals because he had left his inhaler in the hotel room. She had been mortified at the jam they had caused in the narrow leaning corridor. That was in the first months of their relationship and he had at least made it to the top that day. Indeed, although he had swooned to be so high, she had even admired him for his tenacity.

'Wave to me,' he shouted.

On the parapet Orla took in the panorama as the curator gave his commentary. She imagined she was from another age, climbing to spy, to alert or even to throw a heretic to his death.

'There is the cathedral and there the Great House. Below, all the roads lead to Great Island and Cork.'

At the crossroads of the town, a stained statue stood stridently over a modern roundabout.

'The statue below – who is it?'

'That's Royston Lazenby, the landlord here during the Great Famine. They call it the *Vanity*.' He chuckled, 'I'm sure it's the ridicule that stops it being pulled down.'

Orla was seeing a landscape scarred by the unseen history of all those who had passed through. She wanted to know of them all.

'See the forest there?'

She saw a copse on the hillside.

'In there are the ways into Midir's Maze. The caves go on for miles into the ground, right down to the sea.'

'And into the Otherworld,' she smiled.

He laughed, impressed by her joke.

She looked down on to the street below and saw Martin emerge from the newsagent and lean against the Healey reading a magazine and chomping on an ice-cream. He did not look up.

'You're lucky to be up here,' the curator said.

'Why?'

'We'll be closing the tower after this summer.'

'Why?'

'Money. It needs money for renovations and to bring it up to modern safety standards, but the fund for it is meagre.'

She scanned the countryside again.

'There's so much history here, but little interest,' he added.

'Perhaps it needs to be publicized.'

'True, but that costs money as well.'

'Perhaps if it was celebrated more, written about and—'

'You have a keen interest in history yourself.'

'I teach History in Dublin.'

'Ah. Then I need to tell you no more.'

'Oh do. Please go on.'

'Look at the stones here.'

They were blackened and broken.

'There was once a roof on the place but they say it was blown off by a cannon ball fired by the great Juno Byrne.'

'I know about her. She was a friend of Brede Houlahan. They fought the estate during the Famine. I—' There was whistling from below which she ignored. 'Didn't they hide in the cave in Ballyanna?'

'They were true and unsung folk heroes.'

'Didn't they form the secret society of the Black Feather?'

'They did! How do you know these things?'

'My grandfather was Donovan O'Meagher.'

'Well I never . . . I knew Donovan sure. I'm delighted to meet you.' He shook her hand. 'I'm Maurice Aherne. Sure, I've pictures of me and Donovan from way back in our GAA days. He always had a fierce interest in the past like. But wait. I thought Donny was a life long bachelor.'

'He was.' She stared at him.

Maurice was open-mouthed, but began to smile as he realized. 'The dirty old devil! Hah! Isn't the past amazing? You think you understand it and then something comes along and confounds it all. I'm delighted. And you're the spit of an O'Meagher.'

There was another whistle and she glanced over the edge to see Martin beckoning. She waved.

'I have to go. Can I talk to you again?'

'You can, of course, but perhaps not at the top of the tower.'

'But I do feel like a princess up here.'

He, too, glanced down. 'And is yer man your prince?' he asked wryly.

She laughed unconvincingly.

On the street, Martin folded the paper. 'I bought tablets and water. After the boozing last night and getting up early I've another headache.'

'I'll drive then.'

He shifted reluctantly.

'I'm still in shock after you drove it this morning without asking.'

'You'll be right beside me.'

He threw the keys and they landed in the road. She waited for a tractor to pass, retrieved them and they circled the car in opposite directions.

'Where are we going?' he asked.

'Great Island.'

'Haven't you been there before?'

'Of course, but not with you,' she smiled sweetly.

He looked sidelong with suspicion.

In the Great Island Museum on the quayside, no visible vestige of the great exodus or the great ships remained. Orla passed the exhibits of emigration with reverence. Even after years in the classroom, the words and images still haunted her, and to be at the docks where so many were last on Irish soil was always humbling.

She drew away from an absorbing detail about conditions on the coffin ships as she realized she was alone in the darkness. Shrugging, she continued on through the maze of displays for another hour. When she eventually emerged Martin was in the gift shop.

'It's all for the Americans,' he stated, offering no explanation for his absence.

'Would you like a coffee?' she asked.

'I've had two,' he replied.

She said nothing as she immediately went from the place. She was almost in tears in the car-park.

'What's wrong with you?' he pursued.

She was mute with anger and she sat sullenly beside him as he drove back. In Ballyanna she left him in the cottage and walked across the cliffs to Cromwell's Hump. The usual burning confusion after their arguments diminished as she walked. On the headland, in The Hollow, she sat and tried to read. Giving in, she lay back, watched the clouds merge and listened to the sea far below.

In those living moments she felt beyond time and history; as if the place existed of itself. It possessed a terrible beauty and it possessed her completely. For her, history had always been a place she could enter through her mind and imagination, through stories and artefacts. It was for all to know and explore. But here it was within her, a genetic memory, absolutely personal.

She dozed then, warm and safe, dreaming of her grandmother and grandfather and all those before them.

When she returned it was to an uneasy evening, throughout which she waited for him to apologize.

He did not.

The following morning she decided she would speak to him, adamant that she would not waste her time in Ballyanna.

And over breakfast she made to speak, but as she did they both turned to the sound of a tractor over-revving outside and shouts of consternation above the clattering motor.

He followed her through the house and stepped out on to the porch. The tractor was being turned up the boreen where Martin had parked his Healey off the road, in the entrance to the field there. The driver was being directed around the pristine car by another man. There were centimetres to spare.

Martin rushed into the road. The tractor stopped and the two men looked at him in his underpants.

'Watch where you're going!'

'We have it,' smiled the one on foot.

'That's too close,' Martin screamed furiously.

'It's miles away,' he shouted, as he leapt on to the back of the tractor. 'But if you're so worried, boy, find somewhere else to park it. You must be a fucking idiot to park it on a corner in front of a gate.'

The tractor bumped off up the lane and Martin ran to the car and checked the paintwork, running his hand along the side.

'You fucking bogtrotters,' he screamed.

'Fuck off y'Jackeen,' came the derisory reply.

She handed him a cup of coffee when he came in, and stood at the fireplace, peering through the window.

'Is it damaged?'

'No. Thank God. Did you hear that bollocks?'

'You were very aggressive.'

He slumped into the reading chair, spilt some of the coffee, gasped and stared at it. Suddenly he sighed and said, 'And I shouldn't have been . . . I've been an arse, Orla. Can we start again?'

In relief she nodded.

'So what are we doing today?' he asked.

'It's a fine day so we're staying here and going rock-pooling on the strand below.'

'What will we find there except weed and sand?'

She gave him a stern stare and he held his hands up.

'Yesterday,' she explained. 'I found a book about the seashore on the shelf and I have this bucket and those nets. We can expect to find fish, shells, crabs and starfish.'

'That's what children do.'

'And aren't you just a child, Martin?'

'I'm all man,' he growled and grabbed her backside.

'You're a man who needs to be more considerate. I want your full attention today. I'm going to enjoy myself and you're going to make sure I do.'

'Yes, Miss Shea.'

She put on her old floppy straw hat and he sniggered. She shot him a scathing stare and he scurried off to change.

With the tide out, he followed her across the rocks, dutifully stopping when she crouched at a particularly promising pool. She yelped with delight, chasing tiny fish around the pools but he was unimpressed.

Running her net along the submerged rock faces she diligently searched for creatures in the sludge and weed. With wonder, she captured crabs and starfish and shrimps. While she patiently foraged, he quickly became despondent after a few half-hearted attempts.

Eventually, she left him to sunbathe by a large pool and went off on her own. She lost track of time at the water's edge and eventually, when she straightened, she saw McLeavey rowing across the bay. It was then she decided to retreat. Closer to the strand she found Martin stood in the pool splashing water on his bare neck.

'What is it?'

'I've sunburn,' he moaned.

She put her hat on his head and wrapped her scarf about her neck.

There were children approaching across the rocks. When one, a girl, saw Martin, she went into her back pack.

'Do you want some water, mister?'

'No. I'm fine.'

'I think you need some. You caught the sun and that's bad for you. Here, have some of mine.'

'I'm fine thanks.'

She held the bottle out.

'I haven't drunk out of it yet,' she assured him.

'Thanks,' Martin grunted, as he snatched it and gulped down half of it. There were tears in the child's eyes when he handed it back.

Orla intervened. 'Have you seen what we've found?'

All the children crowded round her in wonder.

'Can we have that crab?'

'You can have them all. We're going up now.'

'What's your name, mister?' said the girl with the water.

'Martin.'

'That crab is called Martin,' she declared.

Orla laughed. 'We're staying in the house just there above the strand.'

'That's Donovan's house.'

'Does he have any sweets?'

'No, but he left me some money for any children who want to buy some in the village. If you knock on the door later on I'll find it for you.'

The children thanked her and moved away, slipping and chattering on the weed and rocks. One let out a yell.

'Paddy is here! Let's see what he has.'

They all went running back to the channel. The girl picked out Martin the crab and poured the rest of the bucket into a pool. She looked guiltily to Orla.

'We'll catch them all again later,' she offered.

Orla waved and nudged Martin.

'Look who's coming in,' she observed.

He looked over his shoulder.

'Is that your man you were talking about?'

' 'Tis.'

'Let's go and talk to him.'

'I don't want to.'

'Ah come on. Let's see his attitude when I'm around.'

'You're not going to lose it again, are you?'

'Not at all.'

He took off the straw hat and walked off.

By the time the two of them reached the channel, McLeavey was heaving the dinghy through the shallows and over the sandbank where the children were crowding around and pulling with him. He was complaining loudly about minding their feet but they were ignoring him.

Martin grabbed the dinghy. 'Hello,' he said, leaning on the edge with his weight.

'Hello,' Patrick replied and stood off, glancing at Orla following behind.

In the pause, the children were giggling with glee as they poked and prodded the catch.

'Can I give you a hand?' asked Martin.

'Thanks,' McLeavey replied and they heaved the dinghy on.

Orla followed at a wary distance.

'What have you caught?'

'There's just a few mackerel and pollock and lobsters and a crab. Look there.'

'And what will you do with them?'

'I give them away.'

'You don't sell them?'

When they hit the stones, McLeavey fetched the pulley rope.

'I barter, but for the most part I don't expect anything. Would you like a few mackerel?'

'Please.'

'I'll gut them for you if you like.'

Orla stood behind Martin and listened.

'I can do that,' said Martin.

'Are you sure now?'

'Of course.'

McLeavey leaned in and handed him two large mackerel; they lay stiffly across his palms. Martin looked down at them with revulsion. One of the children sniggered. The girl came round, took the fish and slid his finger under the gills.

'Like this, Crabby.'

There were snorts.

Martin turned to Orla. She took the fish under the gills and held them there.

'I'm afraid we haven't anything to barter,' said Martin, 'so could we buy a lobster?' He picked one from the crate and inspected it. The children watched him intently as he slipped off the elastic band on one of the claws and waved it at them. The claw flexed and he clearly considered it his turn to laugh. They stepped back.

'What are you doing?' demanded McLeavey. 'Put it down.'

Martin turned back to Orla and thrust the creature at her. She flinched and the claw closed and caught her jacket. Martin tried to tug it off but it was firmly fixed on her collar.

McLeavey stepped between them, took out a knife and prised open the claw. He immediately wrapped another elastic band around the claw and dropped it back in the crate. He then turned to Martin. McLeavey was lower down the slope and so face to face.

'Do you know what would happen if that claw had caught a piece of flesh or a finger? It would slice it clean through. You must be careful with these creatures.'

There was no aggression in his reprimand.

'Now if you need any advice about the fish—' Patrick offered.

'We'll be fine,' Martin insisted.

As they walked away, he was strident. 'He obviously changed his attitude when he saw me with you. The man is an idiot.'

It was then that he slipped on the stones and fell on to his backside. The fish swung on Orla's fingers and the fins slapped him across the face as he tried to break his fall by grabbing her.

She helped him up and glanced back, expecting more ridicule, but the children and McLeavey were over the dinghy, inspecting the catch again.

With his free hand he used the palm to brush his backside and gasped.

'What is that? Is that oil?'

'I think it's tar,' Orla said quietly.

'Oh shit. These shorts are new,' he whined.

In An Doras, Orla laid the fish on the draining board as Martin scrubbed his hands and then scrubbed the shorts. He whined again as the tar smeared.

'You'll make it worse. I'll do that later,' she said, taking them from him. 'Are you going to gut these then?'

He looked sidelong.

'Or will I do that as well?'

Martin stiffened, snatched the fish and marched back through the cottage. She watched him tramp across the road and throw the fish over the humpbacked bridge into the stream. He then marched back inside and confronted her. His red face, a deeper shade now, was comical.

'I want no fish. That man is an idiot; this cottage is too small and the valley is certainly no haven.' He slouched in the reading chair and petulantly folded his arms.

She stared down at him as he kicked off his sandals and caressed his neck. 'There is no need for that, Martin. Do you know what you are saying?'

But he wasn't listening. He was looking through the window at his car and his jaw was sagging. He leapt up and rushed back outside. She followed him this time. He stopped on the bridge and started dancing and squealing. She noticed his bare feet on the gravel.

Along the side of the car was a deep serrated scratch and the wing mirror was hanging off. She placed a hand on his shoulder but he shrugged her off. Leaning against the wing his wheezing slowed, and he lamely flicked the mirror.

In tears he said, 'I know it was them. I'll find out which farm it is and I'll demand they pay. This is not right. This is not right. I'll sue them.'

Orla saw that McLeavey was approaching from the strand. She went to Martin and took him firmly this time.

'Come inside, Martin. We'll ask around. We'll solve it together.'

'My car . . . my car,' he moaned.

McLeavey passed.

'Have you seen what they've done?' Martin called.

McLeavey stopped and looked casually.

'You should have parked it somewhere more appropriate.'

'What? Appropriate? I've every right to park it here. Doesn't this field belong to the house?'

Orla saw McLeavey grind his teeth. 'The farmers won't see it that way. They have to work here.'

'They could have asked.'

'I'm sure they'll knock on your door as soon as they realize. Have you gutted those fish yet?'

'No I bloody haven't. I threw them into the stream.'

'Why did you do that?' McLeavey remained level.

'I didn't want the bloody things. I'll pay you for them, if you like and you can swap them for turnips or whatever else you do with them.'

McLeavey stared blankly. 'They were a gift to you both. You shouldn't throw waste into the stream. The rats will be all over it if you do.'

'Do you think I care about rats in a stream when my car is ruined?'

'No. I don't suppose you do.'

McLeavey turned away and walked on, tall and straight-backed. Like a stormtrooper, Orla thought, as she led Martin inside.

That evening they went into Ballybrannigan. The Open Hearts had returned to The Laughing Gull.

She led Martin to the same corner so she could look out across Ballybrannigan Bay and the mountains beyond that were fading into the night.

Though she tried to talk to him, Martin sat morosely sipping his beer. Eventually she gave up but felt no anger or apprehension – she would rather look at the lights in the darkness and every time the door opened, look to see who it was.

When the band began to play Martin leaned to her.

'I thought you said this would be a good crack. You can get this in any bar in Dublin, only better.'

She thought about that.

'You're right of course – perhaps you can, but you don't get this bar in those places.'

'Well I can't be bothered with it. I'm going back. My neck is on fire, I've a headache and I'm flaked after being on that strand.'

'You can't drive; you've had too much to drink.'

'You can drive me.'

He supped the last dregs and stood there shaking his keys. She sighed, smiled and followed him through the crowd.

11

When the Sky was Dark

She awoke to birdsong and snores and lay there staring at the wheat fields swaying up the valley side. They glowed as the sun strengthened. With the window open the breeze stroked the net curtains and she could hear the waves falling on the strand below.

Martin snorted in his sleep, turned to her and exhaled stale breath. His snoring had awoken her intermittently throughout the night. It was why she liked to sleep alone.

She stealthily slipped out from under the blankets and went to the kitchen. Taking her cereal and tea, several of Donovan's notebooks and the transistor radio she went to sit on the stormwall and listen to the news.

The air was cleansed from the night but she could feel the heavy pressure as she sat on the mossy wall with her feet dangling in the long grass on the other side. The radio murmured as she ate, and she was at ease again.

In one of the notebooks she had found a list of places along the Coastal Way: Allann Mor; Ballybrudar; the Ledge of Names; Lir's Tears; Manannan's Fingers; the Thousand Flames and Schull Ban. Each name resounded with a hidden history that she wanted to know.

Martin found her there an hour later. Shuffling and dishevelled he leaned against the wall. He closed the notebook, kissed her hand and placed it against his unshaven cheek.

'You're very patient,' he said. 'I feel much better.'

'You should have stayed in bed,' she said.

'I can't sleep in that sack.'

'I understand that bed was a great luxury when it was bought.'

'And when was that?'

'After the Great War.'

'And I think it's the same mattress. It's disgusting. All those bodies that have writhed around on it. Imagine what's in it.'

'It's a new mattress. Donovan . . . Anyway, how many hotels have you ever been in?'

'But . . . It's not the same.'

'You're right. If anyone else had slept in that bed, they'd be my people.'

He yawned complacently.

'Come on, Orla. They might as well be strangers.'

'I don't think they are.'

'Do you want another cup of tea?' he laughed.

She nodded and he retreated.

She watched the waves fall back and forth and when he returned, found she could not recall a single thought from his absence.

'And what's on today's itinerary?' he asked, slurping violently and gasping appreciatively.

'We're going for a walk to Ballybrannigan.'

'How far it is?' He was trying to calculate.

'Eight miles, there and back.'

'Can't we drive?'

'We'll go along the Coastal Way. They say it's famous for its views and there are places I want to see.'

'Famous? I've never heard of it.'

'Still, it'll do you good.'

She patted his paunch.

'And you wanted me to eat a cooked breakfast,' he scowled.

'And I won't make that mistake again.'

They were setting off over the first stile of the Coastal Way within an hour. Patrick McLeavey was there, repairing a collapsed flat stone wall on the lane.

'What happened?' Martin asked. Orla was mildly impressed that his pride did not inhibit him.

'Staunton struck it with his tractor again. They say he has no place on the road.'

Neither laughed with him and Patrick turned his back.

'So Staunton is the culprit,' Martin hissed with triumphant assumption.

When they reached the ridge on Cromwell's Hump and saw the lighthouse on Lir's Tears, Martin gasped.

'I know. It's wonderful,' Orla said.

'No,' he said. 'Are you saying we've got to walk that far?'

'Yes.'

'Look at the way the cliffs meander there. We've got to walk there and back again?' he whined.

'Yes.'

He sighed and petulantly trudged down the ridge, his arms flapping loosely. She followed behind him, tracing the shapes of the rocks in the shallows, following the easy undulations in the fields and watching the house-martins flying in and out of the cliff sides.

'Can you see the birds there, Martin, shooting away. . . ? There they go. What do you think they are?'

He glanced down. 'I've no idea.'

'I'd like to know,' she said.

'They're just birds,' he added flatly. 'Anyway, I thought you found a book.'

She could not decide if she was more frustrated by his sarcasm or her lack of knowledge.

They passed over the stiles and the stream courses in silence and most often many paces apart, and by the time she reached the gate at the edge of the village, Martin was resting on a bench before the boarded-up restaurant. When she approached he had his sandals off and was massaging his feet.

She sat beside him and he glowered at her.

'That was far more than four miles.'

'How about an ice cream?' she suggested.

'How about a taxi back?' He rubbed his bare legs. 'Those brambles have cut me all over, I've probably fractured my shins and my groin is strained going up and down the hills. Every stone on that path is an injury case waiting to happen.'

She looked back the way they came. The farthest cliffs were obscured by the distance and the darkening sky.

He followed her eye.

'Do you think it'll rain?'

'I think it might,' she decided. 'I can smell it.'

'You've caught the sun that there is,' he observed.

Her exposed shoulders ached as she shrugged.

'I should have worn my hat.'

'I'm glad you didn't. It looks ridiculous.'

'You already said as much. That's why I didn't wear it.'

'Oh.'

Her attention now focused on Ballybrannigan. Off the Coastal Way, on the edge of the village, a short terrace of single-storey concrete chalets had been built. They were garishly grey against the verdant fields. The barren gravel and tarmac was incongruous in its surroundings. Orla imagined some communist haven on the Black Sea Riviera.

'Now that's the sort of property that would be worth investing in,' Martin stated.

'You're joking.'

'You'd have beautiful views and all the modern amenities. What more could you want?'

'It's buildings like that, that ruin the beauty.'

'I don't agree. Look at that place there. Now that's an eyesore.'

She observed the flat-roofed restaurant, built in the art deco style, its whitewash stained and flaking against the sea and the neglect.

'It just needs sprucing up,' she argued unconvincingly. 'Imagine eating out on the front of there on a summer's night.'

'In 1950 maybe, but now – no way.'

They walked together into the village.

'This place is a ghost town,' he decided. 'If it's like this all summer, imagine—'

'I imagine they still sell ice-creams though,' she interrupted.

They bought cones at the shop just opened for the summer, and sat on the pier watching the people passing by.

'All inbred no doubt,' Martin whispered.

'Will you not shut up?' she snapped.

He chuckled, revived after his vanilla swirl.

They then strolled through the village and came to Phelan's Store. Inside, Martin purchased another cone and sat on the wall outside. Orla tried on the straw hats. She found the widest one, far wider than her own, and tilted it on her head.

The tattooed shopkeeper laughed. 'That's a jaunty angle you have there.'

She giggled as she paid for it. Looking at herself once more in the mirror she noticed a display of paintings behind her. They were the usual array of cottages and coastal views, but she had seen one in particular as it was clearly An Doras. She went to it, scrutinizing it, half-recognizing the style of it. There was a flood of sun and outside, sitting on the porch, was an old man holding a cane and staring straight at the artist. Without hesitation she took out her purse again.

'We've many painters here,' the shopkeeper said. 'That one is . . . Ballyanna I'm sure. Yes, I see it now. 'Tis a pretty picture.'

He would have told her more but she hardly heard at all and was out of the door, clutching it, cherishing it.

She revealed the painting to Martin who eyed it apathetically. 'These paintings are all the same. It's not exactly art. The amateurs only paint them for the American tourists. They have no value.'

She snatched it back slid it reverently into her shoulder bag.

The wind was up now and the temperature dropped as they made their way back along the Coastal Way.

It was when they could see Cromwell's Hump was the next headland that the clouds burst and they were caught in a downpour. Martin laughed and so did she as they began to run. The rain against her skin was exhilarating but when she slid on the path, she called to him before he disappeared.

Though he complained, he came back for her, heaving her up and pulling her along as he ran on again. The rain fell more fiercely then, sheeting across the cliff tops. He went faster and she stumbled repeatedly. With no shelter in sight she wrenched her hand away from his. Holding the hat on her head and clutching her bag to her chest she stooped before the rain and walked on at her own pace. Her clothes sucked against her skin and the rain was running down her back. She was no longer laughing.

He strode on, calling to her to speed up but she was miserable now, and then he climbed down through the dense trees and undergrowth in the next stream gully and she lost sight of him. By the time she reached the muddy steps he was up in the next field.

'Wait for me,' she demanded.

'What?'

'Don't go on. Wait for me.'

He turned and walked on.

'Wait!' she screamed.

He stopped and impatiently trudged back down the field to her.

'I'm drenched. I'm cold and I've had enough. Now come on,' he ordered.

'Will you not wait for me?'

'I will of course. I'll wait here. Now move.'

'Help me across.'

'Help yourself.'

'I'm exhausted Martin. I really am.'

'You were the one who wanted to walk all this way and now look what you've done.'

'Well go on then. Don't wait. I don't care. Go on. Go!'

'I will.'

'Well do so!'

'I'm going.'

She stood there watching him stride up the hill. Heaving defiance she stepped down into the gully and immediately slipped on the muddy steps, sliding down into the watercourse. She screamed as she fell, but the sound was muted among the trees.

On the gully floor she rolled across the smooth stones and sat upright in the swollen stream. Dazed and winded she lifted the new hat that had flopped over her eyes and saw the painting was in the water at her feet. For a while she sat there in the shelter of the tangled canopy, out of the wind, listening to the rain patter through the leaves.

When Martin climbed over the stile by the stormwall the thunder was rumbling. Patrick straightened and pulled back his hood and glanced down the path after him.

Martin was walking on when Patrick called. 'Where is Orla?'

Martin stopped in the lane and turned slowly.

'She's admiring the views,' he sneered.

Lightning flashed.

'Don't you think you should make sure she's safe along the cliffs?'

'No, I fucking don't.'

He flounced away. Patrick frowned, pulled his hood up, dropped his trowel and went over the stile.

It was raining hard and the thunder was oscillating through the heavy air when he reached the gully.

He saw Orla shivering beneath the hedgerow on the path. For a moment he watched her snivelling and shivering and holding a sodden painting. Carefully stepping down the path he braced himself on a branch. Orla gasped and tried to stand, immediately slipping on to her backside again.

'Are you hurt Orla?'

'No,' she replied sullenly.

'The views are better up above.'

She remained straight faced.

'I'm going back to the valley. Would you like me to show you a quicker way than over Cromwell's Hump?'

He held out his hand, and for the first time she saw him smile at her. Wide and generous, it was a smile that seemed to ask for nothing.

'Come here to me,' he urged gently.

She hesitated but took his hand and he lifted her up. She pressed against him and reeled away as he turned her on to the path. While she composed herself he took off his raincoat and held it out.

'No,' she said again.

He stepped forward and she stood still clutching the painting, her hat limp over her ears. Putting the coat about her shoulders he led her off the path and up the field. Orla could smell his scent on the coat as she hobbled along. She knew it was a musk, but the scent seemed to invade her senses as if it were her own.

'Have you hurt your leg?'

'No,' she said.

On the field where the Damanta Stones stood at the far end she stumbled on the rivulets and shards and Patrick held her again. She looked sidelong to see the rain soaking through his shirt and then shrugged him off. He waited silently while she rested on the fallen stone before limping on. She could see the valley below and the roof of An Doras.

'I can carry you,' he offered.

'No!' she exclaimed.

'You are in a bad way. I can help you.'

'No.'

'You can't make it.'

She turned to him with her hands on her hips and her hair wet across face and in her mouth.

'I can, I will and I do.'

She spun away and strutted off. She did not see him smile, and he was not smiling because she stumbled again.

Nothing else was said until they arrived on the lane outside the cottage and Orla saw that Martin's car was gone.

She stood on the porch shivering and fumbling for the key in her bag. Patrick stepped forward and opened the door with a key of his own. She frowned at him and went in. Without invitation he followed.

On the stone floor was a sodden pile of Martin's clothes. Patrick kicked them aside. 'Go into your room and strip,' he instructed, and passed a quilted throw to her. 'Wrap yourself in this and get into bed. I will set a fire and fetch some of Donovan's warm clothes and towels.'

She stood there blowing hard.

'I would have done that.'

He nodded and turned away.

She was curled in the bed when he knocked the door. She called him in and he laid the towels and clothes at her feet without looking at her as she peered over the cover.

He was banking the fire when she eventually emerged, dressed and warming.

He held out his hand again.

'I don't think I've introduced myself to you. I'm Patrick McLeavey.'

She took his hand.

'Orla Shea.'

He considered before asking, 'Are you aware of the smell in the bathroom?'

'Yes.'

'It's the cesspit,' he informed her. 'It's worse when it rains. Unless it's seen to it could flood the lower end of the house with sewage.'

She blinked rapidly, surprised by the abrupt advice. 'I assumed the bathroom had been recently renovated,' she said.

'Yes. However the old drain-aways have been blocked in the process. The cesspit fills with the run-off from the fields and has nowhere to go but up through the waste pipes. It should have been noticed but it wasn't. It was an oversight, I'm sure.'

'What should I do?'

'Contact the people who did the job and request they repair it.'

'Thank you. I will.'

He nodded. She looked away.

'There's a cup of tea there,' he indicated. 'I'll leave you now. Can I come back and check on you?'

'Yes,' she replied quietly.

An hour later she was listening to another bout of rain on the roof and trying to call Martin's mobile again, when there was a knock on the door.

She answered and found Anne O'Meagher standing there under an umbrella and holding a tartan camping flask. Her great-aunt bustled past and went to the kitchen.

'You should have spoken. You must always ask. We would have told you,' she chastised.

'Spoken of what?'

'Why do you think we talk about the weather? Because we've nothing else to say? It is because it rules us.'

Orla slumped again into the chair, too despondent to apologize or argue.

'Where are all his things?' Anne called from the kitchen.

'I've boxed them up. I'm thinking of giving them to charity.'

Anne did not reply as she brought her a bowl of steaming soup.

'What soup is it?'

'Pea soup. You will like it.'

Orla sipped it off the spoon. It was thick, sweet and smooth and Anne was right.

'Where is your man?'

'He's gone out.'

Anne raised an eyebrow.

'I don't know where he is,' Orla admitted, unable to resist the admission.

'Well, you know what to say when he comes back . . . And he'll come back.'

'What do I say?'

'That he's a blackguard and no good and that he should go back to the city if that's where he wants to be.'

'I don't think it's any of . . .' she hesitated. 'Thank you Anne.'

Anne looked at her as if seeing more than the forlorn girl and then went to the door.

'That's where Donny would sit and write,' she smiled. 'He was a fierce writer.'

The soup was thick and filling and she ate it gratefully. After a while, she could not decide if she had forgotten Martin was not there or if she did not care.

She awoke with a cry when the front door burst open and Martin swayed in the doorway looking down at her.

'Close the door,' she said.

He kicked it shut.

'Did you enjoy the view?' he slurred.

'You've been drinking.'

'I was depressed.'

'Well I was distressed.'

He flopped down on the settee opposite her. 'And now I'm de-stressed,' he giggled.

'You don't care at all,' she scorned.

'I care, Orla. That's why I've booked us into the Atlantic Park Hotel in Ballybrannigan. We passed it this morning. It's a fine place—'

'Why would I go there?'

'To have some comfort.'

'I'm comfortable here.'

He rubbed his face.

'I'm sorry, Orla. I'm tired and I want a good night's sleep. Come with me and we'll have a meal and we'll talk.'

'Let's talk right now. Let's talk about you leaving me on the cliffs.'

'I thought you were right behind me. I was angry.'

'I fell.'

'And did you break any bones?'

'No.'

'Then don't be dramatic.'

She gasped. 'And the painting was ruined in the rain.'

'It's was worthless anyway.'

'Shut up now, Martin.'

They stared into the fire.

He spoke first. 'I am sorry, Orla. I shouldn't have left you there. That was wrong. Tomorrow we'll buy another painting if they have one.'

She scowled.

'I am sorry,' he insisted.

She shrugged.

'Will you have that meal? It'll be on me.'

She sighed and nodded.

And shortly afterwards she drove them into Ballybrannigan. They took a table in one of the windows with views across Ballybrannigan Bay. She could still taste the pea soup in her mouth. The lighthouse beam scanned the pier and breakwater below.

'This is more like it,' he exclaimed with a mouthful of lobster meat.

'Now this is for the American tourists,' she said.

'You don't have to live like a peasant when you come out to the country.'

'I know that and I don't. I have enough luxury in the cottage.'

He hesitated. 'But it's basic. Wouldn't you say?'

'I would not.'

'Then it's too far out from the city to be convenient and not far enough away to be truly remote. Don't you think?'

'I think it's just the right location to have the best of both.'

'More wine?' he averted.

'No thanks.'

She was grateful that he wiped the flecks of lobster meat from his mouth.

'I thought we could go upstairs and. . .'

'And what?'

He simpered, clearly drunk again.

'What we always do in a hotel in a new place. The romance and the thrill—'

'Shut up,' she hissed. Even if no one could overhear, she flushed with embarrassment.

'Ah, come on, Orla.'

'Not here. This isn't a new place for me.'

'You're joking.'

'I am not.'

With a sneering swig he emptied his glass and poured another.

'I am not joking,' she reiterated, 'and I am not staying here. I'm going back on my own. You cannot drive and I will call in at the barracks and inform the Gardai if you follow.'

Abruptly standing she left him there and strode from the place and out on to the road. He did not follow and she passed through the darkening village in a haze of anger and denial.

The odour of the rain on the lane and in the hedgerows filled her senses with a subtle joy as she walked on, and in the dark and silence she began to think clearly again. Leaving him there was right. She felt no regret or inclination to return. She wanted it to be cleaner, to be polite, even friendly, but it was not and she did not care.

12

Spin, Measure and Cut

She awoke with the sun and as had become her habit she took her tea and toast to the stormwall, feeling the way she had the first time she arrived in the valley. It was a feeling of liberation and relief – she knew it now. Entering the valley for the first time and every time since, she left more and more behind. When she stood there for the first time and stared out to the horizon, unable to see where the sea met the sky, she was looking into the very flux of her being and she liked it.

Later that morning, after packing Martin's belongings and placing them by the door, she returned to the stormwall. On the strand below she saw that Patrick McLeavey's dinghy was upturned and Roberto Cesare was rubbing down the surface. She strolled down to him.

He had his back to her as she approached and was listening to music through his headphones. She walked into his field of vision and he pulled out the earpiece.

'How are you?'

'Fine,' she smiled. 'So what are you doing?'

'I promised Patrick I would clean this old bark.'

'Did you make this one?'

'I wish . . . It's a beauty. This was built by Pearse. He was an excellent craftsman.' He resumed scraping the paintwork as he conversed. 'He was an apprentice of Charlie Bogue.'

She smiled; he told her this as if she should know the name.

'Now there was a boat-builder. His boats are still afloat. I'm told there's even a couple in America.'

'Donovan and Pearse were estranged,' she said. 'What happened?'

Roberto sighed. 'They were both as bad as each other – stubborn and pious. It was probably a word spoken out of turn in their childhood or some forgotten jealousy – they didn't talk about it. Donovan may have said something to Patrick but not to me. I was closer to Pearse . . . Whatever it was, in the end they had nothing to say; they didn't like each other and they had nothing in common. Pearse was one for the ladies and Donovan . . . well, he wasn't, or so we thought.'

She did not know what to say.

He straightened his back. 'So we're related. Isn't it great? You know, Anne spoke to them both. They both knew what the other was up to. They always asked after each other but would never speak. Bloody weird.' His fading accent and strange phrasing were amusing.

'What do you think about me inheriting the cottage?' she asked.

Roberto's eyes narrowed.

'In my view, I think it's yours by right. No one else has a claim to it.'

'Even though I'm from outside and I'd never been here before?'

'It makes no difference. I was born in England and only came here when I was fifteen. Pat found me and brought me over . . . He saved me. But I was treated just the same as he was and he was born here, right up there in Elannat . . . Anyway, it's yours so what can anyone say?'

She shrugged.

'Any news from Mossy O'Sullivan?' he ventured.

'It's a matter of waiting but he assures me everything is in order.'

'He'll see to it no doubt. There's history in that house,' he reflected. 'I understand you're a history teacher in Dublin.'

'I am.'

'You know Saoirse works in Killybeg?'

'I do. I saw her there. It is a fascinating place.'

'There are stories about the Great House that she can tell that they don't like the visitors to be told. I reckon they'd double their numbers if they did. You should talk to her. Ask her about the roses.'

She was intrigued. 'I'd like to.'

'Then why don't you come to dinner. I formally invite you.'

'I'd love to.'

'Then how about Friday?'

She went from the strand feeling elated, but when she got to the top of the slipway, she saw that Martin was waiting on the porch.

'I've come for my things. I'm going home.'

She nodded.

'Have you nothing to say?' he added.

She shook her head.

'Will you come with me?'

'I won't be going back for a while; I want to be alone.'

'It was only supposed to be a week.'

'You lasted three days.'

'Well, I can't waste my time here. There is nothing to do. I'm bored and you've changed.'

She went past him.

'Yes I have,' she said quietly, almost to herself.

'Why?' he implored. 'It can't be this place. Tell me it's not this . . . hovel.'

'You're right, Martin. Without the city and all it has, what else is there we have in common? We go to the cinema, to the theatre, to restaurants and parties, but when do we just sit and contemplate?'

'We're together most of the time.'

'But we don't talk to each other, about each other. I've always got so many other things to think about. It's never just talking and listening. And if I ever do talk, I talk to Bernie. I should be talking to you.'

'We can change. I can change that. We're talking now.'

'No we're not. This place, this hovel, has made me realize . . . You see, I know that you don't care. And now I don't care what you think. When you strip it all away we're left with nothing.'

'You're cruel, Orla. These deaths and this place have made you cynical.'

'It hasn't. It's made me believe in truth and love and wanting something more.'

'That's just arseology. These people don't think. They just live; they just exist. They were born here and won't ever leave. What sort of life is that?'

'And that's why I can't be with you. That statement alone is enough to know what you really are and how different we have become . . . or always were.'

'You know nothing.' He went to the bedroom to pack his things.

She stood in the doorway. 'It's all in here,' she calmly informed him. 'I took the liberty.'

He looked from the bags to her and shook his head slowly, finally realizing her intent. Heaving two of the bags he bustled past her. When he returned she held out the stained shorts.

'I couldn't get the tar from these.'

He snatched them from her and she turned away. The door slammed and she heard the gravel fly as he screeched away.

She made tea and sat in the window, wrapped in the quilt and the quiet of the day, finally alone. She had admitted she did not care but now the realization that she did not love him crept insidiously across her mind. Only now he was gone was it real.

She took a book from the mantelpiece and tried to read, but the words were a wall and she began to cry in a crescendo of release. She thought she did not care but to reject Martin in such a way left her with a dull, aching guilt.

She tipped the tea down the sink, went to the fridge and seized the open bottle of sparkling rosé. Sitting by the fire she gulped back a glass and sat back and absorbed the brief euphoria. For a moment she really did not care at all, but then the rush receded, and she realized she was drinking wine just to get drunk in the afternoon and she cried again.

Blearily, she stared at the glass, wanting to pour it away. Instead she swallowed it in one. She had almost finished drinking the bottle when she telephoned Bernadette.

'It's over, Bernie,' she shouted.

'What has happened?'

'I don't love him and I know it. I finally admitted it. I've known it for ages. I've wasted my time and I didn't know it.'

'Does that mean I can have him now?'

Orla hesitated and then she began to laugh and Bernadette laughed with her.

'You're evil, Bernie.'

'I want to be. I try. Do you think that's why men are afraid of me?'

'I do.'

'Are you drunk?'

'Yes.'

Despite the poor reception, Orla described what had happened over the last three days and felt better for it. Bernie listened as Orla always did but could not resist the scorn.

'He left you in the mud? The bastard. You don't know what you saw in him? You're not the only one . . . You don't know what you'll do now? You'll come out with me again.'

Becoming afraid of the advice, Orla was relieved when there was a categorical thump at the door.

'Can you hold the line, Bernie? I'm going to answer the door.'

She looked through the window to see Patrick McLeavey out on the porch.

'It's him,' she hissed.

'Martin's back?'

'No – McLeavey.'

'Are you going to answer it?'

'I must. There's no reason not to. He can see the light.'

'But you're half-pissed.'

'I'm at the door,' she hissed.

She straightened herself and opened it.

'Hello. I've come to see how y'are,' said Patrick.

'I'm fine, thank you.' She tried to control her words. 'Thank you for your help yesterday. It was . . . kind.'

He looked quizzical when she spoke. He was not wearing glasses and his eyes, now unmagnified, were narrow and hard to see.

'Is your partner here?'

'No. He has gone back to Dublin.'

He considered that.

'I was going to invite you both to my house.'

'Pardon?'

'I'll cook the lobster that caught your jacket. I think I may have been rude to your partner and I'll punish the lobster in apology.'

She stared vacantly as he joked, more through the effort of appearing sober than not finding it amusing.

'Perhaps you would come instead,' he suggested.

She stayed straight-faced.

'I don't think I will.'

'Oh.'

He reddened but held her stare.

'I don't think it would be appropriate to sit alone together all evening, would it?'

'I suppose not . . . It was just courtesy . . . I'm glad you're well. Goodbye, Orla.'

She closed the door and swore silently.

'Did you hear that,' she hissed into the mobile.

'Just about.'

'What do you think?'

'What an oaf,' Bernadette declared. 'There you are in pain and he preys on you. He thinks that if he helps you, you'll owe him something. And what is worse he still asked you to dinner when you told him Martin was gone. He jumped at the chance. He thinks you'll be desperate and he'll have his way with you on the rebound. I think Jack was right about him. He's calculating.'

'Yes,' Orla agreed quietly.

'I saw your mother, by the way.'

'When?'

She came by your flat while I was there.'

'And?'

'I told her where you were.'

'What did she say?'

'Nothing. She just said that she would see you later.'

'Thanks.'

'She's looking her age now mind. Too much dye and foundation. She can't cover it up. It's a pity. She was an attractive woman.'

Orla did not want to say the obvious about her friend's style.

'I'm feeling slightly sick, Bernie. I'll call you later.'

She went to the toilet and stuck her fingers down her throat. It was something she had not done since she was at university. Her gut strained and the bile burned but there was a bitter relief when the wine and toast and tea gushed into the bowl. Although purged she had terrible cramps in her stomach and so she went to lie down and feel sorry for herself a little more.

Later in the afternoon she was composed enough to venture out. She drank water, took the telescope and went for a walk along the cliffs.

First of all she walked up to Elannat where she returned the flask to Anne.

'I was just off for a walk and I thought I'd return this. Thank you. I am grateful, if still a little embarrassed.'

'I did what I had to do,' reassured Anne. 'Sure, how were you to know? You hadn't been shown.'

'Still, thanks again. Is the recipe your own?'

'I suppose it is, but only in that it was passed down to me by your great-grandmother and I'm sure she had it from her mother and so on.'

The connections were irresistible to Orla.

'Will you not come in?' Anne invited.

'I will.'

They sat in the conservatory observing the view.

'I have these pictures,' Orla said, handing over the images of her grandmother and Donovan. Anne perused them slowly. 'I thought you could tell me more about them. They are all I have of the both of them.'

'I haven't seen these since the time they were taken. I thought they were destroyed.'

'Donovan left them for me.'

'I can see that he would. This is on the Hump; this is outside An Doras; this in Andreenmacotter; this down the boreen . . .' She looked up over the rim of her glasses. 'I know as 'twas I who took these pictures. It was Peggy's camera. They arrived in the post months after that summer.'

'There is so much I don't know.'

'That's the way for us all.'

In the silence that followed, they contemplated and as they did so, seemed to breathe in unison with the wind. Still unsure of her great aunt, Orla turned to the view.

'Let me show you my pictures,' said Anne.

Orla followed her through the house. In the living-room, on the sideboard was an array of intricate silver photograph frames.

One at a time Anne selected a frame and revealed the world it had captured.

'This is all of us. I am the youngest there. But there is Rory, Pearse and

Donovan. There is Kathleen and me. And that is our parents Shelia and Tadhg. That was just before the war.'

Orla could see a likeness in them all.

'Here is my uncle, Michael Geraghty – my mother's brother. He was an awful Fenian and was exiled in America. There is his lovely wife Esther. They lived in Boston. I wouldn't know where as I've never been. I still get letters from the family and they've come over a few times.'

'And this one?'

'Ah now. That is outside the Leaping Dolphin. I love this picture.' Orla saw her smile. 'It is old sure. I was just a child and they were getting on. All my grandparents are there,' She pointed them out. 'Eamonn and Catherine O'Meagher and Brenda and Eugene Geraghty . . . Eamonn and Eugene were sailors and shipwrecked. That is how Geraghtys came to the valley. And this old photo you should know is the rarest of them all. That is Brede Houlahan and her daughter Mairead and her granddaughter Catherine who is my grandmother and so your . . . great-great-grandmother.'

Orla imagined the old woman in the photograph as the Phantom Queen, and in her fierce eyes she could see her on the cliffs at Schull Ban, in the night, against the sky, against her fate.

On the wall was a portrait of a boy. The fall of light in the image seemed to bleach his hair and darken his skin. He was looking into the light. The style was vaguely familiar to Orla.

Anne saw her looking.

'That is Patrick.'

'Oh.'

'I painted that when he returned to me. The likeness is there but my hand was unsteady . . . I had been heartbroken when they took him away.'

'Do you still paint?'

Anne coughed and straightened. 'I don't. It's my hands. They're stiff and they shake.'

Orla glanced at the girl in picture and was sorry.

They went back out to the conservatory.

'I'm off for that walk, Anne. Would you like to come with me?'

'I'll stay here. I can see it all from where I am.'

Orla left her there and climbed the hill to the Coastal Way above Gortagort. There she scanned the bay, watching the guillemots hunt off the rocks.

In that living moment she sensed how the instincts of these birds, like a tree in a car-park or eyes in a photograph connecting her to the past.

She panned the lens round and searched up the road to the trees at the centre of the valley where she knew McLeavey's house was situated. She quickly spotted the roof through the canopy and focused on the eaves and the window there.

It took a few seconds to realize what she saw. McLeavey was looking directly at her through a pair of binoculars. She immediately lowered the telescope, more with embarrassment than annoyance, and scurried back down the path.

Rather than retreat into An Doras, which she wanted to do, she decided she did not want to suggest that her snooping was anything more than an accident. She strolled up the stormwall and continued to survey the wildlife, because, of course, that's what she was doing all along.

Although she refused to look, she imagined McLeavey spying on her still so she made her movements deliberate – even grand as she scrutinized the birds and scenery. All the while she was conscious of her profile and posture, keeping her back straight, her stomach taut and her buttocks clenched. It was painful whilst simultaneously bird watching. Only when she thought it was quite clear to anyone watching that she had been entirely enthralled by the wildlife and was now ready to retreat, did she fold the telescope and casually stroll back to the cottage.

Jack Callaghan was standing in the road in full view of McLeavey. She smiled and waved furiously at Jack who frowned bemusedly at her exuberance.

'I've come down to apologize,' Jack said as she approached.

She placed her hand on his elbow and gently led him to the porch. 'For what, Jack?'

'I think I made you feel uncomfortable when I barged in like that and it wasn't my intention.'

'I know that, and there's no need to apologize.'

'Are you well Orla? You look pale.'

'I'm fine. Come in and have a drink.'

He stood in the road as she took to the steps. 'Where's . . . Martin, is it?'

'He's not here. He's gone back to Dublin.'

'Oh.'

'Look, Jack. Come on in. I could do with the company.'

He smiled. 'I will so.'

Over tea he was self-effacing. 'I think I made a fool of myself.'

'You did not.' She flicked her eyebrows coyly. 'I was flattered.'

He hid his face behind the cup. 'I didn't mean to . . . Why has Martin gone back?'

'This place didn't suit him at all.'

'What was it about the valley?'

'It just wasn't the city. He was bored.'

'And yet he was with you.'

'Jack,' she warned levelly.

'Do you mind?'

'No.'

'Then neither do I.'

They laughed.

'But I hope you and Martin can sort out your differences. You been together a while haven't you?'

She instantly recognized the insincerity.

'Does that matter?' she smiled.

'Maybe not. Look. I'll be honest Orla . . . I want to be honest with you . . . You know I like you. I've liked you from the first time I saw you, but I didn't want to give you the wrong idea.' There was an innocence about his hesitant directness. He was flushed with uncertainty and she was aroused. 'Now you know how I feel, I'm just up the road if you need me to talk to or help you. I don't expect you to—'

She held up her hand.

'Could I come to your place tonight to talk?' she asked.

'Of course.'

'I'll bring wine,' she said, immediately regretting it.

'You will not . . . and I will cook.'

He stood and left her there. She watched him bound up the road and sat back wondering if she had done the right thing.

Turning her head this way and that in the mirror, she released and once again plaited her hair. Pinning it up, she patted with the brush until it was perfectly in place. She was wearing the diamond drop ear-rings that her grandmother had left her. She clipped them on and waved her head, liking the pendulous glamour. Then, applying a light beige lipstick, she straightened her figure-flattering black dress, blew herself a kiss and left.

She knew she looked good and it had not taken long; she had fallen asleep after Jack had gone and awoken with half an hour to spare. Feeling much better after the walk and the nap she had opened another bottle of wine. By the second glass any self-recriminations were firmly denied and she had decided that company would be the ideal cure for self-pity.

Warmed by the alcohol, she walked up the lane in the cool evening, imagining that the quiet in the valley could either liberate or madden. For now it allowed her solace; it gave her the space to know herself. Perhaps she would need to go back to the city when she knew enough, but she did not want to think about that yet.

She did want to think about McLeavey watching her this time, hoping he would see her she passed on by.

At the bend in the road the doors to the workshop were open. Within, a radio murmured, a pot-belly stove crackled and the scent of resin was strong. Roberto was leaning against the skeleton of a small dinghy.

She greeted him. She noticed him look her up and down in shock.

'Are you still on for Friday?' he asked.

'I am.'

'Can I invite other guests?'

'Of course. I look forward to it.'

'That's grand.'

'Where are you off to?

'I'm visiting Jack Callaghan.' She was vaguely conscious she was speaking in over-loud declaratives.

'Oh.'

His smiled became fixed. 'What is it?' she demanded.

' 'Tis nothing. We'll see you later.' He put down his tools and went inside.

She stood there a while, unsure of what had just occurred. Back on the lane, she pondered the attitude and decided it was not for her to draw sides.

At Ballygarry, Jack was pacing at the window with the telephone to his ear. When he saw her he replaced the receiver and came to her.

'I've booked a table at Killybeg House.'

'Oh. I thought you were going to—'

'It's expensive, but I don't care. I'll take us there now. And anyway, looking like that, you deserve it.'

He opened the door of the car for her and beckoned her in.

'Aren't you cold?'

'No.'

'You've got goose bumps.'

'Not at all,' she laughed, but after the walk she was frozen.

At the Great House they were led to a table in the grand reception room overlooking the gardens. It occurred to her as the waiter held her chair that determined measures were necessary in order to fully appreciate the surroundings, properly savour the food and to save her blushes, but when wine was offered she accepted.

The meal promised to match the opulent room and they started with potato and wild garlic soup.

'Do you have a problem with Roberto Cesare?' she asked.

His spoon twisted between his fingers.

'Not at all.'

'I passed him on the way. It mighty have been my imagination but his attitude changed when I mentioned where I was going this evening.'

Jack sat back and sighed. 'He thinks I owe him money, Orla.'

'How much?'

'I don't like to talk about it . . . a few hundred pounds.'

'Surely you can afford that?'

'I can, but I won't pay on principle.'

'Oh.'

'He did some carpentry for me and I wasn't satisfied. I refused to pay. He refused to make it right. We argued and we've not settled it since. I regret it, of course, but as I say, it's the principle.'

'Or pride.'

'There's that.'

The main course was a splendid baked Ballybrannigan turbot with champagne sauce.

'Did you ever notice the smell in the bathroom below?'

'No.' He was emphatic.

'In the bathroom – there's an odour. I think it's the cesspit and the rain.'

'Would you like me to send one of the builders down to take a look?'

'Thanks, I would. It's just that you said it was—'

'Donovan was always having problems with the drainage in the place, but he insisted he wanted the work finished for you.'

'Well, if you could have it looked at, I'd be grateful.'

For dessert Jack recommended the carrageen moss jelly with summer fruits and she thought it delicious.

'Perhaps Donovan picked and dried this very weed,' he said.

And it tasted even sweeter to her.

After she alone finished the bottle of wine they left the Great House and sped back through the dark lanes. Although he was confident of the bends and undulations, the jarring bumps made her bilious. But he had been generous and she was reluctant to demand that he slow down.

Only when he failed to turn at the Cross did she ask, 'Where are we going?'

He smirked archly. 'I've something you must see.'

She smiled at his boyish delight. He winked and she had to look the other way, suddenly reminded of Martin.

As they drove through Ballybrannigan she absorbed the beauty of the moon across the water, the light in the windows of the Star of the Sea and the lighthouse beam sweeping across the pier.

By the disused restaurant she asked, 'When did that close down?'

'About ten years ago. I'm looking to buy the place.'

'And what will you do with it?'

'I don't know.'

'You could make it grand again. Bring back the heydays.'

'Those days are gone. Whatever I do it would have to make money.'

The mention of money disappointed her. He pulled up at the gate to the Coastal Way.

She got out, grateful for the air. She breathed gulps and revived a little.

'What is it?' she asked.

He spread his arms wide and she assumed it was the view which was certainly infinite, but he turned to encompass the row of chalets.

'Oh.'

'What do you think?'

'What do you mean?'

'These are the future of homes here. Holiday apartments for city people much like yourself.'

'The view is amazing.'

'Do you want to see inside? One is a show home with all the furniture.'

'I don't need to go in. I can see what I need to see from here.'

'Are you sure now? You can see all the mod cons like.'

Reluctant to offend she shrugged and stepped forward as he led the way. Inside she stood in the darkened room with the blinds apart staring again out over the ocean.

He stood beside her.

'There was a derelict cottage here before I built these homes.'

'Homes?' she absently asked.

'Of course.'

'What family would buy these?'

'Those that want such a view. Two are sold. Two couples from Dublin have bought them. The other two are still available. You know, I could see you here.'

She was appalled.

'And you know if you were inclined, I'd sell it to you for way below what it was worth.'

'You wouldn't have to do that.'

'I know that sure, but I'd insist.'

'I mean I wouldn't buy it at any price.'

'Oh.'

'I have Ballyanna – what would I want with this?'

'It has all the designer fittings. It's built to the highest standards. The view—'

'I'm delighted you've shown me,' she assured. 'I can see it's your passion.'

' 'Tis,' he agreed. 'There's an undiscovered coast here with strands that are only known and visited by the local people. I intend to change that.'

She could not see his face in the shadows but she sensed petulance in his tone.

'Would you like a glass of wine?' he asked.

'I don't think—'

' 'Twould be a toast to our friendship. How can you refuse with the moon over the sea like that?'

'Then I will.'

As she sipped the wine and felt the immediate giddy rush. She remarked, 'I half expect Lir to rise up out of the depths.'

He switched on a lamp and the ocean was lost. They sat at either end of the sofa and she saw how he looked at her with incomprehension.

'The old gods,' she explained.

He shook his head.

'Nuala Phelan.'

'I know her, sure. She wrote stories for children.'

'Yes and no. She collected legends and retold them. I still read them.'

'I'm not a great reader. I've always been too busy. Perhaps she put me off; I don't know.'

'What do you mean?'

'She used to read stories to us in Ballybrannigan School when I was a boy.'

'She did? Wow! What was she like?'

'She was a fine-looking girl.'

'I mean as a storyteller; I mean the stories – what were they like?'

He shrugged. 'All I remember is her voice. I don't remember the words. I probably fell asleep. I didn't care for school . . .' He seemed to realize what he was saying. 'But people say she has a spark so . . .'

She felt the wine creeping like the tide across her senses, but the food slowed the effects and the dulling haze was pleasant.

'Why aren't you married Jack?'

'I was.'

'What happened?'

'She found another fella. I was working all the time and I think she was lonely. We still speak . . . I understand.'

'But still . . .'

'It wasn't right for either of us. It's the same old story.'

He smiled sadly. 'But what about your story?' he asked. 'That's what I want to hear.'

'There's nothing to tell.'

'Tell me about what happened with Martin. Will he come back?'

'I don't know.'

'It can't just be because the place is . . . boring.'

'It's not. It's us. It's me. It's him. I don't know . . . No, like you said, it wasn't right for either of us. I'd known for a while. It was just so easy to carry on and so hard thinking about being alone. Recently, I had nothing to say to him. I didn't even like being with him and when I came here it was worse.'

There were tears in her eyes. Jack got up and fetched the kitchen towel.

'I'm sorry,' she sniffed.

'Don't be.'

He topped up her glass.

'What was it that you saw in him in the first place?'

'That was just it: it was what I saw. He was handsome. You saw him.'

He laughed.

'Not my type.'

She smiled. 'I thought I was lucky. I was proud to go out with him.'

'He should have been proud to be seen with you.'

She blushed.

'I wanted more. I wanted to talk about things and he didn't. In the end it was not enough and then my grandmother died and Donovan left me the cottage and it's made me . . .'

'Re-evaluate?'

'Yeah . . . but then there's all this tension here and I want no part of it.'

'I know and I also try to keep clear of all the envy and gossip. I let them say what they want about me. I want no part of it either.'

'What do they say?' she asked.

'Haven't you heard?'

'No. People don't speak to me about you.'

'They say all I care about is money and that I have no regard for the land.'

'Is it true?'

He reflected.

'I had nothing, Orla, but I made my money, and yes I made it through the land. I think the land is for everyone to share. It can't be for the few who have inherited it.'

'That's me.'

'You know what I mean. I think you can have the beauty but you don't have to live in the past. Don't you agree?'

'You mean have all the modern trappings and still have the isolation?'

'That's it.'

'I don't think so,' she stated.

'Oh.'

'Where does it end?'

'The countryside has to be developed if it is to survive. It can't be left to farmers. I know – I am one.'

He laughed, leaning forward with his elbow along the back of the settee and his cheek against his palm.

'But not in the traditional sense,' she reminded him. 'You said so yourself.'

'All I'm saying is that if I was out in the fields before dawn, as I have been, I must add, I would have little concern for keeping the countryside picturesque or pristine. My only concern was the crop and the cattle.'

'But other farmers recognize their duty.'

'And they suffer for it. That's why I got out of it. That's why these people here resent my views and the way I live. Donovan understood though.'

He touched her hair and she sat still. When he kissed her she tasted him and it was sweet. He drew back and stroked her face as he did so.

'Do you know what was happening when I met you in the road today?' she asked.

He shrugged.

'McLeavey was spying on me.'

'What?'

'He was at his window spying on me through his binoculars.'

Jack did not ask how she knew from such a distance.

'The man is a menace,' Jack declared.

'What do you think he was doing that for?'

'He wants to know what you're up to and who you're with no doubt.'

'He must have seen I was with you.'

He smiled.

'That'll eat him up.'

Orla felt queasy. Her earlier binge had accelerated the surge of the alcohol more than she anticipated and her senses oscillated.

'It's not just that. It's the way he looks at me.'

'He's a queer hawk.'

'Isn't that what they said about Donovan?' she asked.

'Was it?'

'That's what Anne told me.'

'That's what she would say about him. She never had a kind word . . . Are you well, Orla?'

'I don't know.'

'Do you want to lie down?'

'I think I need to go to bed.'

'Here?'

'No. An Doras. Can you take me home?'

He hesitated. 'I can, of course.'

Putting his coat about her shoulders, he held her as she staggered out into the night. He had to fix the safety belt for her.

On the High Road to Ballyanna, he steered wildly about the bends and Orla sat there flopping and heaving. Even so, it was with some surprise that at the Cross again, she watched herself throw-up the meal and much of the wine down her dress and between her legs.

Jack cursed but she was hardly aware.

In An Doras he helped her inside and left her slouched on the side of the bed while he fetched water and a wet flannel. She breathed hard to quell the nausea.

'I'm sorry, Jack,' she moaned. 'I don't know what's wrong with me.'

He washed her face with a flannel but when he reached for the buttons on her sick-stained dress, she lightly slapped his hands away.

He stood off and she did not look at him.

'Thank you. I've been stupid. If you don't mind, I'd like to look after myself now.'

Still without words he left her there.

When she awoke in the morning in the dim light through the narrow windows and the slight taint of damp and vomit, she slowly realized where she was. She moaned and hid her face in the pillow, remembering where she had been.

Her sleep had been shallow and she was tired, but the nausea had eased, if only to be substituted by a headache and thirst.

From the bedside cabinet she grabbed the glass of water and gulped. Getting up to pour more she was dizzied and fell back. It was then that she caught sight of a single red rose on the other pillow; its stem was frayed where it had been ripped from the bush outside.

She hid her face under the quilt and cursed and cried again.

13

Everyone Has Their Own Story

She did not see Jack over the next few days and could not bring herself to call in on him. She considered going back to Dublin but was instead consoled by a trip to Castleford. She took the bus from Ballybrannigan, walking along the Main Street, and in the only bookshop there, and binge again – this time on a fresh selection of detective fiction.

There was something about those Scandinavian homicide detectives, so often recovering from alcoholism or women or both; it was something she wanted to rescue. Perhaps she was as flawed as they were. She smiled to herself – perhaps it was the Viking Dublin blood.

She bought a sweet latte to go, and sat by the river-bank as she had that first morning there. Under the willows she skimmed through the first chapters.

Over the roadbridge that led out of town was a showroom, and under its wide awning was an array of mopeds and bicycles. She was not savouring the thought of the bus back and so strolled over to see what was there.

Her moped in Dublin was yellow and shining, like a sunflower, she always thought. Casting her eye over the colours, was the only criteria she could attach to the purchase of one.

She surreptitiously listened as a mother negotiated the price of a new moped, while her son slouched behind her in petulant ingratitude. Even as she signed the credit agreement the boy was more embarrassed for being with her than grateful for the gift.

Eventually the shopkeeper approached her. His overalls were reassuringly smeared with oil.

'Is it a moped you're wanting?' he asked.

Her mind had wandered as she waited and she also perused the bicycle rack within. It occurred to her that as she had not climbed a tree or swum in the sea since she was a girl, neither had she ridden a bicycle. So she changed her mind. Shaking her head she stepped inside.

'I think I want a bicycle.'

'Then we've a proper range.'

He led her to the rack and gave her the patter. 'This one has a front basket and rear pannier racks; it has mudguards and a chainguard and an alloy sidestand.' He spun a wheel. 'Those are silver alloy rims and hubs with six-speed gears . . .' He glanced at her deadpan apathy and laughed. 'It also has a comfortable saddle designed especially for the more delicate lady's posterior.'

She laughed then.

'So is it to keep fit?' he asked.

'To get to the shops.'

'So you'll want a proper basket?'

'And panniers.'

'And lights?'

'And a helmet.'

'So would you really be wanting a moped?'

She shook her head. 'No. I want that one – the yellow one.'

She found an internet café where she sipped another coffee, checked and sorted her inbox and composed two new emails. She rarely had tea when on excursions; sugary frothy coffees alleviated her aversion to the slog of shopping.

The first message was to Bernadette, reminding her to visit Castle Road and water the plants, and to reassure her that she would return to Dublin to reciprocate the favour before Bernadette went for a week in the Greek Islands. The second email was for Brendan Flannery, arranging a suitable time to meet to discuss the Leaving Certificate results.

Thinking about the meal with Roberto and Saoirse and giddy with caffeine, she decided to buy a dress. Despite her previous city-chauvinism she found a boutique selling quality second-hand, high street labels.

There she found an evening dress in forest green satin. Trying it on she turned in the mirror, admiring the low cut front and crossed back, but not appreciating the woman within. Still, it was long enough to cover her legs, it fitted well so that her shape was preserved, and her auburn hair fell freely across the green.

When she collected her new bicycle, the shopkeeper wheeled out a fully fitted and pristine machine, and she was delighted.

'I've even included a free puncture repair kit and pump.'

'Thank you,' she fluttered, realizing she would have no idea how to repair a flat tyre.

He made the last adjustments to the height of the saddle, and she loaded the panniers with her books, groceries and dress. After ten more minutes of padding out the helmet and tightening it about her chin, she set off, wobbling across the bridge and out of town.

It did not escape her notice that, on the hill there was a college behind a high stone wall and wrought iron gates. Indeed, halfway up, she paused at the kerb and peered down the leafy driveway. It was certainly a contrast to a Dublin Community School.

At the crest of the hill outside Castleford she stopped – the acrid iron bile in her mouth was already strong and the notion that she had misjudged the ease and freedom of cycling was pulsing through her mind with the regularity of every pedal push up the hill.

But after regaining her breath she reconsidered; she had the sun and she was still young, so why shouldn't she ride all the way home?

Anyway, it was downhill for a while so she took off the helmet and placed it in the basket and let the wheels roll. It was easy. She was free. She was in the world.

Despite the slog of the inclines, gliding down the mazy lanes on the other side of hills was exhilarating. The blind bends and high hedgerows made her feel she was entering a different world and it was a world of her making.

By the time she reached Morroe, by way of a mile-long slope along the edge of Killybeg estate, the excitement was still fresh and she stopped at the bakery to buy fresh bread.

She even stopped outside the Imokilly History Society shop and waved to Maurice Aherne. He stepped on to the street.

'And how are things, fine princess?'

'They are good.'

'Where have you been?'

'Castleford,' she preened, still panting.

'And you're riding all the way to Ballyanna?'

'I am.'

'B'Jesus, you're a fit colleen altogether.'

'Maurice, I have many letters and photographs and other objects that Donovan left behind.'

'He was a whore for collecting things and saving stuff.'

'It's just I don't think they should be left to me and for few others to see. I think they are important. There are letters there dating back to Brede Houlahan and Juno Byrne.'

'And Frances Roche?'

'Yes.'

He shook his head in astonishment.

'They would be a fine exhibit indeed, but I don't think my shack could do them justice. Have you thought about the Great Island Museum?'

'I've thought about my own museum.'

His eyes widened.

'Such ambition.'

'I was thinking of renovating the Leaping Dolphin for the purpose.'

'Such vision.'

'What do you think?'

'Is it to make money?'

She laughed. 'No way.'

'Then I'm all for it. I think it's marvellous. Fine girl, y'are.'

By the time she reached the Cross, it was an hour after leaving Morroe; it had not helped that she had more than once been lost in the lanes. Squirming with sweat and gasping, she was grateful that it was all downhill to the strand.

By Annamat, under the avenue of trees, Staunton's tractor came through the dappled light. She clutched her brakes and even had sense enough to ring her bell that chimed feebly, but Staunton was talking to his son and did not notice her shooting out of the shadows and into the ditch.

She veered off the road, the rush of wind in her ears roaring, and as she bobbled over the stones in the ditch, her screams juddered and then the bicycle stopped, lurching forward and thrusting her into the hedgerow. With her face buried in the ivy, she saw Staunton disappear around the bend.

Standing there with her forehead pressed against the leaves, she composed herself before very slowly dismounting.

Roberto came jogging up from the workshop.

'I'll have those idiots,' he declared, lifting the bicycle and helping her back on to the road. 'Jesus, what have you got in those bags?'

'Shopping.'

'Where have you been?'

'Castleford.'

'And you've rode all the way here?'

'Yes,' she said with miserable impatience.

'You're mad.'

She nodded agreement, got back on, filled her lungs, and pushed the peddles, fully appreciating his shove at her saddle as she did so.

At An Doras she skidded to a stop and managed to stagger off and stand the contraption against the wall before flopping on to the bench. There she sat, basking in the sun and just breathing.

After a while she went inside, leaving the bicycle there, hoping it would be stolen, knowing it would not be. She drank a glass of water and flopped flat on the bed.

Her thighs and calves burned and she cried and laughed a little, wondering how many calories she had burned, suspecting it had only just reached double figures.

The next morning she awoke, still dressed and still aching, and remembering she had purchased a new bike, a new selection of books and a new attitude.

Her buttocks were raw and she found it difficult to walk as she stepped out on to the lane to find the bicycle where she had left it.

But she was undaunted. She emptied the panniers, drank more water, showered and changed. Within half an hour she was out on the lane again, tucking her trousers into her socks and setting off into the mist to Ballybrannigan.

Along the High Road she was already regretting it, but it was too far to turn back. She persevered, secure in the decision that she would lean the bicycle against the one in the outhouse and never ride it again.

She stood outside the shop for some time as she recovered, pretending to admire the mist-diminished view. Inside, before she purchased milk, she picked up a paper, but quickly returned it to the rack without even reading the headlines.

On the way back she walked slowly up every hill and spent the rest of the day on Cromwell's Hump, in the hollow on the summit. She turned her mobile off and lay there out of the wind, sipping water, reading her books and letters and sleeping off her exertions. She imagined she could feel the toxins in her blood and the acids in her muscles dissipate.

Among the letters she read Brede's vehemence again. Her passion was appalling and splendid.

> *. . . They call me the Phantom Queen. They say I prowl the streets and I drink blood and possess their soul: that I see all that men fear in their eyes. All I see is the faces of the dead. I know who has done this and I will have revenge . . .*

Orla knew Juno to be fearsome; her reply revealed the terrible blood thirst and ardent friendship these women had possessed.

> *. . . I say do away with them. Make the rest fear you more. I know you can. We know what they would do to you. We know that our lot is nothing and we must make it otherwise. You have your wits and your strength. Show them. If only I was there with you. I would take your place a thousand times . . .*

Distance and time had not diminished the lure of the blood pride, and Orla watched the clouds merge and considered the different skies those women had walked beneath. Though the savagery of it all frightened her, she wanted to believe she could be as bold.

By the time she returned to An Doras she was ready for a different perspective. She had sought to be alone but now desired company.

She checked her voicemail. Martin had still not called and she was annoyed about that. She had expected some resistance but there was nothing. She turned off her mobile again and shoved it in her shoulder bag.

It was time to get ready for the meal with Roberto and Saoirse. Whatever the people of the valley thought of each other, she resolved to remain above it all.

After showering again she put on her make-up and listened to Crowded House. The words of 'Private Universe' resonated with the simplicity of joy and love, but then, she thought, her summer would end and she would still be alone.

Slipping on the satin dress, she pinned up her hair and scrutinized her reflection. She felt over-dressed and it was early. She thought of Jack then and how she had dressed up just to let herself down, and so she unzipped the dress and put on fresh jeans and a blouse. She wound a French plait, applied her lipstick and stepped out into the garden.

The rockery flowers were in bloom now – the pinks bleeding into red and yellows bleaching to white. She sat for a while on the iron bench, just breathing, hardly thinking. In the secluded space the subtle perfumes meandered through her senses, making it easy to believe such living moments could be hers for the rest of her life.

Back inside it took several minutes to decide whether or not to take a bottle of wine to the meal; she succumbed, but was determined to resist it. With the scents still strong about her and the strength of her resolve within, at just after seven she strolled up the lane.

Roberto welcomed her at the door and led her through the house. What from the outside appeared the traditional cottage, with low ceilings and thick slanting walls, was clean and spacious within. The cramped rooms and roof space of the old dwelling had been knocked through and extended to make a wide modern living space.

The mantel of the fireplace was a huge twisted beam. She ran her hand along the grain.

'It was part of the keel of the *Trident* that ran aground on the cliffs below,' informed Roberto. 'It was during the Famine. The captain was a Chinaman with a long pony tail that hung down under his coat. The people thought he was the devil himself.'

The walls were clean and whitewashed, but on the opposite wall was a framed poster of a huddle of youths sitting on flight cases and wearing monkish hoods and boxing boots. It read *Immaculate: Purer*.

'Is that the band with the singer who was shot?' she asked.

'The very same. Patrick and I were obsessed with them. They were beyond rock or pop or politics or anything. They were about pure feeling – soul. I remember when Patrick and me first heard 'You Can Tell Me What You Like' it was like it was about us you know – blood earned, soul burned.'

'Right,' she said, not really knowing. 'You've obviously worked hard on renovating this place,' she averted.

'We have, but if it was up to me the place would look like the workshop – the same as when Pearse had it. This is all Saoirse – she has an eye . . . and Patrick has helped along the way. You know you should see Annamat now; that's a grand house.' She followed him as he explained, 'You know An Doras, Elannat and Annamat were built one after the other. They say three brothers of the Houlahans came into the valley by way of the strand and that's where it began.'

Saoirse was in the kitchen. Roberto put the wine in the fridge and resumed his duties at the cutting board. Saoirse appeared much heavier now. Orla observed the couple playfully nudging against each other and was moved.

'Can I help?' Orla offered.

'There's no need.' Saoirse assured. 'I need to keep active. If I get washed up on the settee, I'll suffocate under my own weight. So what's the story,' she asked archly. 'How are things? What have you been up to?'

'I've been extravagant. I've purchased myself a bicycle.'

'I heard!'

'I have a moped at home in Dublin so I'll keep the bike down here in the outhouse. I think it's ideal.'

It did not occur to her that the things Saoirse referred to were more than bike riding.

'I thought Killybeg House was fascinating. Your work in the gardens is marvellous,' Orla stated.

'I'm only one in a team, but thank you. I've finished there now though.'

Orla looked out on to the enclosed garden behind the workshop.

'Your garden here is beautiful as well.'

'Thank you. If I had more time . . .'

'Donovan left a pretty rockery.'

'He was great with the flowers. He gave me such good advice when I started. There are secrets to certain flowers down here, what with the sea and wind. You have shelter behind the house but you pay for it with the shadow.'

'I'd like to maintain the rockery. I've weeded it and tidied it but I don't know what I'm doing really.'

'I can help you.'

'That would be great.'

'I bought some flowers from Killybeg but they are still in the trays.'

'You shouldn't have done that. I've plenty I can give you. What did you buy?'

'Pansies, lobelias and . . . geraniums.'

'Geraniums are good – you can plant those anywhere and they'll thrive. You'll need other plants that appreciate the shade. I have gardenias, hostas . . .' She considered. 'And you should buy some impatiens – they come in all sorts of colours and are hardy.'

She accepted the wine Roberto had uncorked, remembering too late her determination to resist.

'Roberto said there are tales about Killybeg they don't like you telling.'

Saoirse elbowed her husband and then considered.

'I'll tell you one. Did you see the rose bush above the rockery down below?'

'That blood-red one?'

'That's it. It comes from the estate. There was a steward there during the Famine who cultivated roses. You can find that out in the guide book, but what they don't tell you is that the man hankered after his master's wealth and lifestyle, wanting all the trappings of his birth. But Lazenby, who was the master and landlord in Imokilly, was a terrible blackguard and only interested in the money. Well, the steward, Feltcher was his name, took to wearing fine clothes because his master thought it in keeping, but not only that, just like his master, he wore perfumes.'

'Patrick calls him the gay Malvolio,' Roberto quipped.

'He would make his own from the roses grown in the gardens of the Great House and as the years went by he would wear them more and more brazenly and think he was above them all. Of course, that was his undoing.'

'What happened to him?'

'He raped a girl here in Ballyanna – in the very stream by the hump-backed bridge and left her there to drown. But she lived and eventually remembered things about him. She recalled his voice and the smell of the roses. She was Frances Roche and she and her friends Juno Byrne and Brede Houlahan murdered the man. They say it was Juno who stole the rose and planted it there.'

'I know of the Black Feather, but I didn't know that. They should tell that story. It's far enough away for no one to be connected.'

'But it brings all sorts of tensions still. That place is built on blood, the blood of the wild rose.'

Enthralled, Orla was about to ask about other tales when they heard footsteps on the stripped boards in the lounge.

'Our other guest,' said Saoirse.

Orla turned to see Patrick McLeavey in the doorway. For a nauseous moment she saw him as if through the wrong end of a telescope. The world seemed to retreat from her and she stood in a stasis of shock. She did, however, notice that he was freshly shaven and clean.

Roberto stood impishly between them.

'You two have met, haven't you?'

They both nodded, their eyes fixed on the other.

'I'm sure Saoirse told you who else would be here.'

Both shook their heads.

'I thought you told them,' said Saoirse.

'Come and sit down. Everything is ready.' He led them to the table.

Orla hesitated, wanting to leave, but seeing McLeavey's obvious discomfort she remained courteous. He was flushed and scowling, clearly furious with his brother who was oblivious. They sat at opposite ends of the table, now doing their best not to look at each other.

'You're late,' Roberto chastized.

'I was in Morroe at the timber merchants, ordering the wood for the frames,' explained Patrick.

'Did you do a deal?'

'You know I can't negotiate . . . It's covered. They'll deliver it to me.'

Saoirse brought through oyster soup for the starter.

'Were you at the post office, Pat?' she asked.

'I was.'

'And what's the news?'

'I've no idea.'

'You mean to tell me you didn't find anything out? You're a useless gossip monger, y'are.'

He was indignant. 'I can't be doing with all that. I've too many things to do.'

'He bites every time,' laughed Saoirse. 'If you're feeling left out of the conversation, Orla, they're talking about the Strand of Dreams. They're bringing back The Rest.'

'At Michaelmas,' Orla said.

The men turned to her.

'You know of it?'

'Donovan wrote about it.'

'Donovan tried to keep it going, but the valley was emptying. There were so few people here for many years. It's only now they're coming back.'

'And if you build it they will come,' mocked Saoirse.

'What have you arranged?' asked Roberto.

'I've arranged for the materials to be delivered to Annamat. When we disassemble the platform, it can go back into the far shed.'

'Do you have the musicians now?'

'I've the Open Hearts.'

'You're joking.'

'I met with your man Kennedy and he's all for it . . . and I spoke to Nuala Phelan again.'

'And she'll come?'

'She still can't say.'

'You didn't say our dad would be here, did you?'

'I didn't mention it.'

The main meal was a delicate garlic mackerel. Orla was impressed. Patrick was reticent; clearly familiar with his sister in law's culinary flair.

Orla could not resist. 'Nuala Phelan?' she ventured to him.

Patrick did not respond.

'The author,' Roberto said. 'She's originally from Ballybrannigan. She's in America at the moment. We invited her to read for us, perhaps early in the day, even write a story of the festival.'

'What did she say?'

'She sent a story.'

'You have an original story by her?'

'Of course.'

Orla grinned and Patrick frowned. 'And what is the connection with your father?' she asked.

'They were together once,' Roberto continued.

'Your father and Nuala Phelan?'

'Sure.'

'What happened?'

'It didn't last. They were young.'

'There was a scandal,' Saoirse interjected.

'What sort of scandal?'

'She took the boat to England.'

'You don't know that,' said Patrick. 'And even if she did, what business is it of ours or anyone else?'

'Anyway, there was no bother at Donovan's funeral,' Roberto said. 'They hadn't seen each other in years and they were . . . cordial.'

'The story,' Orla said. 'How will you use it?'

'We hope that it will be part of the celebration as it was in the old days,' replied Patrick. 'We'll walk to Andreenmacotter and launch the candles the way they used to—'

'And then we'll dance and drink until we can't stand,' added Roberto.

'And you've both done this?'

'It's more Patrick. He promised Donovan that he would do it.'

'I would like to help,' Orla stated.

'The plans are all in motion,' Patrick stated dismissively, 'but thanks anyway.'

Orla narrowed her eyes and addressed him directly. 'You know, I wonder if your interest in such a revival risks romanticizing the past for those who don't realize what Ireland was truly like.'

He stared at her. 'I'm aware of how real life was. I've lived like it. Most people want to live in the now – I don't. I am a romantic and I am proud of it. I obviously see this place as so much more than it is to you.'

'That's not—' Orla started to say.

'You mentioned wanting to help,' intervened Saoirse. 'What about the charity? We've set up a charity to preserve the history and traditions of the area and at the same time make it relevant and accessible to all – involve everyone like. If you have stories and music and dancing and laughter – who can resist?'

'I'd be delighted,' Orla said finally averting her eyes from Patrick.

'That's why we want to do this,' said Roberto. 'We remember this place when we first came. Many of the older generation like Donovan and Pearse and Anne, were still alive and so many of the generation in between had left, like our father . . . And of those left behind only a few had children. There was a scourge of country bachelors. Like your man at the end of the table there.'

Patrick shrugged. 'I won't make the same mistakes our parents made. They had children with no regard for each other, for us or for anyone else. We were just lucky in the end. It has to be right or not at all. It's all or nothing.'

'Just don't leave it too late,' Saoirse said, glancing sidelong at Orla.

'As Roberto was saying,' Patrick continued. 'I'm sure Ballyanna was a different place. There was an insular innocence still – a sense of wonder. The world outside was still so far away.'

'I've heard your father spoken of before,' said Orla. 'What did he do?'

Patrick deferred to Roberto.

'Seamus treated both our mothers badly. He was a drunk and a philanderer. He only changed when we escaped England, or rather when Patrick went back and found me. We made him realize what a failure he was. But give him his due, he wasn't bitter; he turned his life around. I suppose we showed him how to. He's a patronizing bastard, but he means well. The best part of it is that he's in England now with Patrick's mum . . . who,' he added, to lighten the explanation, 'I always had a crush on.'

'What about your mum?'

'She died.'

'Oh.'

Patrick spoke then.

'She was beautiful but she was an alcoholic in the end. She never accepted what our father did to her.'

'And yet you have both forgiven him?'

'What else could we do? We could have beaten him or ignored him, but that would have made us as bad as he was.'

'He knows what we think,' declared Roberto.

Orla looked between the two of them as Roberto nodded to his brother for affirmation and Patrick winked. It was a signal of strength not levity.

Saoirse was mischievous. 'So I'm told, Orla, that you've been rescued more than once by himself since you've arrived.'

'Watch out Orla,' warned Roberto. 'She blabs.'

Patrick scowled at her but Saoirse laughed blithely.

'You have a habit of placing yourself in precarious situations it seems.'

'She was irresponsible,' Patrick clarified piously. 'She thought the coast here was not wild and dangerous.'

'They were easy mistakes to make,' Orla defended.

'People have died on the cliffs.'

'I don't think there was a danger of that.'

'Not with me to see to it.'

Orla stared hard, thinking him pompous. 'Aren't I allowed to make mistakes?'

'Not if you put yourself in danger.'

'Was I really in danger?'

'Yes.'

'Well, I've learned my lesson.'

Roberto intervened. 'Don't be so sanctimonious, Pat. You know all about the dangers on the cliffs from first-hand experience.'

'Oh?' asked Orla.

'He fell from them as a kid and broke his coccyx. To this day I can't fathom how he got from the path to the cliff edge. Forty feet straight down. He's lucky to be alive. A few feet either way and it was the rocks.'

Patrick was clearly embarrassed. Orla allowed herself a smug smirk.

'Either way, thank you for helping me, Patrick,' she purred.

He shrugged petulantly. 'As long as you appreciate the place, then I've no issue. And I've spoken to the Stauntons about that tractor.'

Saoirse and Roberto looked at each other clearly delighting in their schemes.

'They're a menace,' he went on, 'the wall; that car and now forcing you off the road. It's too much.'

The tap of cutlery punctuated the silence.

'Donovan knew you would settle,' said Saoirse to Orla.

'He did?'

'When he came back from Dublin he was . . . serene.'

'He was dying,' sneered Patrick, 'and he was desperate.'

Saoirse turned to him. 'But you encouraged him to write the letters and change the will.'

'It was what he wanted.'

Orla intervened. 'He changed his will?'

'Yes. I was the witness. I took him to Mossy O'Sullivan in Castleford.'

'What did he change it from?'

Patrick did not reply.

'It was all left to Patrick,' Roberto said, 'but after your grandmother died, Donovan wanted to reconcile himself to the past and trust his last wishes to the girl he loved. At first he was unsure but Patrick convinced him to. Your mother was to have it but there was some problem there . . .'

Sceptical, Orla looked between them all for signs of conspiracy.

'I thought Jack Callaghan persuaded Donovan . . .' There it was – the look she thought she was waiting for. 'There is a problem between you all and Jack, is there not?'

'Jack showed kindness to Donovan towards the end,' said Saoirse. 'He bought him a few things. He would spend time with him and Donovan was grateful.'

'I think Jack was shocked when the will was revealed and he got fuck all. He had no idea.' Roberto chortled. 'He deserves it.'

'Roberto!' Saoirse was matronly as she and her husband took the plates. Patrick sat looking at the poster of the pugilist monks. Orla traced the grain swirls in the mantelpiece.

They returned with the dessert.

Orla addressed Roberto. 'So what has Jack done to deserve such animosity?'

Roberto blushed under his wife's glare. 'He's all right,' he assured. 'I've known him a long time. We just don't get on, but you seem to get on well with him.'

'I do,' she defiantly replied.

Patrick returned the conversation to the subject of her inheritance, saying, 'The question is, Orla, now you have the place, what do you intend to do with it?'

'What do you mean?'

'Will you sell it, or live in it, or—'

'I don't know.'

They stared at each other.

'If you sell—'

'I don't know what I will do.'

'You don't?'

'I haven't decided,' she declared.

But she had and she had no intention of informing him under interrogation.

'There are some who would buy the place who hold no value in the history, who would tear it down and build again.'

She placed her hand over her glass as Roberto offered more wine.

'That won't happen,' she said. 'My grandfather knew that much.'

14

An Unimportant Distance

She walked back to An Doras in the darkness. There was a cooling breeze eddying off the sea and so she walked down to the strand. The tide was out and the waves hissed in the distance. Huddled on the stones there, the sounds of the place soaked through her senses.

She was there for some time, feeling totally alone and yet equally at one. It was a living moment of purity that she would never forget. She was neither drunk nor guilty, nor confused. There on that beach she knew what she wanted.

Above the strand the light of Elannat cast a ghostly shimmer over the cliff edge and she went up the seasteps towards it.

The conservatory light was on and Anne McLeavey was reading. In the corner was an easel on which a blank canvas was propped. Orla knocked and Anne peered over her glasses and beckoned her in.

'Hello, Anne. Do you mind? If it's too late I can see you tomorrow, but I saw your light and . . .'

'It's all right.'

Anne closed the book and placed the spectacles on them. Her eyes were cold blue.

'I've decided to make the place my own.'

'What does that mean?'

'I want to live here. I don't know when exactly, but when I have settled things in Dublin I will come here.'

'That's good.'

'I found so many things in Donovan's place, so many letters and photographs. I want to collect them and keep them safe. I want others in the family to be able to see them. Will you help me?'

'I will, of course, but are you doing this for Donovan or your grandmother, or for yourself?'

Orla sighed. 'For all of us.'

Anne smiled. 'Then it will be grand.'

'The thing is there is so much . . . stuff.'

'I thought you were going to give some away? Do so – don't be afraid.'

'I have given some away to charity; 'twas some of the clothes and bed linen – is that all right?'

'That's fine, but it's yours to do as you please.'

'I don't want to discard anything that has value.'

'You're worrying about money?'

'Personal value – historical value.'

'It's only a house of an old man. Who will care?'

Orla frowned.

'I care. I want others to know about the place and its past.'

'Isn't it just like any other place?'

'I don't think so. Perhaps I'm seeing it differently coming from the outside.'

'I think you are.'

'There is a story here. A thousand stories and I want them to be told.'

Anne smiled.

Orla took a deep breath. 'Are you testing me, Anne?'

'I am.'

She exhaled. 'In that case, I'm returning to Dublin but when I come back, will you come down and make sure I don't discard anything of value?'

'I will.'

She stood and indicated to the easel. 'Are you going to paint again?'

'The shakes and arthritis aside, I have decided that I have one more picture in me.'

'What will the subject be?'

'I've an idea to paint you.'

Orla blushed. 'I don't think it would be a good subject,' she gushed.

'I think it will be.'

She woke up the next morning ready to confront Dublin again and anyone in it. More so, Dublin was where her things were. For all the beauty of the valley, it was incomplete when she did not have all her things about her.

At the stormwall she noticed that Patrick McLeavey had not taken the dinghy out that day, and though she expected him to call, she had still not seen Jack Callaghan either. She decided to go to Jack herself, to apologize for her behaviour and to thank him for his patience.

Saoirse was pegging out washing as she passed the workshop.

'The meal was lovely, Saoirse. I'd like to do the same for you. Perhaps after the baby is born.'

'I'd love that. I expect I'll appreciate it more when I'm destroyed by the bawling.'

Saoirse leaned against the wall. 'I'm sorry about the two of them,' she offered.

'There's no need to be.'

'I have to keep them apart as much as I can, or else they retreat into their own world. The gang of two, they are. They'd take on the whole world together. I think they may have made you feel uncomfortable.'

'I was ready for them. And it wasn't Roberto.'

'But Robbie will always favour his brother.'

'Perhaps he has always had to.'

'I'm sure Roberto would say so himself if he were here. They've gone off making more deals and arrangements. Anyway, it was good for Patrick to be berated a little. He's a lovely fella but living alone has made him intense and a little insensitive sometimes.'

Further on up the lane she stopped under the avenue of trees before the gate to Annamat, just above where she had ridden the bicycle into the ditch. She glanced up and down the lane and stepped down for a view of the house. Even though she climbed the bars of the gate, she could not position herself to see through the copse.

So she walked on, smiling at her curiosity.

She found Ballygarry empty and taking a card from her purse posted her mobile number through the letter box.

On the way back down the lane she paused again at Annamat and without another thought she opened the squealing gate and crept down the gravelled lane that twisted away through the trees. Where it crossed over the stream she paused, and went more stealthily, feeling mischievous and unsure of her compulsion.

Emerging from the shadows, she stood for a moment to contemplate what she saw.

What had been a farmyard was now converted into a contemporary home. The whitewashed two-storey main house was set back against the hillside, and from each eave dropped two wings, each staggered in the middle to compensate for the shallow slope of the valley. Between the buildings, the forecourt was clean and laid out with pots and climbing plants. The lower windows of the house retained their small shape as the roof was now glass and she could clearly see that it was a studio with an array of easels. From the cliffs, all she could discern was the window and the white walls behind, but this close it was all clear. She climbed the drive through rough grass verges and stood agape.

It was then that the gate creaked and she panicked, instinctively running, scrambling to her left across the gravel and into the tree line. There, trapped by a fence lined with barbed wire, tree trunks and a nettle bed, she leapt up to the lowest bough of the nearest tree and attempted to heave herself up and out of sight. She pulled against the branch, but her elbows would only bend a few inches and she swung there for several seconds before her hands slipped on the slick bark.

Falling back on to the fence she rebounded into the nettles. In the same movement, she pushed herself up with her hands, screamed, rolled away, and ran back out on to the gravel.

Patrick was standing before her as she brandished her hands that were already mottled and swollen. She made to run past him but he grabbed her by an arm and dragged her back to the trees. She could not resist the momentum and was too surprised to even protest. She watched as he seized at a bunch of dock leaves and rubbed them vigorously between her hands.

As the pain partially eased, she released herself and stepped away.

'I could have done that you know.'

'I know.'

'I knew how to do it.'

'I know.'

'I was hoping to see you here.'

'Really?'

She winced at the blatant lie. They stared at each other.

'I didn't expect to see you here,' she admitted.

'And I was hoping you would visit me.'

'It was a mistake. Like I said, I didn't think you would be here.' Her hair had fallen across her face and she puffed it away.

'All the same, now you're here would you like to come in for a cup of tea?'

'I have to go.'

'Please, Orla.' His voice deepened emphatically. 'I'd like you to come in. It's about time.'

She hesitated, then nodded and followed him inside.

He took her to the kitchen and gave her a tube of cream to salve her hands. She sat at the table rubbing with relief as he made tea.

'This table is different,' she observed, determined to make cordial conversation.

'Roberto made it from driftwood.

The glassy varnished top was formed of an intricate cross section of planed ships' timbers, but spiderlike, the legs were as deformed as the day they were combed from the sea.

He saw her surveying the rest of the room.

'This house once belonged to Brede Houlahan's father before they went to America.'

'She's fast becoming a personal heroine for me,' Orla revealed.

He shot a glance at her. 'She was a great woman – like Maureen O'Hara in the *The Quiet Man*.'

Orla smiled tightly to acknowledge the image of fire and will and beauty, and not understanding why he seemed to smile at some private joke.

'The cave you went down into was used by her to hide from the soldiers. She leapt from Schull Ban above it and fell into the waves and swam up over the entrance down there.'

'Isn't that just part of the folklore?'

'I'd say not. I've been down there at high tide and I'd say it's possible if you have no fear and know the place. But most of all there are some stories that don't seem to change and there are the letters.'

'You know I've read them?'

'You have? Well I've some more.'

'You have?'

'Yep. You know you're of direct descent?'

'So we both are.'

'We are. 'Twas Eamonn O'Meagher who went to Boston and married Brede's granddaughter. He had purchased the Houlahan farm here. It had been abandoned after the Famine. It's something that you and I are both in the same house after one hundred and fifty years.'

' 'Tis,' she agreed and they reflected.

Taking a tray with the tea and biscuits he took her through to the living-room. Along the walls, above the low bookshelves, hung family photographs and paintings of seascapes. The deep hearth was cold but was laden with ash. It was a place with the potential to be well lived in and it reminded her of her own flat in Castle Road.

'I see you have a studio above,' she said.

'It's where I work and watch the world.'

She blushed.

'How long were you watching me the other day?'

He was unperturbed. 'I stopped as soon as you looked away.'

'Oh . . . No longer?'

She had half expected him to offer an award for her acting, but instead she smiled through the disappointment like an unsuccessful nominee.

'Why would I?'

'You wouldn't, of course . . . What is it you do up there in the studio?'

'I paint. It's a hobby.'

'But a serious one?'

'I'm serious about it.'

She smiled.

'I wouldn't have known,' she gently mocked.

They laughed together and he took her hands, turning her palms to inspect the rash.

'Are they better?' he asked.

She nodded and he released her gently.

'So what is it you do for a living?' she interrogated.

'Many jobs.'

'You can't make much by fishing.'

'I don't. I'm just keeping the tradition going. The pots along the bay have always been in the family. No, I do odd jobs about the place.'

'Do you sell your art?'

'I have. I don't need to work all year. I work for the farmers. I help Roberto. We did this.' He made a slight gesture with his hand. 'I paint and I teach art in Garrymore. I'm lucky.'

'But it wasn't always that way.'

'What do you mean?'

'What you were saying last night. It was difficult at first for you, having been taken to England and then coming back.'

He breathed hard. 'I expect the way it was for me was not much different to the way you're feeling.'

'How is that?'

'To arrive at a place and suddenly find a world you didn't know existed, and then to find you are inextricably connected to it.' She knew he was deliberately avoiding discussing his disadvantage. 'I remember walking through the lanes and the fields and the village and people stopping me and talking to me as if they knew me, and then finding out these people were my cousins and such. For me, a child from a city estate, it was so . . . alien. People didn't talk to each like that in England. I remember . . . Look, I'm more interested in you, Orla.'

'I'm not interesting at all,' she scoffed.

'Others might not agree.'

She shrugged, suddenly shy.

'Would you mind if I used your toilet?' she asked.

'It's through there,' he indicated.

In the bathroom, she was admiring the two fine prayer plants in jardinières when she pulled down her trousers and pants and gasped in horror. Through the backside of each was a bloody rip. She shuffled to the mirror and contorted to inspect her buttocks. Across both dimpled cheeks was a deep dotted laceration.

It was now, having seen the wound, that her bottom began to throb. She whined and jumped up and down a little in frustration, but that just made it hurt more.

Outside she casually edged towards Patrick against the walls. He smiled. She could not discern if it was cordial, or if he knew the reason for her strategy.

'Thanks for the tea,' she gushed, 'but I'll be off now. I have to pack. I'm taking the train back tomorrow morning.'

'Oh. What are you going back for?'

'I have to mind my friend's flat. She's done the same for me.'

'Oh.'

15

Elusive Agony

Arriving at Castle Road she dropped her bags in the hall and stepped into the living-room. There on the hearth she found a vase of lilies and lisianthus and roses, splayed in shades of pink and red. The insipid odour of flowers was pervasive and sickened her senses.

She took off her coat, opened the windows and gathered the bunch in a bin liner. Martin had, she conceded as she went to the wheelie bin, at least chosen the varieties she liked.

She showered and unpacked her bags and sat watching 24-hour news. Having avoided television, radio and newspapers for several weeks, the news items oscillated between knelling dread and mundanity. She had started sorting through the mail when the front doorbell rang. From the end of the hallway she saw that it was him.

Suddenly she was indignant.

'You have a key,' she shouted.

He pressed the bell again and she went to him. He dropped down a step and looked up at her. Across his forearm he held a second bouquet identical to the discarded one.

He was monotone. 'I didn't want to assume I could just come in.'

'You put the other flowers inside.'

'That was when I knew you weren't here. That was all I did. I thought you would like them.'

'You hardly ever buy me flowers.'

'Because you said you would rather see them in the wild.'

She hesitated. 'That I did.'

He smiled and waited.

'What do you want?' she sighed.

'To talk.'

'Why now? The way you left me, you made it clear we had nothing to say to each other, and you haven't tried to contact me at all: no phone call; no text; no email – nothing.'

'I was wrong. I was stupid and I want to explain.' He looked up and down the road. 'Can I come in please?'

In the living-room she absently shoved the letters under a cushion and sat on the settee. She did not invite him to remove his coat or shoes. Martin lingered in the doorway and then walked to her CD player, checked what disc was in the tray and pressed play.

The clipped chords of 'Don't Dream It's Over' cut in.

Orla was furious. 'What are you doing? Turn it off!'

'I thought it was our song.'

'You hate this music.'

'I don't.'

'I'll not have you doing this. Turn it off now and sit down there.'

She was relieved the chords were cut short before Finn sang of freedom within and without and trying to catch the deluge in a paper cup. This was not the moment for such words.

'If you're going to get sentimental,' she chided, 'at least be honest.'

He sat nervously on the edge of the chair. She did not look at the flowers he gently placed on the coffee table.

'After all this time, we should work this through,' he said.

'You don't realize what's happened do you?'

'Do you?' he rebuked.

'Yes. It's over.'

'Why?'

'You know why. You were not at all interested in what I was doing. You showed no consideration for me down there and in fact you tried to ruin any enjoyment I had. I thought we wanted the same things.'

'We do.'

'Well, what are they?'

He thought. 'To travel . . . To give each other company . . . To be more than friends.'

'I want more than that. I want a home. I want a family. I want peace . . . I want passion!'

'I can move in with you.'

'No! You say it like you'll do it for me. If I have to ask you, or negotiate, or threaten or . . . bribe, then what does it amount to?'

'I said I'd marry you if you wanted.'

'Jesus! Listen to yourself. Are you doing me favour? If you think that well then you can—'

He leapt from the chair and on to his knees. 'Then will you marry me?'

'Get up, Martin.'

He hung his head and stared up at her piteously under his brows, but when she said no more and simply stared he awkwardly slid back into the chair.

She said in a classroom tone, 'You acted badly, Martin, because you don't care and why should you?'

'I was jealous of you.'

'What?'

'I saw that the place had changed you, and I knew I wasn't part of that.'

She was lost for words then, surprised by his insight and more by the truth of it. He continued.

'You seemed so at ease there, with the place and the people. I didn't know what to do . . . Are you going back?'

'Yes.'

'Can I come with you . . . to try again like?'

She shook her head and he was back on his knees, holding his head in his hands. She did not go to him though she wanted to. She knew that to go to him would be disastrous.

He looked at her through tears.

'So this is it?'

'It has to be.'

She was miserable in that moment, but she knew it was right.

'I care,' he said.

'What about?'

'About us?'

'What else?'

'I don't know what you mean,' he whined.

She was desperate to avoid the usual broken logic of the fight.

'I've just told you what I want for myself. Do you care?'

'Of course I do.'

'Then what is it I want? What are my dreams and ambitions? Use your own words.'

He frowned. 'Why are you talking like this?'

It was hard not to be scornful. 'Why haven't we spoken like this before? We haven't because it would mean we would have to face the truth and go our separate ways.'

'Or commit.'

'I doubt it. Look at us now . . .' She offered a more conciliatory tone. 'We haven't spoken like this before because we've both been too afraid to admit we would risk losing the easy life – this single life where we don't have to compromise or apologize at all.'

'This isn't easy.'

'I know, but I refuse to deny anything anymore. Look, if you can't tell me what I want – what do you want?'

'I want you.'

'What for?'

'Because we're good together. Everyone says so.'

'What?'

'We're a couple. Everyone knows we're together. I've had a hell of time explaining where you are to people.'

'Listen to yourself. What do I care about what people think if we've broken up? I'll not be defined by being with you or anyone. I'll be me first.'

'It's been all right up until now.' He was petulant then. 'I suppose I've been convenient.'

'I didn't know until Ballyanna. And don't try to make this just about me. I'll ask you again – what do you want for yourself?'

'I want to enjoy life. I want to travel more; I want to go to the shows, eat great food, buy clothes and—'

'Well, I don't . . . I want more.'

'So you want me to move to Cork with you?'

'No!' She stood. 'Don't you get it? I want you to realize that I want to be alone.'

He stood. 'It's that fella who came to the door that day.'

'It's not.'

'I can tell it is. There you go – you can't even look at me. I know that much about you.'

'Ah, stop your blathering. I have done nothing wrong and I could have. I don't want another man. I want me.'

'I'll wait for you.'

'Don't!'

'I will wait.'

'Do not wait for me, Martin. I'm telling you it will never be worth it.'

He stepped forward and seized her arms.

'Why are you doing this, Orla? You've gone mad.'

'Get off me. I'm not mad.'

He shook her.

'Just like that? You can't do this to me. I waited for you. I thought you were the one.'

'You didn't. I wasn't. I'm not. Take your hands off me!'

He made to kiss her and she squirmed in his grasp, trying to break free. The flowers were kicked to the floor. He took no notice and pressed against her.

She wrenched an arm free and slapped him across the face.

'Get out!' she cried. 'Get out or I'll belt you.'

He shoved her down on to the settee and strode from the room. She seized the flowers and ran into the hallway and heaved them at him. The stems and heads exploded in midair and scattered short of where he turned and threw the key at her. It struck her on the head and she yelped.

'Y'bollocks!' she yelled.

'You fat cow,' he retorted.

As he yanked open the door she ran at him, but slipping on the petals she fell to the floor. On all fours she leapt at the door with all her weight to slam it shut behind him, but it clipped his heel and she heard him tumble down the steps.

'Jesus, you're a brutal bitch,' he raged.

He kicked at the door as she locked it feverishly.

'You balding bastard,' she replied.

'Y'dirty whore!'

'Ah bite my shite!' she screamed, and then sat there sobbing.

The telephone rang but she ignored it. The draught under the door numbed her skin and forced her up and into the bedroom, where, under the quilt, she hid and felt sorry for herself a little more.

When she eventually emerged the day was darkening. She turned up the heating, made herself a hot chocolate in the microwave with milk and sweeteners, and sat in the living-room wrapped in the quilt.

Sipping the chocolate, she checked her voicemail. The first was from her mother.

'Orla. I would like to talk to you. Please call me and I will come to you whenever you are free . . . I love you.'

Orla paused there, stunned by the message, unable to decide if it was merely another ploy; trying to calculate what Maeve could want. She noticed the fitness DVD still protruding from beneath the settee. When she nudged it out of sight her toe smeared the film of dust on the case.

The second message was from Brendan Flannery.

'Hello O.' She smiled. 'Remember you're coming over on results day. We'll have a barbecue and a glass of wine and we can crunch the numbers together. I know how much you like to scrutinize and justify the value added and residuals.'

The third was from Bernadette.

'You're not answering your mobile – why? I'm at the airport. You should have come with me you know. You'll notice your plants are thriving. Please make sure Haughey and Fitz are happy. Change their biscuits and meat and water everyday. Thanks a million and wish me luck. As always, this could be it.'

The fourth was a few seconds of breathing from Martin.

The last message was from Jack.

'Hello, Orla. It's Jack Callaghan. I got your card . . . I'm sorry I missed you . . . I was hoping we could talk . . . Perhaps you could call me. If you don't manage to, I hope it's OK if I call you again later.'

She went to the CD player and pressed play. Neil Finn sang of the liberation and release but her soul reverberated with an indeterminate ache, and in her mind she was still trapped in so many ways.

She spent the week at the flat, gradually caring less about Martin returning. Perhaps she knew him well enough she thought, to know that his pride would not allow him further humiliation.

She arranged her cushions and books on the patio and she settled into a familiar routine again. She was grateful for her neighbour's gardening skills; the walls were draped with honeysuckle and clematis which gave privacy and blocked out some of the traffic noise.

She had purchased an artist's sketch pad and she sat there sketching her ideas for the Leaping Dolphin whilst listening to her CDs of 'This Sceptred Isle'.

She soon developed a daily schedule that she worked through in phases. In the morning she awoke and walked the few streets to Bernadette's flat. There she checked the place through, gathering her letters, checking for leaks and petting Haughey and Fitz while she watched the news. After feeding the cats she returned to her flat and had breakfast.

The next phases were a series of mundane chores, necessary forays to the shops, reading, marking and preparation.

Despite the routine, it was only after a few days that she remembered she had her own letters and found them under a cushion on the settee. With some relish she sat out on the patio, ready with her knife.

First she had to arrange them. By the shape and type of the envelopes she recognized them all except one. She stared at it awhile, realizing she recognized the handwriting style.

She carefully cut it open.

Dear Orla
I am writing to you in the hope that we can talk. You know I don't write well but I must write this letter because I want to see you again. I want to explain so much. When I left you with my mother, I knew you would be loved as I was but I was so prideful and stubborn and thought I knew what I wanted. And when I discovered that I was wrong it was too late to go back. I was too ashamed. I am still ashamed, but now I know that my pride has wrecked everything. I hope you will see me.

Your mother

Orla laughed bitterly. From a scribbled message inside a Christmas card to this. Without further consideration she telephoned her.

'Hello. It's Orla.'

There was the usual cacophony. 'I will call you back straight away.'

The line died and Orla shrugged, not expecting the return call any time soon. Within minutes her mobile buzzed.

'Hello, Orla. Thank you for calling me.' There was no background interference. 'I'd like to see you. I'm moving back to Dublin and I'd like us to meet.'

'OK.'

There was a pause.

'I am sorry, Orla, but I don't want to talk to you over the phone and it's not because I haven't time or anything – I just want to see you.'

'That's fine.'

'When should I come?'

'One weekend after I go back to school.'

'That long?'

'I won't be here for the last few weeks of the summer.'

'Where are you going?'

'Cork.'

A longer pause ensued.

'Then I'll see you the first weekend in September?' said Maeve resignedly.

'Yes.'

'Good.'

'OK.'

'Yes . . . Thank you, Orla.'

Orla was suspicious. Maeve wanted something or something had gone wrong. She immediately tried to forget.

It was while she had fallen asleep in the afternoon, something she did more often lately, when Jack eventually called. Still muzzy with sleep she focused on the caller's number, not recognizing it.

'Hello,' she croaked.

'Is that Orla?'

She coughed. 'Yes. Yes. Hello, Jack . . .'

'How are you?'

'I'm fine.'

'I hoped to see you before you returned home to Dublin.'

'I'm sorry about that. I had work to do before the new term. The leaving cert results arrive tomorrow and I need books and clothes. I need my things you see. I . . . I have to . . .' She realized she was rambling. 'I'm sorry for losing control. Did it clean up?'

'Ah you wouldn't know it happened. Are you coming back down again this year?'

'Oh yes. I'll be down next week.'

'That's grand. Could I see you again?'

'Of course,' she exclaimed too eagerly.

'Perhaps we can go out again?'

'I'd like that.'

That conversation made the rest of the week bearable.

Shortly afterwards, Martin phoned again. She did not answer. He had sent several texts and left voicemails but she had deleted them all.

In the afternoon on the Thursday she broke her routine and travelled across the city to her old mentor's house where they sat in the garden and worked through the statistics. It was the penultimate set of results before Brendan's retirement.

Over barbecue chicken wraps and wine, he eyed her knowingly.

'Tell me what it is.'

'What?'

'What's up with you?'

'You have sauce on your chin.'

'I want to know.'

'I don't know what you mean.'

'Your residuals are good; you've done well by your students; the department remains strong and yet you don't seem at all bothered. It should be me who is indifferent. If I'm to retire next year you will have to do all this alone. What's wrong?'

She sighed and put her glass of wine aside.

'I told you about my inheritance. I haven't told you what I have discovered there, about the people and the past and how I am part of it all.'

'And you didn't know?'

'I knew nothing. It's both terrible and beautiful and I feel I have found something that was always there but waiting for me to find it. I'm in my element down there, Brendan.'

'What does Martin say?'

'Well, there's another problem. It's over between us.'

'And is your world imploding?'

Knowing his opinion of Martin she ignored the cynicism.

'That's just it, Brendan, I think my world is suddenly becoming real to me. I think I know what it is all about.'

'All that after a few weeks by the sea?'

'It's so much more and you know me better.'

'What does this mean for Dublin?'

'I don't know. I truly don't.'

Over the weekend Bernadette returned and she let herself into the flat. She found Orla sitting on the patio in her pyjamas and slippers. She was reading *The History of the Famine in Cork*. She made a note in the margin and put the book down.

'You've lost weight,' Bernadette observed.

'I don't feel like eating.'

'It suits you.'

'What – starving?'

'It's not like you to be sarcastic.'

Orla shrugged.

'You've a tan.'

'I hardly saw daylight all week.' Her eyes widened suggestively.

Orla was revolted.

'Aren't you going to grill me?'

Orla shook her head. 'It looks like you've been well grilled already.'

'So funny . . . His name was Kristos.'

'Don't, Bernie.'

'Who else am I going to tell?'

'I don't want to hear it. It offends me.'

'What?'

'I haven't had sex in months and I don't want to hear about the latest Lothario you've given yourself up to.'

'It's not like that.'

'Yes, it is and you know it.'

She saw tears in her friend's eyes and she was ashamed. She wanted to apologize but could not bring herself to.

'You've caught the sun as well,' Bernadette offered.

Orla closed her eyes behind her sunglasses, sipped water and said nothing.

'Are you preparing for the new term?' Bernadette persisted.

'It's all done. It helped to focus me.'

'Or make you forget.'

Orla shrugged.

'I had Martin on the telephone last night. He says you won't see him. What happened?'

'I went at him like a screaming banshee.'

'You did?'

'Those are his things in the hall. His Playstation, computer games, fantasy novels, DVDs and clothes. He has nothing else.'

'Why were you with him if he was so unsuitable?'

'I thought he was suitable. I didn't know.'

'I told you enough times.'

'You did,' Orla admitted. 'But then I told you about your choices and you took no notice.'

Bernadette smiled wryly. 'He says there's another man. Is it true? Is it Jack?'

'No, it's not true.'

Bernadette sighed in relief. 'Shall I make you a cup of tea?' she asked.

'No I'm fine. I've water.'

'Are you going to give Martin a chance?'

'Why have you come here, Bernie, as a mediator, or as my friend?'

'How can you say that? You know what I think about Martin; I just want to make sure you know what you're doing.'

'Well, I do.'

Bernadette waited and Orla placed the book on the table. 'What happened down there?' she asked.

'What did Martin say?' Orla asked in return.

'He says you changed, that you're a different person.'

'He's right – I am.'

'If that's the case then you need to move on. You need to get back out there. Have you been out since you came home?'

'Only to your place.'

'And don't I know that. Haughey and Fitz hardly moved a muscle when I came in. They're as fat as can be. Where else have you been?'

'To the shops and to Brendan's.'

Bernadette stood up. 'That's it. I'll have no more of this. Get dressed. We're going out together.'

'Where?'

'The nearest bar.'

'What for?'

'We need to have some fun. You can't hang around here with a face like a constipated greyhound.'

'I won't find anything there. I just need my time alone, to sit – that's enough.'

'This is Dublin. You're at the centre of it all. You shouldn't be hiding away here.'

'I don't intend to. I'm taking the train back down to Cork tomorrow. I'm spending the last few weeks of the holiday in Ballyanna.'

'So it is Jack.'

Orla was earnest. 'It is not. I don't need to find a man. I need to find myself.'

16

Soulbabe

She rode to Ballybrannigan on the first day back and there she took the steps up to the Star of the Sea church where she rested in the pews – she needed to after the ride and the climb.

She had last attended Mass with her grandmother and, as she knelt alone, she thought of Margaret and then of Donovan, both pious and failed and tortured by their faith. Father O'Leary would often complain about the young losing their way, but what had she ever had to say to him? It had always been those times when she had the church to herself that she felt closest to God, and she prayed then for both grandparents and for the courage to make good their faith in her.

When she returned to Ballyanna, she sat on the porch feeling exhilarated more than exhausted. Her calves were harder, her thighs were aching but not in agony and she breathed deeper.

It was when she was taking the bicycle from the outhouse the next day that she noticed Jack standing beneath the roses. Emerging from the cobwebs she yelped then blushed.

He went to her then and in one movement embraced her and kissed her. She stood stiffly, unsure if he thought the kiss would indicate anything more than the meeting of friends. He stepped back.

'You know the locals are laughing at you?'

'Are they? Why?'

'They say only tourists and children ride bicycles through the lanes.'

She was vexed.

'People need to find more interesting things to talk about.'

'I think they find you fascinating.'

He laughed then and she was able to smile.

'It's very dark back here, don't you think?'

'The fuchsia needs pruning. It's one of the things I intend to do.'

'I've had the cesspit looked at while you were away.'

'Oh. Who did that?'

'A builder from Castleford who contracts for me; he specializes in drainage issues. He said there's no problem, that it's normal and just to pump out the cesspit. I can arrange that—'

'But isn't it something to do with the drainage and the way the bathroom plumbing was fitted? I thought perhaps the work that was done caused the problem?'

'Not at all. It would take a whole new renovation to make sure it never happens again, but there is no need to do any expensive work like that. The house is not worth that much.'

'It would be if I was to live in it.'

'That's true.'

'So emptying the cesspit will get rid of the smell?'

'It will sure. You have to realize that there was always a smell from the pits.'

She was unsure if he was patronizing her. 'Oh, I didn't know.'

'That's country life. In the meantime keep the plug in the hole and stuff a flannel in the overflow if it gets bad.'

'OK,' she replied slowly.

'You know if it's too much of a problem you should consider selling the place.'

'I couldn't do that. I've plans for it.'

'Have you?'

'I'm thinking of opening the Leaping Dolphin.'

'As a pub?'

'As a heritage centre.'

'Are you now?'

'I was hoping some of the local people would become patrons and contribute artefacts or even money.'

'Of course, that's grand and whatever you choose to do I'll help you as much as I can.'

'I'd appreciate that. Perhaps your building contacts could—'

'Sure,' he dismissed, 'whatever I can do. Where are you off to today?'

'I'm going on a tourist trail along the High Road towards Mourne Head. I'm going to explore the strands along the way. Do you have a bike of you own?'

'I don't. It's a pity. Perhaps I could drive you.'

'Where would be the fun and laughter in that?'

He didn't seem to understand.

'Listen, I'm off to the city at the end of the week. I thought you might like to come with me for company, like. I've a bit of business to take care of but I thought we could make a day of it. What do you say?'

'I'd like that.'

'That's a grand job.'

He hesitated and then kissed her again and this time she accepted it.

The coastal High Road through the valleys was long and undulating but she took water and books and her camera and enjoyed it greatly.

On her previous visit, Anne had drawn a map for her with all the accessible strands clearly marked. At every crossroads she followed the lane down to the sea. Some strands were small and stony while others were wide and sand filled, but each possessed a weary beauty.

Eventually the High Road diminished into a high banked lane and she was lost in the maze that was off the map. At one crossroads, where a solitary derelict cottage stood, the fingerpost pointed down towards Galglass and the Or. She assumed this meant golden. The names echoed in her mind and so she turned towards the sea.

Unlike Ballyanna this hamlet was uninhabited. There was a farm on the hillside, but all else was barren. She rode her bicycle down to the beach which stretched several miles eastwards.

She rested by a flat stone, sipped her water and nibbled a biscuit on which she had spread low fat cheese. Clouds obscured the high sun but the day was warming. In the distance, she thought she could see a dog being walked.

She saw that the Coastal Way, meandering towards her from the east was wide here, leading through a stile in the fence and over the headland to her right. Leaving the bicycle against the wall she took her rucksack and followed the path.

Over the crest of the hill the path dipped down into a deep valley and merged into an unmade lane, along which were scattered the stone foundations of a lost village. She paused to imagine the community, but sensed it was impossible to consider so many hopes and fears.

She went down to the sheltered strand and sat there on the stones for sometime, basking, nibbling another biscuit and reading her book. She was reading of forensics on a body revealed by the spring thaw.

The water before her was clear and she could see shoals of fish in the shallows. Taking a look about her she stripped. Immediately, she felt self-conscious in her togs, noticing with disdain the dimples on her thighs. Tentatively wading in, she was glad the water distorted the image.

The cold exhilaration was acute and she whooped for joy as she fell in. She dived beneath the surface, looking this way and that for the shoal, and seeing the fish dart away through the shallows. She could hear the Song of the Undersea as she floated free.

When she returned to An Doras in the late afternoon she ached again, but after a shower and a light salad she stretched out on her bed and slept solidly until the next morning.

She awoke with the dawn and went to the stormwall with her breakfast and telescope to watch the ships on the horizon and the birds on the cliffs. Before she put the instrument to her eye, she rubbed her thumb across the engraved initials; she was sure now it had been the property of Juno Byrne and she was humbled.

Through the lens she saw that Patrick was already pulling pots in the bay.

By the time she had returned from Ballybrannigan with groceries, she was disappointed to see the dinghy already up on the strand and that he was gone.

That evening, she met Anne coming down the boreen.

'I didn't know you were back,' her great aunt said.

'I've not been here long.'

'Well, then you wouldn't know the news.'

'What is it?'

'I am a great-grandmother.'

'Saoirse's had the baby. That's marvellous. I must go and see her. What did she have?'

'A boy.'

'And the name?'

'They have called him Pearse Francesco.'

'What do you think of that?'

'It's a mouthful and it sounds like a monk but Robbie is only remembering those who have helped him.'

'And Pearse would have been proud.'

'My brother was a miserable and strange man, but he would have been as proud as I am.'

'Would she mind if I went up there?'

'She would not; she would welcome it. Away you go.'

Orla left her there and went to the workshop. Saoirse was sat breast-feeding the baby.

'Do you want to hold him?' she offered.

'I don't think I do. I'm no good with babies.'

'And you being a teacher.'

'I'm just not the motherly type.'

Saoirse held the baby out. 'I think you are. Here. Take him. I need a rest. My arms are dead and my tits are raw.'

Orla was opened mouth at the crudity but found herself laughing uproariously when Saoirse did. She tentatively took the baby and held him against her. He was complete in her arms and his silent presence consumed her.

'Have you seen Patrick?' Saoirse asked.

'I was going to ask you the same.'

'What with the baby, Roberto's not been able to help with the preparations for The Rest. Pat is probably off busying himself with them.'

'If you see him, will you tell him I asked after him?'

Saoirse gave a sly grin. 'I will of course.'

It was several days before she saw Patrick. She had been along the cliffs all morning and had returned to the cottage and taken a nap. His thumps at the door struck hard at her dreams. She stumbled groggily to the porch.

He smiled as she touched at her hair.

'Please come in,' she said, stepping aside.

They stood apart in the centre of the living-room. He stared at her without intimidation but with an intensity that intrigued her. In her mind she sensed some admission was there to be had but he just said, 'How are you?'

'I'm well.'

'Good.'

'And you?'

'Fine.'

He stared; she smiled.

'I . . . I . . . will you allow me to cook for you before you leave again?' he asked.

She was startled.

'I know that last time I asked it didn't seem appropriate—'

'But that was just me being bloody-minded.'

'But all the same I'd like to cook for you this evening.'

The charge of his bold sincerity was amusing.

'Then I'd be delighted.'

'Tonight? Really?'

She laughed. 'Why not?'

He stepped past her with gauche enthusiasm.

'What time?' she asked.

He was already at the door. 'Seven,' he said, ducking back and then disappearing.

She stayed where she was, watching the window where he passed, absolutely awake now and thinking of what she would wear.

She had three hours.

In the bedroom, she laid a dress out over the bed, then selected her shoes, sorted her make-up and ran a bath. She even chose her best lace bra and knickers. Her buttocks had healed and she was confident the bike riding had reduced the cellulite down there.

Three hours later she had been ready for two.

She strolled up the lane in the half light, hoping no one would see her before he did, and when Patrick opened the door she was pleased by his look that lingered too long. The aromas from within were exquisite.

'It's all ready,' he said, as he took the wine she offered and turned away. She watched him, noticing for the first time how he moved with grace.

He led her to the twisted table where two places were arranged at the corner. He pulled out her chair and she took a seat.

The music was low and she did not recognize it.

'What is the song?' she asked. 'I've not heard it before.'

'It's Immaculate.'

'Roberto told me about them.'

'They helped us when we were young, helped us get older, through the bad phases.'

She listened again to the delicate piano and strings.

'This doesn't sound the way I remember.'

'This was much later.'

'What are the lyrics? I can't make them out.'

Patrick began to sing along in a rich high baritone about absolute love believed.

She grinned nervously and she saw him blush.

She wanted to say that it could have been written for her.

He placed the plates between them and then fetched the covered dishes, placing them on the table.

'Can I help?'

He looked at her and smiled, remembering that first day.

'You can, of course. These vegetables are all from the farms here. I had to rush around today to get them. Saoirse or Anne usually cook for me.'

He uncovered the largest oval dish.

'A cobbler?' she asked.

He nodded as she broke the crust.

'What is in it?'

'I'm afraid it's that lobster who had some attitude. I froze the blighter . . . as well as a mixture of other fish.'

'It's delicious.'

He sat back and eyed her.

'It truly is,' she assured, 'but if I ate this well every night I'd never lose weight.'

'You think you need to lose weight?'

'Of course I do.'

'No way,' he dismissed.

She sensed that there was no condescension and she liked that as well.

She placed her knife and fork down and looked at him squarely. He glanced up worriedly.

'Thank you for helping me, Patrick . . . No, for saving me.'

They laughed then.

'Tell me more about Donovan.'

And so he did. The more she discovered, the more she liked the old man and yet the more she pitied him and felt guilty. She gave a sardonic smile at the conflict.

'What is it?' Patrick asked.

She told him.

'I think he was happy at the very end,' Patrick said. 'When he found out who you were he was delighted. He had not loved for nothing.'

'But you were uncertain?'

'I'd never met you. It was an incredible gamble, even foolish, but he was so adamant. I just wanted his place to be cared for, to be kept as it was. A builder would knock it down and start again.'

She gasped.

'That's how I react,' he observed. 'With all that history gone, how many other cottages could tell such a story? You know that the mayor of Cork City himself hid in that place. He was a friend of our great-grandmother Brenda Geraghty.'

'Is it not protected?' she asked.

'No.'

'Then we must make sure it is.'

Tanned and taut, he sat back and looked at her and smiled. It was the same generous smile he had offered when he saved her from the storm. She looked away.

Later he took her into the study and there beneath the shelves he opened his photograph albums. She saw that they were labelled and categorized.

'You know I have many more below,' she said. 'Wasn't it a risk leaving them there?'

He shrugged. 'I didn't know all of what Donovan had. It wasn't my place to look.'

They sat there and he pointed out their common ancestors, sharing stories of shipwrecks, kidnapping, rebellions, transportation and even prohibition gangsters.

'You know more than I do,' he conceded.

'I've been reading the letters and diaries.'

Then he placed his hand down on the next page. 'I've been waiting to show you this,' he said, and then turned the page to reveal a sepia photograph of a young woman with a fur collar and a feathered hat. Orla saw her eyes first of all. They were as all the O'Meagher seemed to be, narrow and piercing. There was nothing innocent about the face and yet she wanted to believe it possessed a vulnerability, that the eyes were as quick to be glad as they were to glare.

'Who is she? She's lovely.'

'That's Donovan's other sister Kathleen. Can't you see it?'

'See what?'

'She looks like you.'

Orla scrutinized the image.

'Yes . . . she does . . . We look very much alike. I see it now . . . but she was a pretty woman.'

He glanced harshly in defiance of her modest denial.

'And I think she looks like a Hollywood starlet,' he declared, keeping his eye on her Orla.

'That's never been said about me,' Orla dismissed with a light laugh. 'What happened to her?' she asked, trying to recall.

'She died at the end of the war. Her hostel was hit by V2 in London.'

She studied the image for sometime, imagining the girl with so much beauty and style, so much more than she.

'And then there is this,' Patrick said, and he opened another album. There was another photograph. Orla recognized it as Brede. 'It was taken in Boston. She must have been over forty years old here, though she does not look it. She only had two children, you see, so she was not old before her time. She could have no more after the second child and then her husband was killed.'

'That was Jack.'

'Yes! Anne has another picture taken much later but this one shows her nearest her prime.'

Orla was silenced by her incredible likeness to these women. Brede stared into the lens, the Phantom Queen, as hard and defiant as she had to be. She had fled all she knew and fought for and made a life in another world. Orla thought she understood. She wanted to believe that somehow Brede had returned.

'I see it too,' he said, as if hearing her thoughts.

She pressed the image between her fingers. The thick card was tangible and tantalizing.

'I have a selection of photos I've scanned for distant cousins who're tracing their roots like . . . I'll send them to you.'

'I'd appreciate that. Are you not going to show me the rest of this place?'

In the gallery where she had seen through the telescope she saw easels, wicker chairs and his binoculars on the sill.

'It's the same as Elannat,' she observed.

'I want it that way. It reminds me of when I first arrived. I use these binoculars for watching the ships and the weather.'

He handed them to her. She saw a ship, silent and serene on the horizon.

'There is something about the lights fading over the curvature of the Earth,' he said, 'some despair but hope as well. There is not much more to show you. Can I walk you back?'

'Please.'

'Would you like to borrow one of my coats?'

'Yes.'

He slipped it over her shoulders and she inhaled again his subtle scent.

As they walked apart in the darkness she spoke more of how the place had affected her.

'You know, I've been around Europe and across the world; I've seen so much art and architecture and I've been awed, humbled – even crushed, and then I come here and it seems like that was all so . . . insignificant . . . and I'm not sure why.'

'It's because it's yours.'

'I don't believe that.'

'It's how I see it,' he stated. 'For this one life this place is mine.'

She pulled up the collar of the coat. 'As a girl I would love to imagine myself in history, as if I was part of it, but I knew I wasn't. I used to think I could travel in an invisible bubble that allowed me to go anywhere through time and just watch.'

'Where did you go?'

'Ancient Greece, Egypt, Elizabethan England, Rome – most of all Rome. I love the politics and the power.'

'What about the wars?'

'The fighting didn't interest me. It's the senate or the court or parliament that I'm drawn to.'

'It was always the wars for me – the strategy and the heroism and the luck.'

'And the futility?'

'Where would your kings and caesars be without blood?'

She laughed.

'But you see, in my time-bubble,' she reiterated, 'I'm still detached from what I see, just a voyeur with no stake in the objects. I'm just looking. And when I actually go places, I'm no more than any number of millions who have seen what I see. The monuments and museums and the caesars and scholars are all necessary for me to know, but I don't know, they're also just . . . academic, and still I'm just looking.'

'I think of all the thousands who have passed this way,' said Patrick, 'and it makes me feel closer, knowing I'm one of them. I'm part of it all. It makes me necessary. It's in the blood. I see the past all around me, alive in every living moment.'

She was glad he could not see her tears, but perhaps he sensed it. What she could not say yet was that here she was no longer looking, she was living.

'When I first returned,' he said, 'I knew this was my home – immediately, intrinsically, in my blood.'

They passed An Doras and stood at the stormwall together. She could not see him in the night but his presence ebbed in her, too dangerous to fully admit; if she did so she feared it would be a deluge. She felt a subtle elation with the sound of their breathing in unison with the fall of the waves.

He spoke quietly.

'I thought I remembered the sun across the curve of the bay. It was the valley of my dreams, though I couldn't have remembered it. They had taken me to an estate in the city and I thought that that was my world, but when I returned it was all here. You know the memories actually hurt when I remembered them; they were so pure and clean and real again. And then I began to know the place once more. Donovan and Anne and even Pearse, who was a difficult man to know, saw it in me and showed me the places. Perhaps I can show you.'

'Yes.'

They stood and listened.

'When I walk across the cliffs, I feel connected,' she said. 'In the city there are just too many lives to know – it drowns you. Here I am free. I want to be part of that. In the city, growing up, I always felt the world was indifferent.'

'But do you think these cliffs or waves care about us?'

'It's different. I know I am nothing to the geology, but in the city people don't want to know when they should. It's just I've only realized now that it can be different. If you'd have asked me last year, or even a few months ago, to explain how I felt I would not have even understood the question. I'd had nothing to judge my life against, but now I know I was incomplete.'

'So you feel complete?'

'I feel different; I feel part of something.'

'You always were part of it and like me you didn't know it.'

'But isn't this place just an escape?' she fretted.

'I expect so in some way,' he conceded, 'but isn't that the city cynic in you? Don't we all want to belong?'

'I think it is because I am an historian. Perhaps it's all just my predilection for the past.'

'What use is anything Orla, if we don't have the wisdom and strength of our past generations? When I look back to where I came from, I find the strength in them to take things on. I think we're only complete if we live with the past, in the now, for the future.'

She chuckled then but was still considering the cliché when he left her outside An Doras and he faded into the darkness.

She paused on the porch, looking around her; seeing the lights across the hillside and the meagre hue of the moon on the sea. There was an intimacy in that dark peace and again she thought the place could be hers. She glanced up the lane and wondered if Patrick was watching her.

Inside she turned the bellows to revive the fire and thought about what had been said.

17

Heart Cartography

On the morning Jack came to collect her, Orla had made the decision to ask him again about his relationship with Donovan. She wanted to believe that both sides were to blame, and that her conciliation would resolve it all.

With her denial intact she looked forward to her excursion by making a list of items for the cottage, including curtains, throws and towels. She also intended to investigate internet access via satellite.

She had been to Cork City a few times for conferences but then, only to and from hotels. She had visited once as a student and had taken in all the sites of interest, but it seemed so long ago. Jack promised to show her the back streets and old shops that was the true face of the city.

When she got into the car, his acrid cologne was vaporous and she opened the window for air. He looked sidelong.

'I've air conditioning,' he said.

'Oh I know. It's the rush of air that I like.'

She could also smell a hint of tobacco.

When she showed him the list Jack was sceptical. 'Will you have time to relax with me with all that to carry?'

'But I'll have you to carry it,' she countered.

'Of course,' he quickly assured.

By Castleford the conversation had ceased and Orla tried to convince herself that he was concentrating on the road and that they were at ease together.

On the dual carriageway now she watched as they passed the marshy flats of Cork Harbour. The mist was still wisping across the water and she was reminded of the world of Nuala Phelan where gods and men lived between our realm and the otherworld. She thought of her grandmother then, reading to her in Wellington Street, and tears stung her face.

'Are you well?' Jack asked.

'I'm just imagining the way this area must have looked to the people in the past.'

He raised an eyebrow.

They were nearing the city and along the banks of the Lee, the cranes and scaffolds dominated the skyline.

'They wouldn't recognize the place anymore I'm sure.'

'But this is the new Ireland,' enthused Jack. 'The Celtic Tiger still roars.'

'It's a pity.'

'What?'

'I hate to see it.'

'And you want it the way it was before, with all the young leaving like I did, crippled by religion and duty and drink.'

'We could have grown differently. It didn't have to be about money.'

'This is the real world; it's always about money.'

'I don't think it is.'

'That's because you've never had to go without, Orla.'

She resented that but she suspected he was right.

'I still think that concrete isn't always the solution.'

Having clearly won the point, Jack shrugged indifferently.

After parking he followed her up St Patrick's Street, idly standing aside while she browsed for the items on her list.

Laden with bags and barely stifling his irritation he asked. 'How about I buy you a dress to crown the day?'

'Is the day over? Do you have to go back?'

'Not at all if you've more to do. It's just you've not been into any boutiques. Don't you like shopping for clothes?'

'Not especially.'

'Oh.'

'No, I don't care for it. I'd rather shop online.'

'Jesus, you're strange.'

'It seems like such a waste of time and the fashions are never appropriate.'

'But you look good.'

'I try.'

'They've reopened Central Mall at the end of St Patrick's Street. Perhaps we could go there.'

'I try to avoid places like that. They're over-priced and soulless.'

'I'd say they were convenient.'

'And crowded.'

'But they have loads of fashions.'

'You don't have to buy me anything. Really, I've enough clothes.'

'But I want to. How about perfume then?'

She feigned looking at her list. 'How about a new ironing board?'

He blew his cheeks in consternation. 'Orla, I'd just like to buy you something special.'

His insistence was annoying her and she wondered if he ever truly gave gifts.

'OK, but why don't we have lunch before that and I can compose myself?'

They deposited the bags in the 4x4, and went for coffee in the restaurant at the bend on St Patrick's Street. They took a table at the window and looked down across the wide parade.

'Did you ever take Donovan out for the day?' she asked.

'He didn't want to go. He was bred in the country. You, though, were born in the city. Now you're here, I can see it's where you belong.'

'I've spoken to Patrick McLeavey,' she stated.

'You have?' He splashed his coffee and mopped it with a sleeve. 'Why did you want to do that for?'

'He is my cousin.'

'Second cousin. And after all his carry on with you – and him giving it the big I am all the time.'

She sneered at the jealousy. He opened his palms, sighed and sat back.

'What else can I say, Orla? I only know what Donovan told me. He said they'd argued about the inheritance.'

'I don't think he resents my inheritance at all.'

He shook his head with hurt. 'And he told you that?'

'It began badly between us but now . . .'

'Now they see who you are and how you've settled, they don't want to cross you. You're an educated woman. They don't know anyone like you. You frighten them.'

'Are you sure?'

'Look, what can they do now? They might as well accept it and make the most of the situation . . . I feel like I'm in detention, Miss Shea.'

She smiled mirthlessly. 'I don't want to hear any more about it. Whatever it is between you and them I want no part of it.'

After a few minutes of silence he flipped open his mobile and turned it on and the ringtone immediately sounded; it was 'Eye of the Tiger'.

'Speak!' he demanded.

She sipped her latte and did not listen to the conversation or the others that quickly followed; she was remembering the old postcards her grandmother had of the city.

Back outside, she followed him towards the Central Mall. Despite the tension, it felt good to walk beside him. She was conscious of other women checking him. It made her wonder what he saw in her when the eyes of those other women would slip to her with obvious surprise. On passing a side street she spied a bookshop.

She touched his arm and he was startled.

'I'd like to go in there.'

'Oh, of course . . . I forgot you like to read.'

Inside she immediately began scouring the shelves for books on local history. As she crouched and leaned and stood engrossed, Jack absently leafed through random tomes.

Only after half an hour of browsing did she realize he was not there; he had retreated to the pavement where he paced the shop front, laughing into his mobile.

He saw her and returned.

'Have you found something?'

'No. I'm still looking.'

'When will you be finished?'

'Soon,' she stated, resenting being rushed.

'There's a burger bar in the Mall. I'm famished. Do you want one if I get one?'

'No, but you have one. Have two.'

'Can I get you anything?'

'Have your burger first and then come and get me. I'm happy here.'

'Well, I've also that business I've to attend to. I've just received a text and . . . Could I meet you in an hour or two?'

'Of course,' she replied in relief.

'Where should I meet you?'

'I'll make my way back here if I go elsewhere.'

'I may be a while.'

'So might I. You have my mobile if I get lost.'

As the door bell chimed his exit, she sighed and set upon the shelves once more.

Three hours later he returned to the shop. She had been reading since she returned an hour before. He helped her carry the books she had purchased. She thought she could smell booze through his cologne. On the way back to the car-park they passed the Grand Theatre.

'They've *Much Ado About Nothing* here,' she observed. 'I'd like to see it.'

'It's Shakespeare,' he stated. 'Aren't you tired?'

'We could walk down the river-bank and take an ice cream and come back.'

'We could have a drink and rent a hotel room,' he suggested casually.

'Jack!' she admonished, despising the insinuation even though he merely laughed at his daring.

'Wouldn't you rather go out to the new multiplex in Castleford and see a film?'

'No, I wouldn't.'

'I've never been to see a play before.'

'Then you'll have some culture.'

'How about a compromise?'

'Which would be?'

'I take you to the Laughing Gull to see the Open Hearts and I'll bring you back here another time and make a night of it. I'll even take you for a meal if you'd allow me.'

She considered the offer.

'The Laughing Gull it is.'

At the pub, even as the band began to play, she sat watching the light fade over the mountains.

After another bout of silence, Jack had gone for drinks. Again she watched him slip through the crowd, stopping at intervals to take a confidence or share a joke, laughing and nodding sincerely and looking her way with a wink.

She was thinking about the chalets and cranes and multiplex cinemas and it was making her angry.

She studied Jack as he laughed. He reminded her of Martin with all his charm and beauty and she was suddenly ashamed and a little afraid.

The band finished the first set with 'Irish Love of Mine' and although they performed the song beautifully, Orla was ready to leave. The chatter of the crowd oscillated in the distance and Jack was again waylaid on his way back with a fresh pint.

'I'd like to go back now,' she stated when he sat back down.

He almost spat out his drink.

'You don't mind, do you?' she asked.

'Of course not,' he claimed.

The following morning she arose early; it was hard to sleep and she did not know why. Despite the restlessness, she was thankful that she only had two glasses of wine and returned early from the village. At least she was not enduring nausea as well.

As usual she took her tea and toast and book down to the stormwall. She was thinking about Jack and some realization was imminent.

It was then that Patrick approached down the lane with his oars over his shoulder. They were alone in the grey morning. She smiled nervously.

'Hello,' he said, clearly surprised to see her.

'Where have you been?' she asked.

'I've been working.'

'I thought you would come and see me.'

'You've been busy.'

'I thought . . . I was just looking at the cliffs over there.'

He followed her gaze to the ridges along the cliffside.

'They call that Gortagort. It's where the people grew their crops in the Famine.' Although she knew, she wanted him to tell her. 'Their land and gardens were just below here and they starved up there. There were hundreds here once. It must have been savage . . .' He leaned the oars against the wall. 'You know there was to be a road over the cliffs there. The boreen was the first stage, but the cliffs further along fell away and Lazenby ran out of money and then he was killed.'

She was struck once more by the desperate tenacity of the Famine people. Her mind could rationalize with statistics and dates and names, and she could even apportion blame, but it was always the mass graves, the roads to nowhere and the grey ruins and such visible remnants as the inconspicuous ridges that offered a truer sense of the scale of it all, and made her want to weep.

She wandered where her blood flowed through the story, wanting to be part of the survival against such oppression, such deprivation and such bad luck.

'I think I am lucky when the lives of those people contained so much toil and pain, and I am able to return to the valley in luxury.'

'I think as long as we know what happened then we should not feel guilt. They would not want that. And I've work to do. I don't idle and I don't think you do either.'

'Of course,' she said. 'Can I help?'

He laughed. 'If you like.' He paused. 'If you like, you can come out with me one day.'

'Really? I'd like that.'

'If the weather's fine you can come tomorrow.'

'Oh yes.'

'Can you swim?'

'Ah, yes.'

She could probably float, she thought.

The following day she was waiting when Patrick called for her at first light.

'See I'm wrapped and warm and weatherproof as advised.'

'And the wellingtons are good.' She was pleased that he seemed impressed.

'But if you fall into the sea slip them off or you'll go straight to the bottom!'

'Oh. OK.' She assumed he was joking. Still determined to do well, she pointed to the oars. 'I can take those.'

He handed them to her. She struggled to lift them to her shoulder. Taking one end he lowered the oars and they carried them together.

On the verge above the slipway, he opened the secure box and from it heaved up an outboard motor. With its exposed parts and the sharp blades, Orla was slightly intimidated. The feeling was made worse when he handed her a grubby lifejacket.

The tide was in and they dragged the dinghy down the stones. She watched as he fixed the motor to the stern and set the oars in the rowlocks.

Wading through the weed bank he held the dinghy steady and she rolled in. After considerable squirming she sat herself on the bow board. She looked sidelong at him, baiting him to comment, but he just grinned.

In one swift movement, he was in, standing behind her and pushing hard against the stones with an oar.

And then they were out in the channel and Orla gripped the sides. She flinched as Patrick gently took her fingers and prised them loose.

'Just look around you,' he said.

And so she did. As the blades slapped on the smooth black surface she watched the land recede and a new perspective unfurl.

'The place seems so small from here.'

'It is.'

When they had eased through the channel he put the outboard down and powered eastward towards Cromwell's Hump. She could see Lir's Tears three miles distant.

With her hair tousled and the wind against her face, she looked back at the bay and shouted, 'I love this place Patrick.'

He nodded.

She traced the Coastal Way as it wound along the bays and strands. With confidence now, she leaned over and thrust her hand in the water, sensing the power of it.

When Patrick cut the motor, they were at the three islands. The swell was perceptible, the sun was strengthening, and she began to feel nauseous. He saw her blanch and handed her his water. As she sat heaving, he began to sort the fishing tackle.

'I don't need to fish,' she said.

'Oh. I thought you'd like to see what I do.'

'Just being here is enough.'

'I'll have to check the pots.'

'Of course, but can we just float downstream so to speak.'

Deep breaths and light sips helped quell the nausea and from inside her bag she took out her straw hat and placed it on her head. Patrick grinned again.

'What?' she challenged.

'Very Betty Davis.'

'What?' she asked again, remembering Margaret and the man from the Ministry of the Sun.

'Sorry,' he offered.

'No, you misunderstand; how did you know?'

'It's just there's a resemblance.'

'Did Donovan ever tell you about my grandmother?'

'Only that he loved her and about you and your mother.'

'And no more?'

'I think it was too painful for him, and when he returned from Dublin it was mostly about you that he spoke of.'

She considered that and with mock haughtiness said, 'I think I look more like Katharine Hepburn.'

They laughed then and were laughing and talking still when he rowed into the narrow strand on the far side of Cromwell's Hump.

Before them was the gully of dense trees and undergrowth through which a stream trickled down through the rocks.

'Beyond there is where I found you in the rain,' he explained.

He jumped into the shallows and she followed. Together they pulled the boat up and tethered her. He then led Orla up on to the rocks to their right where there was a series of raised grassy ledges which eventually and precariously led back on to the Coastal Way.

Arranged on the ledges, in several square beds, was a spread of dry serrated seaweed.

'This is the carrageen moss,' he informed. 'Saoirse collected this.'

'So this is where it dries.'

'This was Donovan's spot. He liked the seclusion.'

She slipped on a clump of long grass.

'I used to warn him about coming down here as he got older but he took no notice, and that sister-in-law of mine was just the same even when she was pregnant.'

'And Donovan would sell it?'

'Oh yes. In the past there would be piles of the stuff but in the end it was just pocket money.'

'So it's spread out to dry out?'

'To be bleached by the sun and the rain and the dew. I have to take it in now. We're due storms and it would be a waste for it to be blown away.'

She helped him fill the shoulder-bags.

'Here. Try some,' he said.

She chewed a sprig.

'Rubber and salt – a delicacy.'

They returned to the dinghy and when they reached Cromwell's Hump he cut the motor and rowed over to the series of bouys set across the guileen.

She saw him looking to and fro into the water as he rowed.

'What is it?' she asked.

'Manannan's Fingers. There. See the auld grabber.'

She peered into the water and discerned the jagged towers in the gloom.

'The pots are on the other side so that no one else steals them.'

'People would do that here?'

'Of course,' he frowned. 'And who would catch them? But Manannan here has taken down a fair few ships. He doesn't care if you're a robber or a saint.'

Once through the submerged rocks, he steadied the dinghy as she hooked the pot line with the gaffe. When a wave slapped the dinghy, she lost balance and fell back against him.

They remained together for a moment, neither knowing how to react. Then they silently withdrew and he held his hand out for the gaffe without looking at her.

She watched the pot emerge through the water. Inside, a turquoise lobster was slowly revealed. He heaved the pot aboard in a shower of water and weeds and pulled the lobster and gave it to her, its flapping tail first.

'Throw it back,' he instructed. 'It's too small.'

She took it between her fingers. Its shell shone and she could feel the convulsive strength of it. Placing it on the water, she watched with satisfaction as it sank out of sight.

'Would you like to row back?' he asked.

'Do you think I can?'

'Have a go.'

He stood and stepped back and she shifted nervously to sit between the oars. Standing behind her, he held her hands and guided her strokes. With a steady rise and fall she became confident and guided the dinghy back towards the strand.

He stepped past her and leaned back against the stern, taking his turn in admiring the view.

By the time they reached the channel and he took over she was exhausted and elated. Her nausea was gone now.

At An Doras she invited him in for a warming drink. She made tea in the kitchen and when she came in with the tray, she found he had walked through to the old pub.

'Do you know why it was called the Leaping Dolphin?'

'I assumed it was because of the Laughing Gull in Ballybrannigan.'

'That was named after this pub. It was for the dolphins that followed the boat that Eugene Geraghty and William O'Meagher sailed in. They were shipwrecked in Africa and saved each other. Eugene returned with William and bought this property and started the pub.'

'I've had this idea,' she said. 'I would like to open this place as a heritage centre.' She glanced to him for some approbation. He was looking about, nodding and calculating. 'Donovan has left so many artefacts and letters,' she went on. 'I am sure it could be done. I could do research and it would help the community.'

'And I would help you,' he immediately offered.

'Thank you.'

'Me and Roberto could make cabinets and shelves. You could even have glass in them.' He cast his eye about the room. 'The bar there could be made into a fine desk or booth. What do you think?'

He was silhouetted in the window now with the fields and the boreen to Elannat in the background. She was seized by the desire to go to him but still she was so unsure if for him it was anything more than kindness.

That night, when Jack called, she sat by the fire feigning illness.

'I don't know what it is; I just need to rest. I'm thinking about going to bed early.'

He hovered in the doorway offering no consolation. Without a word he approached her and placed an envelope on the table. She opened it. It contained two tickets to see *Much Ado About Nothing* in the following week.

'Oh, Jack.'

'What is it?'

'I'm to go back at the end of the week. I have to finish my preparations for the new term.'

'Oh.'

'But thank you. That was so kind. Perhaps I can pay you for them.'

He remained looming there and she wondered if he was deliberately doing so.

'Are you going to The Rest?' he asked.

She looked up and nodded.

'Would you come with me?'

She hesitated, wanting to refuse.

'Yes, I will. Of course, I will.'

He stepped forward. She sat still as he kissed her. When he was gone she could taste his acrid aftershave.

But she did indeed go to bed with a hot chocolate and her book, but only so that she could arise early the next morning to join Patrick again. She had arranged with him to explore the fields together.

As agreed he was waiting in the lane when she emerged.

'Have you got your telescope?' he asked.

'Yes.'

'And water?'

'Yes.'

'And armour?'

'What? Oh. Yes.' She smiled though the joke was weak.

He turned and started back up the lane.

'Where are you going? I thought we were walking to Ballybrannigan.'

'We are. There are other ways.'

Before the workshop he turned into the field and she followed him up to the valley edge. She could see the Damanta Stones to her right. At the crest of the hill they paused to look back across the valley. It was golden in the sun.

'I'll take you straight across the fields and we'll go by the Coastal Way on the way back.'

'What about trespassing?'

He laughed. 'No one will mind. This is the old way and sure, what harm will we do, and who else knows these ways through the fields?'

She felt secure as she walked with him and they spoke of the crops and the hedges and more of the past. He told her the names of hamlets and houses and families and farms through time. The words were quickly lost but they wove an intricate web across her soul. Still he was reluctant to reveal much of his own history but she persisted in asking when it seemed appropriate.

He bought her an ice-cream in the summer shop above the pier. He caught her eyeing the cracked chocolate coating of his lolly and offered her a bite. She hesitated and then bit as delicately as she could.

On the way back he named the birds and they sat on a small beach.

'This is perfect,' she said.

'It's rough in the winter; it's a barren place then.'

'I can imagine, but I would see it in the same way. I'm not here for the sun, Patrick. I'm here to stand over there on Cromwell's Hump and touch the sky.'

He laughed. 'When I first returned I stood there and spun around and around and screamed until my voice was gone.'

'That's extreme.'

'Then I fell into The Hollow and twisted my ankle.

She laughed.

'That's what I felt,' he continued. 'I was released. I had returned and all the rage and confusion roared.'

'Was it bad where you came from?'

'I escaped is all,' he said. 'I was lucky to have this place to come to . . . I was lucky.'

'And you brought Roberto back.'

'That was later but, yes. I'm more proud of him than anything.'

She was moved by his words and the understanding made leaving for Dublin a deep regret.

'I'm going home tomorrow.'

'I know.'

'You know Dublin will always be my town, but Ballyanna is where I belong now, I'm sure of it.'

She did not need to look at him to know he believed her.

18

The Road Never Ends

Back at Holy Cross the talk in the staffroom was of holidays abroad, DIY and weddings. As she listened to the anecdotes Orla smiled and even laughed, but she could find no words to describe where she had been. She just felt the sickness of her soul and a feeling that she was beyond it all.

Her new timetable was fair and she enjoyed meeting new faces and old. Her early lessons were dictatorial, establishing her routines and expectations, but she soon relaxed into her usual digressions and self-deprecations. She remained proficiently eccentric in her delivery and the pupils in her care knew no better, but she knew she was acting as an automaton. The planning and preparation was uninspired and uninspiring. She regurgitated the old formulas and presentations and thought no more of it.

Sinead McAuliffe came to Orla while she was on duty in the playground. The girl slipped her arm into hers and Orla noticed how her clothes were crisp and her skin clear. She surreptitiously checked her hair for nits but it was washed and combed through. Sinead leaned into Orla, her wide eyes looking up.

'I've had the best summer ever,' she whispered.

'What did you do?'

'I flew in a jet.'

'You did not!'

'I did. We went to Costa . . . Costa . . .'

'Spain.'

'That's it.'

'And did you see your ma and pa?'

Sinead's brow creased.

'They want me to come home,' she replied flatly.

'And what do you want?'

'I want to stay where I am.'

Orla thought she understood what that meant and hugged the girl.

Sinead looked about then to ensure she was not being watched, and placed a pen in Orla's hand. A flamenco couple danced on its barrel.

'That's you and your fella when you find him, miss.'

Later that week she was standing among the split acorns and empty cups and cigarette ends beneath the Old Man. She traced the roots into the earth and noted how the tarmac swelled and cracked with the strength of them.

As she placed her bag in the pannier of her moped Martin stepped out from behind the tree.

She gasped.

'It's the only way you will speak to me,' he reassured. 'I need to say I'm sorry.'

She breathed and considered. 'And I am sorry,' she offered. 'Losing my temper like that was not me.'

'You had reason.'

'Perhaps.'

'Orla, I don't want it to end like this.'

'Martin, I didn't want to hurt you, but it's no use. I know my mind.'

'Do you? You seem so sad.'

'I am. I'm here and I don't want to be.'

'I told you I would wait.'

'Please don't do this. You must leave me alone now. Move on with yourself.'

'I've changed, Orla. I think I know what went wrong. I was selfish and stupid. I've changed.'

It was with him there, pathetic and indignant, that she finally realized the fundamental change that had occurred in her. She knew absolutely he was not the right one.

When she spoke it was with resignation. 'I was thinking about what I would say to you if I saw you again and I just couldn't think of a thing. Now I wonder why I'm not in tears or angry or . . . Well, there's just nothing to care about. Before I met you I wanted love in my life . . . I wanted intensity and respect and passion and I never found it. And then you came along and by that time I was thinking it would be too late for me if I didn't find it soon.'

She turned her crash helmet to put it on.

'Wait!' he exclaimed.

'I have to go.'

'Please!'

She relented and held the helmet ready.

'Please.'

'No, Martin.'

It was then he screamed, 'Who are you to do this to me? You think I'm the one who's losing you? You think I can't get on without you? You can't cook; you're always on a period; you can't make a decision on your own and—'

But she had slipped the helmet on and was smiling bitterly; he was making this decision easy.

He stepped closer and she could hear his muted tirade.

'You West Brit bitch. You have no taste in music, or film and the books you read—'

She switched on the engine and though his mouth opened and closed he said nothing.

All the doubts and confusion were cleared and she flipped the visor down.

She wanted to believe that what he said was merely spiteful pride, but too much of it was true.

For the rest of the week she tried to forget the verbal assault. He did not call and although perturbed she was pleased.

More often she took lunch alone at her desk, looking out across the car-park to where the oak tree seemed to shudder with the weight of dying summer leaves and the fear of the winter.

Danny Mulroney found her there.

'I've done it, miss.'

'And what is that?'

'I've made a family tree and I have it here in my bag.'

'I must see it.'

He unrolled it across the desk. Several pages of A4 lined paper had been taped together.

'It's marvellous,' she exclaimed.

He had coloured in the lines and taken great care with the names and dates.

'My ma and pa loved it. I went round all my family and they told me all sorts of names. I even have photographs.'

She questioned him about the people and he enthused.

'And what about you, miss? What did you do over the summer?'

'The summer's not over yet,' she said.

And when Danny left her there, her thoughts returned to the valley and the kiss Jack had given her before she left. She could still taste the hardness of it, still troubled that she had allowed him to believe he could come so near.

Thoughts of Patrick seemed to exist amorphous and indecipherable in her every thought.

She looked down on the tree. She saw her life as a map, not a tree. The tree was in stasis, the roots were firm and immovable; it could be cut down at anytime and the branches seemed to reach but never achieve. On a map she could trace roads that led somewhere but also returned.

One night, halfway through the term, she trudged through the rain to her moped. Sighing, she shoved her books into the panniers. She had endured a particularly tedious pastoral team meeting in which the head of year had insisted on reading every bullet point of a particularly turgid handout, as if they could not read it for themselves. She shook her head; too often it was such incompetents, too eager to escape the classroom, who became the managers. And merely to justify their positions, they wasted time and resources on futile initiatives and number chasing. To be a teacher, she thought, should be honourable and simple, and yet it was complicated by these mediocre bureaucrats who spoke for no one but themselves.

As she made to put her crash helmet on she saw a figure approach through the school gates.

'I will get the Gárdaí if you do this again.'

But when he passed beneath the lamp she saw it was Patrick McLeavey.

'What?' she gasped. Her heart raced and she thought he could surely hear it. 'What are you doing here, Patrick?'

'I was in Dublin anyway.'

'You were not.'

He looked startled and she sensed it was true.

'Why?'

'I have some of my art in a show here. It went on to a gallery.'

'Was it the provincial exhibition?'

' 'Twas.'

'I saw it. It was at the Municipal, wasn't it?'

'Yes.'

'I had to leave before I saw it all.'

'It wasn't much, just rural artists given a pat on the head, but I've sold some work.'

'That's brilliant. You should have said something.'

'You know I paint and didn't we have other things to talk about?'

'We did. Would you like to come back to my flat to catch up?'

'I've got to get back to the station.'

That he had not made time for her made her ache with disappointment.

'I couldn't leave without seeing you,' he explained. 'I wanted to talk to you.'

She drew out of the rain beneath the tree.

'What is it?'

'I wanted to ask you to come back with me.'

'What?'

'Come back to the valley and stay with us . . . with me.'

In the living moment she was dazed. A blood rush soared through her senses. What she said was not what her soul screamed.

She stammered, 'My life is here, Patrick. My work is here.'

'I think your life is there.'

'I didn't expect this, Patrick.'

He turned from her and began to walk away. She went after him and seized his sleeve.

'Patrick, it's just not as simple as that.'

'It is,' he said.

'You can't just expect me to give up everything and go with you. It's naïve to think it could be so simple.'

'Is it?'

'Yes. I've not even told you how I feel . . .'

But before she could he had turned away again.

'Patrick. Come back, Patrick.'

But he was gone.

At the flat she threw her helmet down, stripped, showered and changed into her pyjamas. She then sat on the settee and cried. The lights were off and the rain fell and she was miserable and afraid.

After a while she calmed and went into the hallway. There on the mat was the post she had stepped over in her frustration. On top was an envelope that had been hand delivered. She opened it immediately. It was a blank sheet of paper. She walked back into the room, collapsed into the chair and cried no more.

In the departmental meeting the following week she was distracted and said little. Another initiative was to be abandoned and replaced by a strategy she recognized from teacher training twelve years before. Brendan looked about the table, but he was clearly trying to bait her.

'So what are the new ideas for units of work? I think we should introduce more about the English monarchy. We do far too much on the martyrs of the Easter Rising.'

But she smiled and nodded and thought more of her plans to leave.

Brendan was pragmatic in his summation. 'So students must learn dates and names and be tested regularly. An empathetic approach must be avoided so that linear understanding is acquired. Interpretive skills should be developed but only when facts are known. My question is why do we teach History and why do we teach at all?' He raised his chin and waited for Orla to respond but her face was fixed in an absent half-smile. 'Because,' he continued, 'of the love of the subject and the joy when a child understands. Our students will continue to empathize, interpret and learn the facts as they have always done . . . I think this initiative has been instigated.'

Afterwards he called her into his office. She was evasive about her apathy.

'What has happened to you?' he asked.

'What?'

'I expected a fight in there.'

'It's fine. We'll adapt. Like you said, we'll do what we always do until it changes back to the way we started with.'

He laughed. 'Yes, but as I say, you've changed.'

'I have not.'

'You have. You're no better than one of these mooning teenagers who prowl the corridors.'

She was demure.

'If I'm going to lose you,' he added, 'what will this school do?'

'I'm just a teacher.'

'You're not, Orla. You love history, but more, you love the children and they know it. You know I've told the head that he shouldn't look for a replacement when I retire.'

'I'm sorry.'

'Who's going to fight for the subject when it's squeezed out of the curriculum?'

She shrugged and smiled.

He attempted a different approach. 'How is Martin?'

'I don't know.'

'Oh. So he's definitely out of your life?'

'We broke off the engagement.'

He narrowed his eyes.

'Well I'm glad. You can do better.'

'Brendan, I was going to add that even though we're postponing the marriage plans we're making a go of it again.'

He was ashen.

'Serves you right,' she chastized. 'What if we had been?'

He shrugged mischievously. 'Perhaps I have a chance now.'

'Now I think you could do better!'

Shaded beneath the coppice, she waited for her mother in Fair Hill Cemetery on the benches that commanded a view over Dublin Bay.

From where she sat, she closed her eyes and in her imagination was lifted up, rising above the cemetery to look back on herself.

She could see herself alone; she could see her grandmother's grave and she could see her mother approaching through the stones.

She was a place on the map of her life and all the roads went away from her. With Margaret gone, she thought, she had nothing in Dublin now. It was her town, her home and she had thought she would never leave, but it was empty now.

Maeve sat beside her on the bench. They did not speak or touch. They stared at the grave. Orla could smell her spiced perfume; it was unusually subtle.

It was Orla who spoke first. 'So what is it you need me to know?'

'I need you to know that all my anger, all my . . . needs . . . it's all gone. I'm sure of it. The more I've thought about the life my mother led – since she died, the more it doesn't matter to me.'

'She led a life with true love in it.'

'I think I know that, but I couldn't forgive her being unfaithful and for lying.'

'She was the most loyal person I've ever known . . . And one lie—'

'And what a lie! Wasn't it the worst thing she could do? To discover you are another person.'

'I did discover that.'

'But for me to discover it in such a way at that age. I was stupid and pig-headed anyway. It just made me worse. I couldn't stand there and see her lie to Bertie every day. I knew it would destroy him if he knew, so I left. I couldn't forgive her for it.'

'And now you want forgiveness for all your betrayals?'

Maeve shook her head. 'I know I have made so many mistakes, but I was so full of anger and pride that I just carried on doing it again and again until I learned not to care. I couldn't admit I was wrong.'

'What about leaving me?'

'Perhaps that was the worst thing of all . . . I'm so sorry.' The apology was a whisper.

Orla nodded mutely and they silently stared out over the bay until Maeve stated, 'I have no one, Orla.' The revelation was flat and emphatic.

Orla looked at her then. She saw for the first time her mother's age and how she resembled Margaret. Her mind screamed to judge her mercilessly but instead she felt only pity. When she said, 'It was the life you chose,' she said it without any malice.

Maeve nodded.

'I've been back here several times since the funeral.'

'A funeral you didn't attend.'

It was then that her mother cried and though she too had tears, still Orla could not go to her.

Maeve coughed. 'Is it too late for me and you?'

She felt like that fifteen year old again, hating her for leaving and adoring her when she swanned away so garish and glorious.

'What do you want, Mum?'

Maeve looked at her with wide watery eyes.

'I don't know. I don't know what I can have.'

Orla held her mother's hands on her lap and her mother rested her head on her shoulder and she sensed it would be enough, that they could have more.

19

Infinite Parallel Theory

In the shortening days before Michaelmas, Orla thought less of school and more about returning to the valley. On the Friday, after lessons, Bernadette arrived at the flat and they took a taxi to the station.

Bernadette made good her promise and said no more about Martin. She, too, understood that her friend had changed and the only task now was to understand her. She insisted however, that Orla telephone Jack for a spin from Castleford.

It was darkening when they arrived in the valley and they strolled down to the stormwall to see that the platform for dancing had been erected on the strand.

'The summer is all gone,' Bernadette shivered.

'If it's like this tomorrow, there won't be a crowd,' Jack sneered. 'The two brothers will be laughed at.'

'I won't be laughing,' said Orla.

She did not look at him.

'If you freshen up we can see the Open Hearts at the Laughing Gull,' he suggested.

'I'm in,' exclaimed Bernadette.

'I don't think I will,' decided Orla.

'Ah go on.'

'You two go.'

'I couldn't,' declared Bernadette.

'Jack. Will you take her away and have a bit of fun?'

'Well . . .'

'I'd really appreciate it,' she urged.

'I'll not go,' declared Bernadette.

'Yes, you will. I insist. Will you take her, Jack?'

'I will.'

Bernadette needed no further encouragement. While she was in the bathroom, Orla stepped out into the road where Jack was sullenly slouching against his 4x4.

'How have you been?' he asked.

'Well,' she lied.

'How are things in Dublin?'

'You mean Martin?'

He nodded.

'Martin is gone.'

He straightened. 'Am I still taking you to this dance?'

Still she could not refuse. 'If the weather is not too cold.'

'Don't mind me, Orla. I'm just sour because all I've been hearing is talk of this dance.'

'If everybody's talking about it, then it will be a success.'

He shrugged. 'About tonight, I—'

Bernadette came out on to the porch then. Her day's make-up having faded, she looked better for just having tied her hair back and applying fresh lipstick.

'Here I am – the one minute make-over queen. Bring on the night.'

Back inside Orla unpacked and arranged more books on the shelf. She also arranged a line of her favourite CDs and finally, set about building some folded cardboard storage boxes she had purchased in Dublin for the purpose of filing the letters and photographs.

She was in the reading chair thinking herself very fortunate to be left behind when the door was struck with a familiar thump. She leapt up, straightened herself and answered the door to Patrick.

He remained on the porch, facing the road.

'Hello, Orla.'

He would not look at her.

'Hello!'

'I've had the cesspit pumped but the drainage will need to be looked at. Did you discuss it with Callaghan?'

'I did.'

'And he said?'

'That the work was unnecessary and too expensive and that it was always that way with these old places.'

He sighed.

'If you like, Robbie and I will rectify it when we get time over the winter. We've had a look. We can do it.'

'I'll pay you.'

He looked sidelong and shook his head.

'Would you like to come in?' she invited.

'I thought I'd say hello – that's all.'

'Do you need any help?' she offered.

'I'm glad you came,' he said.

'It looks like it's all ready.'

'I'll see you tomorrow.'

He stepped off the porch and left her there. She laughed in bemusement and slowly closed the door.

She was in bed and still thinking about him when Bernadette arrived back at midnight. She staggered in and grabbed the end of the bed as she removed a stiletto. Wobbling there on one heel she fell forwards on to the bed and did not move.

Orla covered her over and went into the lounge to sleep on the settee by the embers of the fire. Her sleep was intermittent. She couldn't decide if it was the anticipation of the celebration or because of Bernadette's snoring.

By six o'clock she was up in the half-dark and standing by the stormwall. She looked back up the valley and saw through the trees that a light was on in Annamat.

She decided to go there.

From the gravelled forecourt she saw that Patrick was painting in the studio. She rang the bell and stood back. With a sheet, he covered what he was working on and descended.

'I got your letter. You had so much to say. It was difficult to take it all in,' she said.

'Would you like tea?'

'Please.'

She followed him into the kitchen.

She recalled again the words she had spoken to him, and wanted to explain how she felt now and that he was not wrong to go to her and ask anything of her, but instead she said, 'I really appreciate you arranging for the cesspit to be pumped out. I really should pay you.'

'Not at all. It should have been done before you came. I was led to believe it had been.'

'Did Jack tell you it was?'

'It doesn't matter.'

'I'd feel better if I could contribute.'

'I won't hear anymore about it.'

The kettle rumbled.

'I hope you don't mind me asking,' she said, 'but why were you arguing with him that first day I was here?'

'It doesn't matter now.'

'It does to me, Patrick. You know, I feel like I'm a child here and no one will tell me the truth for fear of my sensibilities.'

He poured the boiling water.

'The man had a surveyor out to the place not a week after the funeral.'

'What for?'

'What do you think? He wants the land for himself.'

'No.'

'Before Donovan died Callaghan drew up plans for a series of chalets on the field above the cottage. He convinced Donovan that it would revive the community. He knew it was what Donovan wanted to hear. He wanted your grandfather to sell him the field above the cottage so that he could extend the complex and have uninterrupted views of the bay.'

She listened.

'When Donovan told us, we were livid and told him that any such development would meet resistance. It was all I could do to stop Donovan selling him the land instead of leaving it to you to make the decision.'

'And you think this is why he . . . befriended me?'

'I know the man.'

'I can assure you, Patrick, that the field will never be sold. Why didn't you tell me this before, instead of . . . instead of acting the way you did?'

'I didn't know you. How could I ask such personal questions?'

Still she did not want to believe it. 'We were just friends, just as he was Donovan's friend. He and Donovan were intimate.'

'They were not. What could the man tell you about Donovan that anyone couldn't?'

She shook her head. 'Donovan trusted him.'

'He trusted everyone. Why do you think he waited a lifetime for a woman who would never be his?'

'That's cruel.'

'It's true. When I was away working was when Callaghan befriended him. Before then Callaghan hadn't been down here since he was a child. Look, if you won't take my word, don't ask me about such things – ask him instead. Better still ask anyone else who's had dealings with him.'

She shook her head.

'You're making me say these things when I only want to say them to his face,' Patrick complained.

'If he's that bad I needed to know. I've been made to look a fool for not knowing.'

'You're no fool, but I could not tell you.'

'Others could.'

'Ah come on. You hardly believe me now.'

He looked at her then and saw the tears in her eyes.

'Jesus, I'm sorry, Orla. This is not what I meant to happen.'

'No. It's not you, Patrick. It's me. Please. I'm fine.'

He sighed. 'How about we watch the sunrise upstairs?'

'I'd like to.'

She followed him to the studio where the deep purple night was fading through red into blue.

'Can I see what you have covered there?'

'No.'

'Oh.'

'I can't bear people seeing my work before I've finished it. It has to be right.'

She looked down through the valley and over the bay. 'It's a beautiful view,' she said. 'I can see where I stand at the stormwall.'

'There was once a house at the bottom of the boreen but that was pulled down to build that Famine road. The view has remained unchanged since then. Can you imagine building more houses there?'

'No, but I can imagine Juno Byrne standing there with her telescope.'

'You know that Chinese sea captain Roberto told you of? He gave it to Brede Houlahan who in turn gave it to Juno.'

She looked at him and laughed.

'I'll make it a centrepiece of my collection.'

'I spoke to Maurice Aherne about your idea for the Dolphin.'

'And what did he say?'

'He said you'd already mentioned it and that it was madness.'

'And what did you say?'

'I said I agreed. He also said that you could use whatever resources he has.'

She clapped in delight and Patrick was startled.

That evening Maurice Aherne stood with her at the hearth in the Leaping Dolphin. She had taken the boards down and the fading light washed through the room with dust dense amber hues.

'And Roberto and Patrick are to make glass cabinets,' she enthused, 'and I've made enquiries about the damp and heating and—'

'Then you have all that you need.' He absorbed the space, seeing through the evernow. 'Can you imagine this place as it was? They were hanging out of the doors and windows here. And Brenda Geraghty would be over there at the bar. Jesus, she was a battleaxe and no one would give her any bother, not ever. She was as wild as the Fierce Eye herself.'

Orla held on to one of the ceiling rungs.

'And do you know what they're for?' Maurice pointed.

'I don't.'

'That was for Eugene. He lost the use of his legs in the jungles of Africa and here he was swinging around the pub like Tarzan.'

Patrick came to the door.

'What a day, boy,' shouted Maurice from a few feet away.

'Aye. It's fine enough.'

'You did well.'

'I've someone here for you to meet, Orla.'

A woman entered the bar, her eyes adjusting to the hued gloom. Orla knew her immediately and stepped forward holding out her hand and almost curtsying.

Nuala Phelan let out a little laugh and held her hand firmly. She touched the flush of modesty that erupted across her throat, but all Orla saw in the lengthening shadows was eyes that seemed black as caves.

'Maurice, can you help out here,' asked Patrick. 'Mossy O'Sullivan says that the Ranageanna Militia took orders from the Lir Boys against the Black and Tans.'

Maurice bustled out with Patrick in tow. 'Where is he? Take me to him. The man knows nothing.'

Orla could not speak. Suddenly all the stories were there in her mind, vying and crying for attention.

She watched as Nuala also looked about the place, remembering and reliving.

'I sometimes think I have a time bubble,' Orla managed to say.

Nuala laughed again.

'Like you can actually go there.'

'Yes,' Orla blushed and was glad of the poor light.

Nuala still held her hand. When she spoke it was soft and precise, like a true storyteller.

'I loved Donovan, Orla. I knew about you. I remember when you were born and he was so proud and so very sad.'

Orla wept then and Nuala embraced her.

'I have something for you, Nuala,' Orla said eventually. 'It's through here.'

At the bar, Nuala watched as Orla took the journals from their box.

'These are among the things Donovan left. I think they are meant for you.'

'His stories!'

Nuala kissed her then and Orla was overjoyed.

They then sat out on the porch, not drinking tea as Donovan did, but with a glass of wine each.

'Do you know that he was the one who believed in me?' Nuala explained. 'My parents loved me completely but they did not understand about the writing. It just wasn't the thing for a girl to do. I used to come here and sit where we are now and he would tell me stories of the place and . . . well, the rest you know. In my very first book there is a dedication to him.'

'I haven't seen it.'

'But it's there.'

'It's like he knew I would meet you.'

Nuala giggled. 'He did indeed.'

People were passing on their way to the strand and many stopped and introduced themselves. Bernadette returned from below for a few minutes, but after an indifferent introduction to the author she was off again to see the band.

As the light faded completely, the swirl of fiddles and bodhrans erupted. Nuala went on down as Orla realized she had forgotten to change her clothes or apply her make-up.

Standing before the mirror she decided lipstick would do in the dark, and then turned to see Jack at the door. He was all smiles.

'You look great, Orla,' he offered, then seeming to see her anxiety, asked, 'What is it?'

'I know what you want from me,' she stated.

He blanched and then angered. 'Then it doesn't matter what I've come to say?'

'What have you come to say?'

'Ballyanna is my home. I love the place.' His words were like broken stones. 'But progress can be made without ruining natural beauty.'

'You had plans and you didn't tell me.'

'I submitted planning proposals with Donovan's permission. He wanted you to understand the value of what you were inheriting.'

'I do. You're no better than a land grabber.'

'I am not. Yes, I have made money from the property prices but someone had to. I was lucky, that's all.'

'You only buy coastal locations.'

'I purchase prime property. It's business.'

'History and family are not business.'

'It can be.'

'What?'

'Don't be naïve.'

'I have been naïve. Now I know what you were arguing about when I first came here.'

'With McLeavey? He thinks he owns this place.'

'He does not. He lives here. He believes in it. What do you believe in?'

'In you.'

They stood staring at each other.

He spoke quietly then. 'Look, of course I want to make money but if you said no then no bother – I have enough. I'm not here for that; I'm here for you.' He stepped towards her. 'I want us to walk on to that platform together and not care what others think. I don't want to get involved . . . Donovan knew this. That's why he spoke to me because I did not want to know about the gossips.' He stepped closer still and touched her arm. She lifted his fingers off and as he made to speak on she held up her hand.

'Don't come any closer. Go alone. I'll have none of you.'

But he did say one more thing. 'I don't live in the past, Orla and neither should you.'

She did not reply and he went from the place.

She actually laughed when he was gone, but waited a while before joining the passing crowds and following him down.

When they turned off the slipway she saw that the strand was thronging. The platform was lost in the smoke from the fires and dancers were on the boards where the Open Hearts played.

Orla saw Roberto and Saoirse dancing gently to one side. She looked for Patrick and found him with his grandmother over by the seasteps. With them stood a couple she did not recognize. She approached.

Anne kissed her and Orla was surprised. She stood back as her great-aunt introduced her companions.

'This is my son Seamus and his wife Elizabeth. They have come over from England for The Rest.'

Orla realized. 'This is your father and mother?' She could see it clearly.

As tall as her husband Elizabeth was a presence to be reckoned with, Orla thought. Seamus was holding her as if he would not let her go.

'Donovan wrote to me and invited me here tonight,' Elizabeth said. 'I was sorry not to have spoken to him again before he died, but you are here and that's what he wanted . . . When I came into labour with Patrick, Donovan was with me. It was almost where you are standing now. We were here watching a meteor storm and the contractions came.'

'What did he do?'

'He shouted a lot and took me up to Elannat and that's where this specimen was born.'

Patrick smiled boyishly.

The children who had tormented Martin ran to Patrick. 'You should be dancing, Paddy.'

'I don't dance,' he declared.

They grabbed his hands and led him away through the crowd. Seamus too drew his wife away to the platform.

Orla was left with Anne.

'It seems you are truly making this place your own with your plans for the Dolphin.'

'I am, but not yet; not until I come to stay.'

'And that won't be long I think.'

Patrick was dancing with the children but she saw that he was looking her way though the flames.

By the water's edge she saw that Roberto and Saoirse were lighting the candles for the march across the cliffs, and already a procession of people was making its way up the seasteps. Anne handed her a candle and they joined them.

As they went she listened to the laughter and the stories and the joy of it all.

Above Gortagort she sensed Patrick at her side. In Andreenmacotter a generator hummed and lights were strewn across the ruins and over the waterfall.

'It is beautiful.' Orla gasped.

'They used to say the stream flowed over the souls of the dead, washing them out to the seamother,' Patrick said. 'Newly married couples would come here and the groom would douse his bride under the flow so that their children would each take on a part of the departed souls.'

'And yet Margaret and Donovan were never married.'

'But they came here that summer and he held her under the water.'

She laughed.

They were close and she could feel his breath on her.

'Your friendship means so much Patrick,' she whispered.

But she was unsure if he heard because he was retreating up the path to the ruined chapel.

She followed.

'The chapel is called the Annunciation. It was burned by the army in the troubles,' he said. 'They were after Michael Geraghty and the Ranageanna Militia. There has not been enough of a community since to build it again, and there are no roads that come here. There are tunnels underneath. Me and Roberto dug them out when he first came. I'll show you.'

He took her hand and led her down a series of stone steps into the tunnel through which she had to stoop. Their breath echoed and he held her close to him.

When she saw the lights at the end of the tunnel, she was disappointed, wanting to stay there longer.

Stepping out on to the crowded strand they saw Nuala step forward to speak. Her face flickered in the flames.

Orla realized Patrick still held her hand.

'When the hidden people escaped from the otherworld, it was after years trapped in the labyrinth. They had travelled thousands of miles before they found the way through The Deep and out into the sun. It was the first time they had seen the sky and though at first they were afraid, when the warmth touched them they lay on the grass and basked and knew they had found a true haven.

'From the cliffs they named Schull Ban; they looked down on the waves and thought it terrible and wondrous. They ran through the fields rejoicing and claiming the land as their own. Walking from the hedgerows to the streams to the seashore again, they ate what there was and cared for nothing.

'But then the sun faded in the sky and the winter came and the earth refused to yield up any more nourishment, and the hidden people knew pain again. Some crawled into The Deep, but they could not find their way back through the tunnels. It had been too long and they perished in the dark. You can sometimes hear them still.

'Many of the people followed the sun, fleeing to other lands and of those we do not know what happened, for they were never seen again. Those that stayed remembered what the land once was and their hope was not lost. Many died in their homes but some lived to witness a stranger walk among them.

'He came out of the sea and out of the night holding his candle before him, and though they had no food, they welcomed him as was their way. He saw that they were starving and showed them how to nurture earth and make her yield up more of her gifts time and time again. At first they did not believe him but when the first seeds grew and he patiently tended them and they tasted them, they understood at last and rejoiced, for they knew they would never go hungry again.

'And so at summer's end when they came to the stranger to thank him they found him gone. And so they came to the strand where he first emerged from the night with his flame before him and they set their own flames on to the water, hoping he would find them and know that they remembered all they had lost . . . and gained.'

She bowed slightly and the people quietly clapped and then took it in quiet turns to walk down to the water to place their candles on the waves. Some took off their footwear and strode out into the shallows. Orla took off her sandals, lifted her skirt and was the last to do so.

She felt a hand on her back and was comforted that Patrick guided her up the steps and into the vibrating haze of the generator lights. As she slipped on her sandals he flicked the switch and the lights faded.

The people were making their way back but she stood watching the flames drift out to sea. She saw the souls leaving and returning.

They were the last to return to Ballyanna and even before they reached Schull Ban they could hear the music erupt again. They said nothing as they walked together. She was enjoying the grass against her bare legs.

Back on the strand the people were dancing again; some were dancing in the sea.

Again Patrick was drawn away to be congratulated and she was content to stand watching, just glad to be part of it all. When he returned he said, 'Would you dance with me, Orla?'

'I thought you didn't . . . I don't . . . Yes.'

He took her hand and led her to the platform. She felt many eyes on her. She could not look at him and closed her eyes.

The band was playing 'Irish Love of Mine' and, as he held her she breathed him in and remembered the day of the summer storm. He smelt raw and real against the fire smoke and the sea air, and in that living moment she cared for nothing else.

20

The Romantic

When Patrick was taken from her by congratulations and cheers, Orla withdrew to An Doras. Inside, she immediately noticed Bernadette's bags were gone and considered phoning but decided not to – she knew what had happened.

Instead, she lay in bed thinking about the evening and listening to the people passing by outside. Despite the raucous shouts and screams there was a calm in it all and she eventually slept easily.

In the morning she awoke late to the sound of her mobile's ringtone. It was Bernadette.

'I want to apologize. I was flutered. I'm sorry.'

'So what did you do?'

'I got him to drive me to Castleford. I took the first train this morning.'

Orla laughed. At least she had avoided the sordid details. Bernadette protested.

'I made a mistake, Orla. I shouldn't have. I was disgusting.'

'It was for the best.'

'You are my best friend and I've ruined our friendship.'

'You haven't. He bamboozled us both.'

'What?'

'I think you saved me.'

'It doesn't make me feel any better.'

'And you shouldn't – I want you to suffer a little longer. Anyway, what do I want with a man like that?'

'Or a friend like me?'

'Oh, Bernie. What do you want with him?'

Bernadette was silent.

'He is every other man you've been with,' Orla pursued. 'When will it end?'

Still she did not respond.

'I just think you're better than you think you are.'

'Can I call you in the week?' Bernadette asked quietly.

'You can.'

Orla walked down to the stormwall. On the strand, all that was left of

The Rest was the bare platform and scattered piles of chard driftwood.

As she breathed she felt free again. She was thinking of what she would say to Patrick, when Jack Callaghan suddenly appeared against the wall beside her.

She stood straight and silent.

'It's not what you think,' he said.

'You have no idea what I think. You don't know me and I don't want to know you, now go away.'

'We're neighbours.'

'Well, find another place to live.'

'Who do you think y'are?'

'Someone who values this place and people.'

His lip curled.

'You're an idiot. Do you think this place matters at all? Do you think the people who were here a hundred years ago would recognize it? Do you think in a hundred years' time anyone will care?'

'I'm not angry with you, Jack. I'm angry with myself. You're right, I was an idiot.'

Stones were scraped on the lane behind them. They both turned to see Patrick standing there with a bicycle at his feet.

'Away with you,' Patrick ordered darkly.

Jack looked from him to Orla and back again. He blinked slowly.

'Now,' Patrick stressed.

The wider man, Jack reared up and charged at him, but Patrick stepped aside and Callaghan tripped on the bicycle frame, staggered and rolled in a spray of gravel and dust. Orla winced as he knelt there staring at his ripped palms and tattered jacket.

Patrick stood waiting, but Jack got up and walked away without looking back.

Patrick turned to her and spoke fast. 'I saw you from the window and I saw him walking down—'

It had happened too quickly for her to be afraid. 'There was no need—' she began to say.

'There was. He shouldn't be talking to you at all. I'm being honest. I couldn't bear it. I'm . . . I'm sorry . . .'

'Aren't you afraid he'll do something desperate now?'

'He won't. He's a coward.'

She was reassured.

'So you were spying on me again?' she asked archly.

'I think I was.'

'I enjoyed our dance,' she said.

'And I.'

They stood there in silence for a while, just watching the birds. A crow flew down and hopped across the long grass.

'That's the Morrigan,' he said.

She laughed. 'She's after the casualties of the battle.'

'Maybe she's here after the battle between us?'

'I thought that was over.'

'It is,' he assured. 'Are you going home today?'

'It's half-term so I thought I'd stay for most of the week. I'm going to be sorting and arranging. If you have time, I could do with the help.'

'I'm all yours.'

They looked out across the bay.

'If you have time I'd like to show you something more of the place,' he said.

'If you wait awhile I'll get dressed.'

They walked back to the cottage.

'You know where the name comes from?' he asked.

'An Doras – no.'

'They say it was the first house built here, and that it was a door to paradise. Others say it is a door to the otherworld. I say the O'Meaghers married into a family by the name of Dawes.'

His quips were worsening. She laughed and went in to change. Soon they were walking along the Coastal Way towards Cromwell's Hump.

'Will your mother and father return for good?' she asked.

'I don't know. I hope they do, but he has so much to prove.'

'It's not too late though.'

'I don't think so. What about your parents?'

And she told him of Maeve.

'Is it too late for her?'

'No. I think she knows what to do now.'

On the headland they stood in The Hollow.

'This is the fire pit for one of The Thousand Flames to warn of invading pirates and the English.'

'Were there that many beacons?'

'There were a few dozen a least. I would sit in here—'

'Out of the wind,' she interrupted, 'and feel as though you are out of the world.'

She watched him step up and offer his hand. He stood above her, like a poet on a crag she thought.

'But this is not what I brought you here to see,' he said.

She followed him down the slope to the small strand of the guileen, opposite where she had fished with Martin. He took her hand and they traversed the rocks, following the tide on its way out.

Beneath the summit he stopped on a wide ledge and she looked down with him to his feet.

It was then that she saw it; not a pitted eroded rock face but coarse carvings, like runes, where the rocks had been carved and worn and carved again.

'Here.' He pointed to his own name and that of Roberto. 'And there.' She saw Anne and Pearse and then Donovan. 'This is The Ledge of Names. Donovan used to say it was the gravestone of the children that were cast down by Cromwell's men. I think he knew it was just a way in which the people here marked this as their own place; as something more permanent than life. To be part of it is a powerful thing.'

She touched the rock and felt his words.

'Your name should be there,' he affirmed.

They walked back together. At Annamat he prepared lunch and he invited her to eat it in the studio.

'You're wearing perfume,' he suddenly stated.

'Oh yes, I am.'

'You've not worn perfume before.'

'Have I not?'

'No.'

'Do you like it?'

He breathed her in. 'There's flowers there and oranges and spices. It suits you, Orla.'

The blinds were up and she sat on a wicker chair and looked out through the canopy of trees, trying not to look at him.

'You have a huge and beautiful house here, Patrick.'

'It's true.'

'But it must be lonely.'

'It can be, but I am free, just like you. That's the single life.'

'Free but lonely,' she mused. 'And what do you think the married life would be – compromise and company?'

'You might as well remain friends for that.'

'Then what?'

He looked at her. 'What about infinite love? What about joy? What about dying for the one you love?'

'Hah,' she scoffed.

But she thought about it as she nibbled her sandwich and he went to his easel. It was serene with only the sound of their breathing, the rattle of a paintbrush in the waterpot the brush of the leaves against the glass.

And then he took the canvas from the easel and went to her. Turning it in his hands he placed it across her lap.

She saw immediately it was the painting she had lost in the storm. She did not look at him but sat studying it, relishing the strokes and the simplicity of it. The paint seemed to pulse with the heat of the day that Donovan had sat there. It reminded her of the sun on the ruins at Pompeii or Delphi, and how she saw beyond it all, how she saw everything alive again.

She stood up and put it in the seat and put her arms about him and kissed him.

He stood static with shock.

Rain tentatively rattled across the panes, the sky darkened and without words she led him through to where she hoped the bedroom would be.

When she awoke the following morning the rain was heavier and he lay beside her studying her. Her mind screamed with the joy of it all and yet her soul ached.

'My grandmother called this place the valley of her dreams,' she said. 'Do you think she could have dreamed this Patrick?'

'Could we have?'

She smiled and kissed him.

'I want to get inside your head,' he said.

She touched his face. 'I want to be inside you completely, to stay there, to be safe there. If you would have written anything on that letter what would it be?' she asked.

'Still I would write nothing.'

'Why?'

'Because I would rather speak to you everyday for the rest of my life.'

He kissed her and she cried.

'What is it?' he asked.

'I didn't think this could happen?'

'I am sorry.'

'I feel sick.'

'Why?'

'It hurts.'

'What does?'

'The way I feel. This ache. I never knew . . .'

Still she could not say it.

'I have to go.'

'Where?'

'To be on my own.'

He sat staring at her as she dressed hurriedly and left. Below she took one of his coats from the peg and went.

By the time she was out on the lane it was raining harder, and the rain cleansed her. She half-ran towards An Doras, but when she reached the boreen, she did not go in; she turned over the humpbacked bridge and strode up the hill.

All the way she was grateful for the rain and the hour. She sobbed with joy and confusion.

High on Schull Ban by the windblown tree, she looked back across the bay and out over the ocean.

She thought about the Postman capturing the sound of his world: waves, big and small, the wind on the cliffs and through the bushes, a beautiful starry sky, a heartbeat. Like him, she could hear everything.

And she could feel everything. Even the touch of rain and the pressure of the air against her skin made her feel alive, as if she were there in an invisible multitude. She could feel them all around her. She knew they were there. It was all in her imagination but she needed no bubble.

'You could be Brede herself on the cliffs here.'

Patrick approached along the path. She leaned into him as he embraced her.

'And if I jump will I escape and never be seen again?'

'No. I will catch you.'

She turned to him and kissed him, shuddering with fear and trust.

'Has the pain gone away?' he asked.

'It's just I didn't know what it was to feel like this. I thought I did, but I never have. I know what it is now to live.'

'And love?'

'Yes. Now I'm doing what you do.'

'What.'

'Making small talk about the meaning of life.' She sensed him smile. 'I thought my life would always be the way it was.'

'It was a good life,' he said.

'Sometimes I think it was no life at all. I thought it was over for me, Patrick, and now—'

'And now you know I was waiting for you.'

'I've travelled so far and in the end it's all here. I don't want to go back.'

'You don't have to: it's that simple.'

They kissed for a long time then, breathing in each other, their minds engaging, their souls coalescing.

She turned and leaned back and he said, 'You'll never see the end of the road while you're travelling with me.'

She put her cheek against his heart and it beat so fast.

The rain had stopped and the sun was rising as an orb through the clouds.

MERCHANT ID : 2100181[illegible]

AID : A0000000031010

APP NAME : VISADEBIT

VERIFIED BY PIN

FOLLOW US ON TWITTER

@HOLLISTERCO

011108620623030610380988

SOUTHAMPTON SO15 1QB UK
0-238-023-7024

Reg	Trans	Date/Time	Cashier
006	8331	2012-06-30 12:17	01564593

605643076 ACCESSORIES £32.00 £32.00

Total £32.00

VISA £32.00
************8801

Change Due £0.00

VAT £5.33

AUTH CODE : 466137
CARD INPUT METHOD : ICC
TRANS TYPE : SALE
CARD NUMBER : ************8801
EXPIRY DATE : 1211
START DATE : 0911
PSN / ISSUE NUMBER : 00
TERMINAL ID : 27515378